CHERRY BLOSSOM LOVE

Beth was in love with her boss, but he could only dream of the brief passionate interlude he had shared with a Japanese girl long ago, and of the child he had never seen. Beth agrees to accompany him to Japan in search of his daughter. There perhaps, the ghost of Madame Butterfly would be laid, and he would turn to her for solace . . . Her loyal heart is lead along dark and dangerous paths before finding the love she craves.

MAYSIE GREIG

CHERRY BLOSSOM LOVE

Complete and Unabridged

LINFORD
Leicester

First published in Great Britain in 1974 by
Robert Hale Limited
London

First Linford Edition
published 2008
by arrangement with
Robert Hale Limited
London

British Library CIP Data

Greig, Maysie, *1902 – 1971*
 Cherry blossom love.—Large print ed.—
 Linford romance library
 1. Love stories
 2. Large type books
 I. Title
 823.9′14 [F]

 ISBN 978–1–84782–262–8

Published by
F. A. Thorpe (Publishing)
Anstey, Leicestershire

Set by Words & Graphics Ltd.
Anstey, Leicestershire
Printed and bound in Great Britain by
T. J. International Ltd., Padstow, Cornwall

This book is printed on acid-free paper

FOR MY SON
ROBERT
who wrote the song
included in this story

1

Beth Rainer knew the moment her boss, Tom Dillan, came into the office on that fateful Monday morning that there was something different about him. Usually he came in with that infectious smile of his that was almost a grin, cheerful, looking relaxed after a weekend when he would undoubtedly have played several games of golf, saying exuberantly, 'Well, how are you, Beth, on this grand morning?' Or if the morning wasn't so grand, he'd mutter, 'It's hell outside, but the sight of you, Beth, is enough to make it seem as though the sun were shining.' And then they would both laugh and for a few minutes before they got down to the usual Monday morning routine there would be friendliness and even a certain intimacy between them.

Beth had come to treasure those

minutes. Often she thought they were the most precious in the whole day; they seemed to establish a bond between them. She wasn't just the efficient personal secretary, the girl who had worked closely with him for over three years, she was someone who meant something in his life, on whom he had come to rely for so much.

But then for a long time now he hadn't treated her as just an ordinary secretary; he looked to her not only for efficiency but for advice. Often he'd break off in the middle of dictation and say, 'What do you think, Beth? Do you think I've put that too strongly?' Or he'd smile, and when he smiled like that he'd look years younger and she could see in him the mischievous boy he'd undoubtedly been.

'Do you think I'm holding my hand out too wide, Beth?' he'd say. 'Greedy, huh?'

He had started calling her Beth two years ago. They had been working late and he'd suddenly asked her if she'd go out and have dinner with him, and over dinner he'd said with a laugh, 'May I call you by your first name, Miss Rainer? We Americans aren't used to formality. I'd feel much happier if you'd let me call you Beth.'

A faint flush had risen to her cheeks and she'd been conscious of her heartbeat quickening. 'I'd be glad to have you call me Beth, Mr. Dillan.'

Two years ago and her heart still beat faster whenever she saw him. Her main happiness was in working for him and being with him. She had come to know all his moods and instinctively she responded to them. But the mood he was in that Monday morning was different from the others she had come to recognise. He was glum, pre-occupied and aloof, as though he had something of great weight upon his mind.

'Hallo, Beth,' he said, and he scarcely seemed to notice her rejoinder: 'Hallo to you, Mr. Dillan.'

Instead of going over to his desk as

he usually did, he crossed to the window and stood staring out into a bright London early spring morning. The large office, high up in the building, looked down over Piccadilly. Already the pavements were full of pedestrians hurrying along. Most of them had already discarded their winter clothing. The spring suits of the women were multi-coloured and gay. Here and there on the opposite buildings you could see window boxes with bright yellow daffodils. The sunshine glinted on the tops of the buses, on the limousines and sports cars. Spring had definitely arrived.

'It's a lovely morning, isn't it, Mr. Dillan?' Beth said tentatively. But in his present mood of detachment she wasn't even sure that he had heard her.

She stood there beside his large mahogany desk with the letters in her hand she was going to give him, watching him as the moments slowly ticked by and he made no movement. He was a large, powerfully built man of thirty-seven or eight, with a finely shaped head, strong regular features, a cleft in his chin, dark grey humorous eyes, and brown hair, inclined to curl, which he kept resolutely slicked down. He was purposeful and dynamic and essentially masculine. She knew that he played golf regularly but otherwise she knew very little of the social side of his life. What social life he had he didn't bring into the office. She had never been asked to book theatre seats for him nor to order flowers to be sent to any woman, and yet it was incredible there shouldn't be other women in his life. Physically he was still a young man in every way; sometimes when they were together she scarcely noticed the difference in their ages.

But this morning as he stood by the open window, gazing down on to Piccadilly, she watched him fearfully. What had happened? She was well versed in all the aspects of his business and she knew that nothing was wrong there. The firm was the Hyman,

Landour Company, manufacturers and distributors of every kind of plastic article. Their main office was in New York but they had another branch in Tokyo. Tom Dillan had been manager of the London office for five years. He had come from Boston and had easily fallen into the English way of life.

Presently he turned away from the window, but there was still that glum, preoccupied look on his face.

'Here are your letters, Mr. Dillan,' Beth said.

'Oh, yes.' But he still made no movement towards his desk.

'Beth, would you dine with me tonight?' he asked abruptly. 'Or am I interfering with some date you have?'

'I haven't an engagement, Mr. Dillan. Do you mean we shall be working late?'

'No, but I want to talk to you as a friend. I have something very special to ask you.'

Her heart missed a beat. It couldn't be . . . But then it might! When you are in love there are so many things you cling to hopefully.

'I'll be delighted to have dinner with you, Mr. Dillan.'

'Shall we dine at the Savoy? I'll come out and fetch you in the car.'

'That's very kind of you, Mr. Dillan.'

He brushed that aside. 'It's the least I can do. I'll pick you up at seven.' He added, 'Is there anything in the mail?' but still he made no movement towards his desk.

'Nothing very important, Mr. Dillan.'

'Good. I'll go through them presently and give you a buzz when I want you to come in and take dictation.'

'Very well, Mr. Dillan.'

She left him and went into her own office, which adjoined his. She glanced at herself in the mirror. She gave a provocative little pout. She was wearing a new spring suit of green flecked tweed. It was the first time she had worn it and she had been hoping Tom Dillan would remark on it. Usually he did notice her clothes, especially if she was wearing anything new. He'd say, smiling, 'That's a new dress, isn't it, Beth? Rule me out if I've seen it before, but somehow I don't think I have.' This morning he had said nothing. 'As far as he's concerned, I might have been wearing sackcloth,' she thought with a wry twist to her lips as she continued to stand before the mirror.

She wouldn't have been human if she hadn't been appreciative of the picture she made, and Beth was far from a vain girl, but the green flecked tweed suit complemented her bright red-golden hair that she wore cut fairly short, swept high up in front in a pompadour effect, and which curled naturally around the base of her neck behind. The eyebrows were a darker red and the long lashes verged on brown; her amber eyes held humour and as often as not a suggestion of mischief. The mouth was wide and generous, and the square-cut chin showed that she had as much determination as is wise for a woman to have. She had been called many things — striking looking, arresting, fascinating — but no one had ever described her as being merely pretty, probably because her small mobile face held too much character and determination. Her mother bewailed this determination and blamed it for the fact that though Beth was nearly twenty-four she was still single. Her mother, a widow who had married early herself, was a firm believer in all girls marrying young.

'Once a girl gets past twenty-two she gets too choosey and settled in her ways,' she would grumble to her cronies over a cup of tea. 'I can't make Beth out. In the past few years she's had plenty of opportunities to get herself married to a nice young man; she doesn't only discourage them, she's plain mean to them — at least that's what I think. She's so darned fussy. I've never met a man who could live up to all the absurd ideals she has. After all, a man is only human.'

Beth knew quite well her mother's viewpoint and would laugh at her affectionately: 'You think any moment now I'm going to be tabbed that extra woman, don't you, Mumsie? You're an old fashioned darling; you think a bad marriage is better than no marriage at all. I even believe you think the word spinster is as bad as a swear word.'

'What if I do?' her mother had grumbled. 'I hate to see you throwing away all your opportunities, Beth. You're young; you still have a chance to find a nice boy to marry you. But soon it may be too late. I know you like your job *and your boss*.' She underlined that rather cruelly. 'But where is it going to get you? He's years older than you are, and if he had a mind to marry, my opinion is he would have married long before this. Some men are born bachelors and no matter how hard a woman chases them it avails her nothing. Be warned, Beth.'

But Beth had merely laughed and rumpled her mother's shingled head. 'Don't worry, Mumsie, I'm perfectly happy with my single state. Maybe there are women, too, who are cut out to be bachelor girls.'

'I don't hold with this bachelor-girl nonsense,' her mother retorted. 'They're spinsters and should face up to the fact. I wish you'd leave that office with Mr. Tom Dillan and get yourself another job.'

'Nonsense, Mumsie.' Beth's voice had sharpened. 'I wouldn't dream of leaving my present job. I'm as wrapped up in the business as Mr. Dillan is himself.'

'Hmm,' her mother commented, but one look at her daughter's face warned her it was best not to pursue the subject.

This morning as Beth moved away from the mirror and crossed over to the small table where her typewriter was, she was remembering some of those conversations with her mother. Was her mother right? Should she resign and try to find herself another job? Would that be the answer to the restlessness she felt and the sense of frustration which so often came over her lately? Often she, too, had the feeling she was bashing her head against a stone wall. She knew Tom liked her; she guessed he was even fond of her, but never by word or gesture had he led her to believe that there was more to it than that. Would it be better for her and her own self-respect if she left? But at the very thought of leaving, of not seeing Tom Dillan five days of the week, her heart would close up and she would feel a sense of sheer terror. No, she decided, no matter what happened in the future it was better to go on like this. At least she saw Tom all the week days. And she knew if she did leave him he would always be in her thoughts; she would be worrying about what was going on in the office.

'You're a fool, Beth Rainer,' she said to herself as she sat down before her typewriter. 'But you'd rather be foolish this way, no matter how much heart-break it might bring you, than be anyone else in this world, even' — she gave a small laugh — 'the Queen of England!'

The rest of the day passed off without incident. She left on time for once to go home and bath and change. Since Tom was taking her to the Savoy she wanted to do him proud. What was it of importance he wanted to ask her? But she shut her mind down on that thought quickly. Time enough to find out about that later. 'Don't be a silly little fool,' she admonished herself sternly. 'Whatever it is he has on his mind is probably something to do with the office.'

2

Beth's home was in Putney; a fairly large old Georgian house with a small but attractive garden which her mother tended lovingly. It was too large for their needs but her mother, who was nothing if not sentimental, clung to it because she had come here soon after she was married and Beth had been born there. There were four stone steps and then a small covered porch before you entered the front door.

Beth opened the door with her latchkey and let herself in to the square front hall.

'Mumsie!' she called.

Her mother's voice floated out from the lounge which opened out into the hall: 'Hallo, darling! You're home in good time tonight.'

Beth stepped into the room. Her mother was lying on the couch, reading

14

one of the numerous women's maga-
zines she never seemed to get tired of
reading. She was a small bright-faced
woman with eager brown eyes, a face
which had once been round and soft
and pretty; but the features had
sharpened with age and the hair, which
had once been the same red-golden
colour as her daughter's, had faded.
But she was still bristling with energy,
and she sprang to her feet directly she
saw Beth and crossed the room with
quick nervous steps to embrace her.

'You're home in good time tonight,
darling,' she repeated. 'I'm glad that old
boss of yours didn't keep you working
late. I've been making a shepherd's pie;
you like that, don't you, pet?'

Beth embraced her affectionately.
'Oh, Mumsie darling, I adore your
shepherd's pie, but I'm terribly sorry I
won't be in tonight. I'm going out to
dinner.'

'A date?' her mother asked excitedly.
'Someone new, Beth?'

Beth laughed affectionately. 'No,

Mumsie. I'm sorry, but it isn't one of the hundred-and-one swains mooning around after me; I'm going to dinner with my boss.'

'Oh,' Mrs. Rainer said disappointedly. 'I suppose that means he'll want you to go back and work late at the office?'

'I don't think so. He's taking me to the Savoy. Oh, Mumsie.' She hugged her mother in excitement. 'We may even dance.'

'What's happened?' her mother asked, with a slight touch of cynicism. 'Has he pulled off a big deal or something?'

Beth held her away at arm's length. 'Don't be mean, Mumsie. Maybe he just wants to take me out to dinner for fun. Besides,' she added, her eyes shining brightly, 'he said he had something important to talk to me about.'

'Then if it's what you think it is, darling, he's been a mighty long time coming to the point,' her mother said cryptically.

Beth laughed. 'Don't try and marry

me off too soon.'

'Too soon?' her mother snorted. 'I don't want to have a spinster for a daughter.'

Beth shook her affectionately. 'You think of nothing but falling in love and marrying, Mumsie — even at your age. I'm perfectly content as I am, thank you. And now I must rush upstairs, shower and change. Mr. Dillan is calling for me at seven.'

Her mother hovered in and out of the room while she dressed. She noticed, this time without commenting, that Beth had put on her one and only evening dress, a gown she had fallen for in the sales but had not yet worn. It had a tight-fitting golden brocade bodice; the skirt was composed of layers of tulle in varying shades of gold and amber.

'You look really lovely,' her mother said, with a small sentimental sigh. 'Good enough for any man to . . . ' But she broke off.

'You mean good enough for any man to propose to. But somehow I don't think that Mr. Dillan has a proposal on his mind. It's something more important.'

'There's nothing more important than marriage,' her mother said sententiously. 'If you don't marry you're only half alive.'

'Well, if it's any consolation to you, Mumsie,' Beth smiled back at her, 'I shall certainly do my best tonight.'

'You don't mind him being considerably older than you are?'

Beth shook her head. 'Tom may be in his late thirties' — she called him Tom to herself and to her mother — 'but in spirit he's as young as any man I know, and he has the advantage of experience.'

They heard a car draw up before the gate and both went over to the window.

Tom Dillan drove a black Bentley. It was a magnificent looking car and dwarfed every other car in the street.

Mrs. Rainer chuckled. 'My, but this will give the neighbours something to talk about.'

'Please go and let him in, Mumsie. I haven't quite finished putting on my make-up.'

It was a lie. She was perfectly made up for the evening; mascaraed eyelashes; a faint suggestion of blue on her eyelids; well powdered to hide the few freckles on her nose.

She gave her mother a little time to talk to Tom. This was the first time they had met. But she didn't wait for long; her mother was notoriously outspoken; she was afraid of what she might say if left alone with Tom too long.

A few moments later she stood in the doorway of the lounge, poised, looking younger than her years, and quite lovely in the gown of varying shades of gold, with a silver-squirrel stole draped over one of her arms.

Tom Dillan, who had been talking with her mother, was wearing an immaculate dinner suit of Savile Row cut.

'Why, Beth,' he exclaimed, a surprised undertone to his voice, 'what's happened to you? You look completely different.'

'You've only known my office self,' she smiled at him. 'This is my other self.'

'All I can say is I'm mighty proud to be taking you out this evening.'

Her amber eyes smiled back into his grey ones. 'I'm mighty pleased to be going out with you.'

'Well, get off, both of you,' her mother chortled, making a motion as though she were shooing chickens. 'There's never too much time on a night out — at least that's what I felt when I was young. I always wanted it to last until breakfast time — and sometimes it did.'

He opened the door for Beth and she climbed into the front seat of the limousine. It was delicious settling back into her corner. The cushions were so well sprung. There was a delightful aura of luxury.

'I never had such a shock in my life as tonight when you walked into the drawing room,' he remarked presently. 'Why haven't you shown me your other self before?'

She laughed happily. 'I haven't had the opportunity, kind sir. When we've dined together before it's always been because we were working late at the office.'

'I've been a fool. I ought to have asked you out like this — often. As you know, I have a nice apartment in Curzon Street; it's well furnished and the service is good, but by no manner of means could you call it home. Often I've felt lonely of an evening; several times I've thought of calling you up and asking if maybe we couldn't take in a late supper date and then go on to some nightclub. Guess I was scared. And then our relationship in the office is so perfect, I was afraid that if I did try and date you it might spoil it.'

'But you don't mind spoiling that relationship tonight, Mr. Dillan?'

'I had no alternative. I had to talk to you personally, Beth. I didn't want to talk to you about it during office hours.'

She looked at him, wondering, not daring to let her hopes rise too far. But did this something personal coincide with the dreams and hopes that had lived with her all day?

They had crossed Putney Bridge and were driving through the heavy London supper and dinner traffic. He apologised for the slowness of their progress, but she flashed him a bright smile. 'Don't worry, I'm enjoying every moment of it.' And she was. She felt as though the comfort of this limousine was her metiér. She would like to have driven on in this comfort, sitting beside Tom Dillan, into eternity. The workaday efficient Miss Beth Rainer, who caught buses, often strap-hanging in the rush hour, or dived deep underground into equally crowded tubes, seemed a different person from the girl who sat beside Tom in the limousine, someone with whom she had a nodding acquaintance, but that was all.

'Perhaps I'm a schizophrenic,' she thought.

She still knew that her boss had something on his mind. His frown of concentration couldn't be wholly attributed to the thick traffic; but now she hoped and prayed that it was she herself who was on his mind.

'The manager of our Japanese branch, Chris Landour, arrived over the weekend,' he told her abruptly.

She was amazed.

'You mean Mr. Landour is here in London? But — I didn't even know he was coming!'

She saw a faint grin twist the corners of his lips. 'You don't know everything, Beth, though I'm sure you think you do.'

'But how? Why did he come?' She was stammering slightly. 'There's been no correspondence.'

'No. It was a surprise visit, though he did cable me on the Saturday morning at my home address. He flew in at midday yesterday. He's joining us later tonight at the Savoy.' He hesitated and added, 'He had a great deal to tell me. We talked till half into the night.'

She smiled. 'No wonder you looked glum when you arrived at the office this morning, Mr. Dillan.'

Again she saw the slight grin twist the corners of his lips.

'Did I look glum? I suppose it was because I had so much on my mind. I still have, Beth. But I must say that the sight of you has cheered me up. I've taken out many women in the past, but it's a long time since I've felt so proud of one of them.'

Her cheeks flushed; her amber eyes sparkled. 'Thank you, Mr. Dillan.'

'When we're out of an evening, couldn't you call me Tom? Or,' he added, looking at her critically and searchingly, 'do you think I'm too old to have you call me Tom?'

'What nonsense!' She gave a small throaty laugh and the happiness surged up into her heart. 'I never think of you as older than myself — at least not much older — and I'd love to call you Tom — outside the office,' she added quickly.

He nodded. 'I suppose that's best. It wouldn't be wise for the other clerks to hear you calling me by my first name.'

She gave a small shudder. 'I'd never live it down. They'd believe — ' but she broke off, her colour heightening.

'What would they believe?'

The flush in her pretty, high-boned cheeks deepened. 'All sorts of things, probably. Silly things. You must know what office gossip is. For eight hours a day an office is like a small world, everything is noticed, everything talked about.'

'I guess so; only the boss is the last person to hear the gossip.'

'But I should certainly hear it. It would make me most uncomfortable.' She added, suddenly daring, 'I might even have to resign.'

'No, don't dream of doing that,' he said quickly, a horrified note in his voice, 'I wouldn't know how to get along without you. I depend upon you in so many ways, and tonight after I've told you what I have to tell you, you'll see how much I do need and trust you.'

Her heart sank a little, but then she told herself she'd been a fool to hope.

As they drove down the Strand towards the Savoy she tried to think of other things. She had often heard of Christopher Landour, representative of the Hyman, Landour Company in Tokyo. Tom had once referred to him as a right smart young fellow. She wondered how young he was. Not too young, she supposed, to have risen to such a responsible position. She had typed numerous letters to him but she had no clear idea what he might be like. It would be nice to meet him in the flesh. But why hadn't Tom asked him up to the office? Why spoil this evening, this, their first real evening out, when she didn't feel like his secretary or he her boss, when they were man and woman out for an evening's enjoyment together, learning to know each other in a purely social way?

The foyer of the Savoy Hotel was a world of movement. Women in chic evening clothes, many of which bore the hallmark of famous designers, passed with their dinner-jacketed escorts down into the main restaurant, where the band was playing the latest popular tunes and where there was dancing on the polished floor; others in street clothes passed into the Grill or into the large cocktail bar. Everyone seemed gay and scintillating, looking forward to an evening of pleasure and escape.

Beth didn't need to leave her wrap and she and Tom went down the long flight of carpeted stairs together to the dance floor and the main dining room. A mirror on the side wall caught his reflection and she thought for the second time that evening how handsome he was. It was strange he had never married, for she didn't believe he was indifferent to women.

She had thought at times there might have been a love tragedy in his past, but if there had been, surely there had been time for him to have got over that? And then she reminded herself that she knew very little of his personal life; what he did of an evening after office hours, where he went in the weekends. She hadn't even known that Christopher Landour, manager of the Tokyo office and nephew of one of the directors of the firm, had arrived in London.

The head waiter showed them to a table reserved for them. It was in a corner, slightly isolated from the other tables, a table at which they could talk without the danger of being overheard. She wondered if because of its isolation Tom had especially stipulated to have this table. But there was a good view of the dancefloor and the raised platform where the band sat, and where the cabaret entertainers would perform.

The waiter presented two immense menus offering a wide variety of choice.

Beth laughed. 'I'm always at a complete loss when confronted with a menu such as this. I'm so greedy; I want to taste every single dish.'

'Then may I do the ordering?' Tom

took the menu from her. 'And if you don't agree with my choice you can always send it back and order something else.'

She gave a little mocking sigh. 'It's all in your hands, Big Boss. Did I ever tell you that I adore masterful men?'

His lips twisted in that smile that was half a grin. 'You think I'm masterful? Do I browbeat you? Do I make your life a misery, Beth?'

She looked straight back at him, her amber eyes aglow. 'You make my life wonderful,' she said with quiet sincerity. 'I think you're tops.'

She had never seen him look discomfited before, but for the moment he did look embarrassed, though pleased at the same time. 'I'm glad I have such a loyal little secretary,' and then he raised his eyes and looked directly into hers, 'and such an attractive one.'

The flush in her cheeks deepened. She kept her eyes fixed upon her plate, and then the wine waiter was there with the champagne, which stood slantwise in its silver-plated ice bucket, and a moment later the waiter was serving them delicious slices of smoked salmon. The preceding minutes had been tense, but now she raised her eyes and smiled across at him naturally.

'I adore smoked salmon. This is certainly going to be some meal.'

'I don't know why I haven't done this before, Beth,' he said when the waiter had left them. 'Maybe I was scared.'

She raised her head and looked across at him. 'Scared, Mr. Dillan?' She flushed slightly and added, 'I mean Tom.'

'That's better.' He smiled approvingly back at her. 'Yes, scared,' he reiterated. 'I was scared to know you in a more personal way. You see, I was afraid I might fall in love with you.'

She took some smoked salmon on to her fork, but her hand trembled as she raised it to her lips.

'But why should you be afraid, Tom? Am I an ogre?'

'You're the sweetest, dearest girl,' and then he broke off. He put down his fork. 'Shall we dance, Beth?'

This was the first time they had danced together. He danced smoothly, conventionally; he didn't do any of the latest steps and she was glad of that; it showed he didn't often go out dancing.

They didn't talk, but she looked up at him often as they danced. He was a full head taller than she was; taller than most men on the floor, and far more handsome. The rhythm of the band was pounding in her ears, seeping into her heart. Her feet seemed to have wings upon them; she wanted to keep dancing . . . keep dancing.

They applauded for an encore and the encore was an old-fashioned waltz. Tom was in his element. He swept her round the dance floor. She felt like a leaf blown by a strong wind. They whirled and twisted. This gipsy waltz tune might be old-fashioned dancing but it was something which got into your blood; you whirled and whirled, your head throbbed, your heart spun, but it seemed as though you were dancing on air. You were exhausted and yet you couldn't bear the waltz to end. But of course it did end and they stood looking at each other, panting a little.

'That was truly something. You won't believe me, Beth, but sometimes in the office, when you've been taking my dictation, I've dreamt of holding you in my arms like that, whirling you around the dance floor, feeling your body close against mine.' He broke off. 'I shouldn't have said that.'

'But I enjoyed hearing it. I should have enjoyed it even if in the office you'd suddenly stopped dictating, taken me into your arms and whirled me around the floor in an old-fashioned waltz.' She laughed a little hysterically, 'Even if we'd knocked down files and tables, it wouldn't have mattered.'

He said, his voice slightly unsteady, 'I'm beginning to learn you're not a very conventional girl, Beth.'

'No,' she agreed. 'Conventions don't

make for happiness. All that matters is what you feel.'

'I'm glad you're not conventional, Beth,' he said soberly. 'It'll make it easier for me to tell you what I have to tell you.'

They had fillets of sole with tartare sauce and then pressed wild duck with sliced orange. The food was perfect and while they ate they talked casually. But as they talked she was conscious of an undercurrent. They were both tense; this desultory talk was but an interlude.

Finally the coffee and the *petits fours* were brought. The waiter held up the champagne bottle and then tipped it upside down in the ice bucket.

'We'll have some more presently,' Tom said. 'For the moment we don't want to be disturbed.'

The waiter bowed and withdrew. The dance music went on, a throbbing background to their own thoughts and emotions.

Tom emptied his coffee cup and pushed it aside. He leant across the table and said very quietly, 'I'm going to let you into my life, Beth, and I couldn't do that unless I cared for you deeply. I'm even going to ask for your help, for I think you may be able to help me. That is, if you are willing, and if you care for me enough.'

She brushed aside all the trite phrases that came to her mind. Instead she said simply, 'Yes, I care, Tom.'

She felt his hand reach for one of hers under the table and clasp it tightly. 'Bless you,' he said hoarsely.

He withdrew his hand; he rested both his elbows on the table and leant closely towards her. 'I want you to think back to the time of the German blitz over England, and later, the V-2 bombs. You remember it?'

She shook her head. 'I'm afraid I don't.'

He continued: 'I was barely twenty, but I was already a pilot in the American Air Force when the war against Japan ended. I was one of the first of a fleet of flyers to be sent in. We were the conquerors and were treated as such. It was devastating to our egos. I was a lad but I thought of myself as a man. I strutted about intent upon showing my superiority, and then suddenly I came up against a girl — one girl, who frankly laughed at me. She was really lovely, I thought her the most beautiful girl I'd ever seen in my life.

'She was very slim, dark haired, with a lightish complexion. Her father was a Japanese professor of the old school, but she worked in an office. At the end of the war most of the young women who had been secluded in their homes had come out and worked. She wore a European business suit to work, but at home she always wore the kimono and obi. She was eighteen and I fell violently and passionately in love with her. I asked my colonel for permission to be married, but he turned it down flat. I was too young, he said, and at that time the army didn't approve of American Army and Air Force men marrying Japanese girls. Anyhow, he said, since I was under age I must have my parents' approval first. But at that time, with the hatred of war still in everyone's mind, and especially the Americans' hatred towards the Japanese, I knew they would never give their consent. But for all that we had an idealistic love affair. We went for a weekend to Fujiyama and stayed at the famous Fujiya Hotel. We were both sublimely happy; it was spring and all the cherry trees were in bloom. There was a lake with the fabulous snow-covered Mount Fuji in the distance. We would walk around the shores of the lake, telling each other time and again how much we loved each other . . . ' He broke off abruptly. 'Am I boring you, telling you all this, Beth?'

She gave a small laugh that had tears behind it. 'Not boring me, Tom.' But she was deeply hurt. Each word he uttered was like a knife wound in her heart. But could she have expected Tom to have reached his present age without any love affair or to have remained a bachelor for so long if there hadn't been some hidden love affair in his past? She told herself she had been starry-eyed, hoping for the impossible. Was Tom still in love with this Japanese girl he had known so long ago?

She clenched her hands tightly under the table and murmured, 'Please go on, Tom.'

'I was ordered back to the States. I think it was the colonel's doing. He was a friend of my parents back home and was distressed at my love affair with Eiko. I think he imagined that once I got back home I would forget all about my little Japanese sweetheart. I had no alternative but to go, but I swore that when I became of age I would go back and marry her. In the meantime we promised to write to each other regularly. My parents, who are now both dead unfortunately, were a stiff elderly couple, typically Bostonian. They had been in their late thirties when I was born. They had rigid ideas and principles. They would have been horrified had they known I was in love with a Japanese girl. I could expect no help or sympathy from them. And then one day Eiko wrote me she was going to have a baby. I was desperate to get back to her, but I was still in the Air Force and when I applied for leave it was refused. I think my old chief had written my present one that on no account was I to be granted leave to go back to Japan.

'I wrote Eiko nearly every day, reaffirming my love and swearing that directly I was twenty-one and it was humanly possible I would go over and marry her. She wrote me that her mother and father were taking her to one of the islands at the north of Japan, Hokkaido, to have the baby. I suppose they were afraid of local scandal if she had it in the suburb where they lived.'

There was a long pause and then he said: 'That was the last I heard of Eiko. I wrote and cabled her old address, but all my letters and cables were returned to me. One day I read in the newspapers that a fierce typhoon had struck the Island of Hokkaido; nearly all the buildings on the north-east coast had been destroyed, thousands of lives had been lost. I was in a desperate state. I wrote and cabled, but there was never any reply. About that time my father died. My mother was desolate; she became a semi-invalid. All she lived for was to see me whenever I could get leave. Often I longed to tell her everything and beg for her understanding, but I knew she would never have understood. It might have been her death-blow. Almost a year after my father's death, she died, peacefully, thank heavens, in her sleep.

'My military training period ended about that time. After I'd settled my parents' affairs I flew back to Japan. The only address I had was Eiko's old home in Tokyo. I learned from the neighbours, with the help of a guide who spoke English, that after the Seis had gone to Hokkaido, a sister of Mrs.

Sei had moved into the house for a while, but after she had learned of the Seis' death in the typhoon she had sold the house. No one knew her present address.

'I was more desperate than ever. This was the first I had learned of Professor and Mrs. Sei's death. I questioned the neighbours for news of Eiko, but they knew nothing. I flew up to Hokkaido to see if I could get any news on the spot. But, apart from the fact that the police believed that two of the bodies which had been unearthed from the fallen masonry of the destroyed hotel building were those of Professor and Mrs. Sei, they could tell me nothing. They had no idea whether one or other of the bodies, too mutilated to be identified, had been that of their daughter.

'It was a fruitless, heartbreaking mission, and after six months, when it became necessary for me to return to the States to see to some of my late father's financial affairs, I believed the best thing I could do was to try and put everything behind me as a closed chapter in my life. But before I left I interviewed one of the biggest private detective agencies in Japan. I put everything before them and asked them to do all they could to find out if Eiko had been killed at the same time as her parents and what had become of the baby, if indeed it had been born. They promised to do everything in their power to assist me, but it was some years before I received any information and then I was already working my way up in the Hyman, Landour Company in New York. They wrote they could not confirm the news they sent me, it had been picked up from local gossip; but they believed that Professor Sei's daughter had given birth to a baby girl just before the typhoon had struck the island.

'You can imagine how I felt. I wanted to fly straight back to Japan. But then I asked myself, what could I do? The inquiry agents had written that they had no idea what had happened to the baby. I knew it would jeopardise my chances of promotion if I left the firm at that special time. I could only urge the agents to pursue their inquiries at no matter what cost. But though I waited eagerly, desperately, for news, the years passed and I heard nothing. In time I gave up all hope, believing that Eiko and the baby had undoubtedly been killed when the typhoon had struck the island. I threw myself into my work and as the years passed my youthful love for Eiko died. She became remote, like a dream figure. In fact with the passage of years, my whole affair with her seemed like a dream fantasy.'

He paused and signalled to one of the waiters to refill their coffee cups. When this was done and the waiter had departed, Beth said quietly, 'And yet you never married?'

'No,' he said slowly, stirring the sugar in his cup. 'For a long while I didn't consider myself free to marry and, then afterwards, when I had brought myself to accept the fact of Eiko's death, I became too immersed in my work to give myself time to form any sentimental attachment. Oddly, it's only recently I've thought of marriage.' He broke off again.

The silence was embarrassing, almost painful. Beth's heart was thumping violently. Certain things he had told her had dismayed and hurt her at first, but she knew, in that lengthening pause, that it hadn't altered her love for him. What had he meant by saying he hadn't thought of marrying until recently? Could that be the reason for the strange mood he had been in all that day? Had he met someone he believed he could love, someone new in his life? But then why should he tell *her* all this . . . ?

Again in spite of all her efforts to keep calm she found herself trembling.

Tom Dillan took up his story:

'I had made a great friend in the office, Landour's nephew, Chris. He was some twelve or thirteen years younger than I was but all the same we were very close. Apart from you, he is the only living being to whom I have confided the whole story. Some years ago I was sent over to manage the London branch, and about two years ago Chris was put in charge of the Tokyo branch. He wrote me that while he was over there he would do all he could to see if he could find out what had happened to the baby. But, of course,' he smiled slightly, 'she would no longer be a baby. She would be sixteen years old. I replied I would be very grateful if he could do anything to help solve the mystery. But I had long since given up hope that I would ever hear anything of either of them again, and then . . . ' But again he paused.

She broke in, unable to control herself, her voice sharp, almost staccato: 'You've found out something in the past two days? You said Christopher Landour had flown into London.'

'That's so. Chris said he thought of writing me but as business is fairly slack at this time of the year, he decided to fly over and tell me himself. Besides, he was partially educated in London and wanted to come back and see the old town.'

She leant forward tensely: 'What news did he bring you, Tom?'

'He thinks he may have found my daughter.'

She gave a small stifled exclamation.

'You see, through a new inquiry agent, a Mr. Oswara, he managed to get on the track of the aunt, Sabrino Hanko. She was very ill and expected to die at any moment. It may have been the knowledge of her approaching end which made her finally tell the truth. It was she who had intercepted my letters while Eiko and her parents were up in Hokkaido. Instead of forwarding them to Eiko, she had sent them back to me. Apparently she had done it because of her hatred for Americans. She called them pig-dog conquerors; she would have gone to any lengths to have prevented her niece from marrying one of them.

'After the inquiry agent traced the aunt, he got in touch with Chris, who went with an interpreter to see the old lady. She told them that Eiko was dead; she had been injured in the typhoon and the birth had been premature. She had died, but the baby, which she had asked to be called Michiko, was alive.' Suddenly he burst out almost explosively, 'Do you realise that, Beth, I have a daughter — Eiko's and my daughter, and she's alive!'

'I'm awfully glad, Tom,' she whispered. 'Has Mr. Landour found her? Does she know you're her father?'

'He's traced her,' Tom said. 'But she doesn't know I'm her father. Apparently she was given to a family named Ito to rear.'

'Has Mr. Landour been in touch with the Ito family?'

He nodded slowly and took a sip of coffee that had grown cold in his cup. 'He has, but not with any satisfactory results. As a matter of fact . . . ' But this time he broke off to exclaim, 'But here's Chris now. He can tell you the rest of the story in his own words, Beth!'

3

A very tall slim young man, who looked about twenty-five or six, had approached their table. He was dressed in a faultlessly cut dinner jacket and his lean face with the sharply etched features was smiling. He had very dark hair and surprisingly blue eyes. He had a high intelligent forehead and a rather pointed chin. He wasn't exactly handsome but there was something arresting about his appearance. You felt, having once met him, you wouldn't forget him easily.

'I'm sorry I couldn't get away earlier, Tom, but I was dining with two Japanese business associates over here and they were full of formalities.'

'Chris, I want to have you meet Miss Rainer — Beth Rainer,' Tom said.

The newcomer's hand shot out and when Beth offered her own hand he grasped it warmly. She was aware he was looking her over quickly and with a surprising concentration. Surprising because, she asked herself, why should Christopher Landour, who had only just met her, be interested in her? It was natural that she should be interested in him; not only was he the big boss, Edward Landour's nephew, but Tom had mentioned that despite the difference in their ages he was by way of being his best friend. He must be a very good friend since he had made this flight all the way from Japan especially to tell Tom about his daughter.

It was too early for Beth to know yet just how she felt about what Tom had told her. His revelation of his deep love for the Japanese girl had been hurtful, and yet she told herself it had all happened many years ago. She had suspected for some time that Tom must have had some deep emotional attachment in his early life. It was the only way she could explain to herself why he had never married. Now she knew that he had not only had a past love; he had a daughter.

While Tom was asking the waiter to bring up another chair for Chris, she asked herself how the knowledge that Tom had a teenage daughter affected her. But the story Tom had told her was too recent for her to know exactly how she felt. She did know, however, as she looked across the table at him while the waiter served them some fresh coffee, that the knowledge had in no way interfered with her love for him. In a curious way it appeared to have strengthened it, for he seemed suddenly in his perplexity to be more human, a man who needed sympathetic under-standing.

The waiter had brought an extra glass for Chris and was hovering expectantly about the table with the wine list.

Tom grinned across at Chris. 'Do you still like champagne?'

Chris smiled back at him. 'I'll say. Do you remember those bottles we used to crack in New York whenever either of us got a rise in pay?'

Tom returned enthusiastically, 'We certainly had some grand old times together.'

'You were darned nice to me when I first came into the firm. You showed me all the ropes and never once made me feel an incompetent youngster.'

'Nonsense. I only did what any other fellow in my place would have done.'

'But you didn't treat me as a juvenile,' Chris insisted. 'We were pals.'

Beth looked towards Tom, a warm appreciative smile in her eyes. Yes, he would be nice to a junior suddenly thrust into his department, in the same way as he had been nice to her when she had first started working for him. He would go to unlimited pains to make the youngster feel confident and at ease — that was in his nature. Some men might have been jealous of the fact that the young man was Edward Landour's nephew, his closest living relative and naturally destined to go high in the firm. But she knew that Tom was incapable of such an attitude of mind. He would always be understanding and generous, thinking of others rather than of himself.

The band had struck up a new tune, one which had just made the hit parade. The vocalist came before the microphone and began crooning:

'I stood in the moonlight and
    watched the lights flicker,
Flickering on the water of Tokyo
    Bay;
Alone there I stood, for I was a
    stranger,
I came in a steamer that arrived
    that day.'

'This is all the rage in the nightspots of Tokyo,' Chris commented. 'Would you care to dance it with me, Miss Rainer?'

Instinctively she glanced towards Tom. His dark grey eyes smiled back at her: 'Go and dance with Chris, Beth.

I'm sure he's much more expert on the floor than I am. I suppose I'm getting too old.' He said it in a half-disgruntled, half-humorous way and they both laughed.

'Nonsense, you'll never be old, Tom,' Chris said, 'You're far too dynamic.'

Beth agreed with him. It was ridiculous for Tom even to suggest that he was getting old. All the same, in a curious way, she wished he hadn't made the suggestion.

Chris Landour danced effortlessly and faultlessly, Beth felt he might have been born on the dancefloor. She had some little difficulty at first in following him, for since she had fallen in love with Tom she hadn't encouraged other men to take her out dancing. But soon she was at home with the easy rhythm of his style and was able to follow his steps without concentration.

The vocalist was singing again. It was odd, Beth thought, the song should be about Tokyo when Tokyo was so much in her mind.

'Out of the darkness a girl came
  walking,
I stood there and stared at the
  Japanese lass.
I went up to her and we started
  talking,
And faster than sound the time
  seemed to pass.'

While the vocalist had been singing, Chris had been humming the tune under his breath. Now in an attractive deep baritone voice, he sang very softly the words of the last verse:

"'Twas love at first sight, I knew
  from the start.
I never thought love could come
  that way;
For right then and there she cap-
  tured my heart
As we watched the dawn break
  over Tokyo Bay.'

'Like the song?' he asked. 'It's all the rage, even in the U.S.'

'It's pretty popular here,' Beth added quietly. 'It's queer how popular everything about Japan is becoming. I suppose it's because Japan offers quite a different civilisation for us, and we all seem to want to escape. We're so restless.'

Chris nodded: his thin intelligent face concentrated in thought. 'You're right there, Miss Rainer. I guess it's because we all know we're living on borrowed time; we want to cram as much experience and diversity as possible into our lives while we have a life to live.'

'Is Japan very exotic and exciting?'

He nodded slowly. 'It *is* exciting. It isn't only its picturesqueness, its centuries-old shrines and palaces, nor its strangely beautiful scenery; to me its main interest lies in the state of mind of the people, the tremendous clash which is going on between the old Japan with its thousands of years of tradition and the new modern Japan which has sprung into being since the last World War.'

'Is the new Japan very Americanised?'

He nodded. 'In some ways very much

so. At least,' he added pensively, 'on the surface. Sometimes I think you have only to scratch the surface and you will find the old Japan as deeply rooted in everyone's heart as it was before sky-scrapers, air-conditioning, rock 'n roll and brassy nightclubs were ever heard of. A great number of the modern generation, especially the young ones, behave exactly as American teenagers — at least they appear to. But I often wonder what will happen to them as they grow older; will they go back to the culture and ideals of their fore-fathers? Sometimes I think it's inevitable. There is a very strong movement afoot to preserve Japanese nationalism and to resent the influence and presence of foreigners in their country, no matter what benefits they may derive from their presence.'

'I've read something about hostile demonstrations against visiting V.I.P.s; especially . . . ' But she broke off and a warm flush of embarrassment crept up her cheeks.

'You mean especially against visiting American V.I.P.s?' he said with a chuckle. 'And don't be embarrassed talking about it, please. We Americans who live there are well aware that there is a group — and unfortunately a very large group — of Japanese who not only resent us but hate us and everything American with an almost fanatical hatred. And it isn't only the elder generation who, remembering the destruction of the war, especially Hiroshima, may have cause to hate us; a number of the younger generation, especially the intelligentsia and the student bodies, feel the same way. They are even more fanatical than their parents; they are well organised and seem to be amply supplied with money. One can only guess at its source.'

'You mean the money is supplied by Communist interests?'

'It could be.' And then with that sudden change of mood which she was to learn was characteristic of him, he laughed. 'But why are we talking so seriously, especially on a first meeting? I wanted you to talk about yourself. I've heard a great deal about you from Tom.'

She laughed, too, and her bright amber eyes twinkled. 'But I think you already know something about me, apart from what Tom has told you. You were certainly giving me the once-over when we met just now at the table.'

He smiled and when he smiled his face took on a slightly lopsided slant. 'That's a bad habit of mine, trying to sum up a person at a first introduction.'

'Does your first judgment usually prove correct?'

'At least I know whether I'm going to like them or not.' He added in a lower voice, which all at once was surprisingly serious, 'I know I'm going to like you, Beth. Tom has always called you Beth when he wrote me personally and when he talked about you yesterday.'

She felt a warm glow of pleasure.

'He wrote you about me?'

'Certainly. I've been looking forward to meeting you for a very long while. I knew instinctively that we would have a great deal in common.' He looked down at her in a curious way and almost imperceptibly his arm tightened about her waist. 'Of course I mean what we have in common is Tom,' he said aloud.

The band had ceased playing after the encore. She and Chris had stopped by the huge windows that looked down over the Embankment. She half turned to lead the way back to their table, but he put out his hand and caught hold of her arm.

'Don't go for a minute. I noticed when we danced by the table that Tom was talking to two men, undoubtedly friends of his. I love the Embankment, especially at nighttime. It's so quiet and mysterious and inevitable somehow. You feel that no matter what may happen to the world, the Thames will go on quietly flowing. When I was over here before I often used to wander along the Embankment, especially at night, watching the lighted ships and

the barges glide by in the moonlight.'
He added with a short laugh, 'Does that
sound silly to you?'

She shook her head. 'Of course not. I
love the Embankment myself, especially
on a night like this when the grey
waters are almost silver. But then I'm a
Londoner born.'

'My mother was also a Londoner.
England has always seemed a second
home to me; but then I was up at
Oxford.'

'I suppose you have relatives over
here?'

'I must go down and visit them. My
maternal uncle lives in Sussex. I
thought of taking Tom down with me.'

'Why don't you? It would do him
good to get away from the office for a
while. I don't remember when he last
took a holiday.'

'Tom was always a demon for work.
I'm glad he's found another interest.'

She said involuntarily, 'You mean
what he's learned from you about his
daughter?'

'I wasn't thinking of Michiko. So he's already told you about her?'

'Yes. He was telling me tonight before you arrived.'

'How do you feel about it, Beth?' There was sympathetic understanding in his voice.

Suddenly for some reason she felt very close to tears. She supposed it was the result of the emotional shock she had received that night learning about Tom's dead love and that he had a daughter alive.

'I'm awfully glad for him if it brings him happiness.' Her voice faltered slightly.

'Only time will tell that,' he answered gravely.

'Have you met her?' she asked urgently. She was consumed by a great sense of curiosity, but of course it was a deeper emotion than pure curiosity. Even now she felt that this unknown half-Japanese girl was very much bound up in her own life.

'No, I haven't seen her. I was

forbidden to see her by Michiko's foster-parents, Mr. and Mrs. Ito.'

'You mean they don't want her to get into touch with her father again? But surely that's a very selfish attitude. And anyhow I feel that the decision should be up to Michiko.'

He said gravely, 'From what I gathered from them, she has already made her decision. You remember we were talking previously about that section of the Japanese public that is strongly anti-American? The Itos belong to that fraternity and have apparently brought Michiko up in their own ideas. They told me point-blank that she, as they, hates all Americans and wanted to have absolutely nothing whatsoever to do with them. When I pleaded that it was only fair that the girl should have at least a chance of meeting her father, they said it was her own wish that she have nothing to do with the man whom she blamed for her mother's seduction and ultimate death. I argued with them but could get nowhere. I tried writing to

Tom but found it too difficult to put everything I wanted to say down on paper. That's one of the main reasons I flew over. Besides, I wanted to see England again.' And he added more quietly, 'Also to meet you, Beth.'

4

She made no comment. Instead, she half turned and said, 'Shall we go back to the table?' And this time he made no attempt to stop her.

Tom was sitting alone, moodily sipping a glass of champagne.

'I wondered where you two had got to,' he said.

Christopher answered easily, 'We saw you had friends and thought we had better make ourselves scarce until they had gone.'

'Some business friends of mine. But we didn't talk for long. They're here with their wives.' With a noticeable effort he tried to lift himself into a more jovial mood.

'How is Chris as a dancing partner, Beth? He used to be pretty hot on the dancefloor when we were together in New York.'

Beth smiled as she sank down on to the seat he was holding out for her. 'I don't think he's lost his ability to dance in Japan. I thoroughly enjoyed it.'

'You must take Beth out dancing while you're over here,' Tom said. 'I'm afraid I've been selfish keeping her working late too often in the office of an evening. I'm not much of a dancer.'

'Nonsense,' Beth said heatedly. 'You dance awfully well.'

'For my age,' Tom said, and dragged down one side of his mouth in mocking self-pity.

'You're not a Methuselah, so don't start imagining you're one,' Beth said angrily. This was the second time tonight he'd made a comment on his age. 'You're not even in your prime. Isn't that supposed to be forty?'

Christopher laughed. 'Tom needs someone like you to pull him out of himself. I happen to know that the firm has offered you several trips back to the States, but you've refused. I'm sure that you've organised the business so well over here that it will carry on effectually without you for a few weeks — or even a couple of months. It's conceit to think that any one of us is indispensable.'

Tom grinned slightly. 'I guess you're right. But if we didn't hang on to our small sense of self-importance, what would there be to live for? I know we're none of us indispensable, but we don't like to admit it.'

Beth nodded slowly. She liked to feel she was indispensable to Tom in their work in the office. She would like to have felt she was the same in his personal life. At times she had felt that she was, even if he didn't realise the fact. Could he be made to realise it? Would she find an ally in Christopher?

'I'm going to drag you down to the country next weekend,' Christopher told Tom. 'My uncle is a parson and has a large rambling vicarage in Alfriston, Sussex. There's plenty of room and I know they'd be delighted to have you.' He turned towards Beth:

'Why don't you come along, too,

Beth? I'll put through a phone call to my uncle in the morning, but I know he'd be pleased to have both of you.'

She glanced towards Tom, but he made no sign whether or not he was glad of her inclusion in the invitation. He had relapsed into the same preoccupied mood he had been in previously.

'I don't think — ' she began uncertainly.

'You *do* think. And what you do think is that you're coming,' Christopher broke in with a laugh. 'My uncle will welcome you — that is, whenever he realises you are there. He's shockingly absent-minded; and my aunt is one of those energetic souls, always on the go from morning until night, cooking, doing housework, visiting the sick and the poor, and sitting on committees — eternal committees. When I wasn't travelling on the Continent I used to spend my vacation with them while I was at Oxford. Well, how about it, Beth? I'm not going to take no for an answer.'

'You two seem to be getting along pretty well. It took me over a year to call her Beth,' Tom commented with a wry smile.

'But I felt I knew her even before I met her,' Christopher said. 'The perfect secretary.' He added with a laugh, 'That slays you, doesn't it, Beth?'

She made a faint grimace back at him. 'Very well, I'd love to come, if you're sure I won't be a nuisance to your aunt and your uncle.'

'That's as good as settled,' he said. 'Say we have another dance on the strength of it?'

Again she glanced towards Tom, hoping he would say, 'It's my turn to dance with Beth.' But he merely nodded: 'Go ahead and dance. I like to see you young people enjoying yourselves.'

'Tom makes me mad when he talks about his age,' Beth said explosively as they started dancing.

He smiled understandingly. 'I can see that it riles you. Maybe it's a defence mechanism.'

She glanced up into his thin-featured face sharply. 'Just what do you mean?'

'Maybe he harps on his age to convince himself he's too old for you.'

'But that's nonsense. He's not more than thirteen or fourteen years older than I am, and he looks much younger. He doesn't look much older than you.'

'Ah,' Christopher said, grinning slantwise. 'That's because he's led such a virtuous life, while I, I regret to say, have led anything but a virtuous one. I'm glad I came over here. Between us we've got to make Tom forget he's in his late thirties. I can see you badly need an ally. Will you have me as one?'

He seemed to think he could take control of the situation and she felt faintly resentful.

'Why do you think I should need an ally?'

'Isn't it obvious? You've worked for Tom for three years; you've probably been in love with him for at least two. How come that you and he haven't married?'

Beth flushed hotly. 'You can't marry a man if he doesn't ask you to.'

'Oh yeah,' he grinned down at her. 'I always thought the little lady had a great deal to do with a marriage proposal. But perhaps you English girls are more reticent than our girls back home. Our girls usually decide on the man they want and go out and grab him.'

'I don't want to be brutal, but it would seem that none of your fellow-countrywomen have wanted *you*,' she flashed back at him.

He laughed in genuine amusement. 'One up to you. I'm afraid I'm a wily old bird where lovely ladies with matrimony in mind are concerned. But Tom isn't like that,' he added more seriously. 'Tom's an idealist. And besides, he's damnably stubborn. If he hadn't been both of those things he wouldn't have clung to the memory of a boyhood love affair all these years. And now the knowledge that his daughter is alive and has grown up has thrown him right back into the past. Yes,' he added, with a half-confident, half-mocking smile, 'you'll certainly need me as an ally, Beth.'

★ ★ ★

Beth's mother hovered about her in the bedroom as she packed for the weekend on the following Friday evening. She kept offering to help Beth but merely succeeded in getting in the way. Beth treated all her unnecessary efforts with affectionate, amused tolerance.

'I'm so glad you're going away for the weekend, darling,' Mrs. Rainer breathed. 'And don't worry that I shall be lonely. I shan't be in the least lonely. Goodness knows I have so much to occupy me here; I can use the time turning out the linen closet and patching those sheets which have gone in the middle. Then I can go through your clothes and give your suits a good brushing. No, don't fret about me; I'll be busy and occupied every moment of the day.'

Beth stopped her packing. She turned towards the older woman and hugged her. 'Don't do anything like that, Mumsie darling. Go and see some of your friends or go to the movies.'

'I don't know anyone to go with on a Saturday afternoon,' Mrs. Rainer said. 'All my friends seem to be busy at home with their families.'

'I know,' Beth said with a sigh and turned back towards the opened suitcase. She adored her mother, but she was undeniably a problem. Her mother and father had been supremely happy together. They were so content with each other's company that they had neglected their friends. As a result, when Beth's father had died quite suddenly of heart failure when she was very young, her mother had had few friends to turn to and centred all her activities and emotions entirely upon Beth. She was always urging Beth to marry, and yet Beth often wondered, if she did marry what would become of her mother?

She knew that her mother hated her widowhood, but what chance had a woman of meeting someone attractive and companionable? — and he would have to be romantic. Mrs. Rainer was still incredibly romantic, as much so as she had been as a young girl.

'It's all nonsense to believe that you lose your zest for romance as you grow older,' Beth thought. 'In some types of women, of which my mother is one, the yearning for romance never dies. Widowhood is a cruel thing. It leaves a woman at a loose end when she most needs sympathy and companionship.'

Were elderly spinsters any happier? she wondered as she went on with her packing. If you had never known the love and companionship of a man, was it easier to endure a lonely old age?

'But I don't want to be a spinster,' Beth thought passionately. 'I want to be married, be bossed about by my husband — even if he's in the wrong;

have a home and babies. Surely every man should want the same thing — a home and children, a wife whom he could adore but at the same time dominate when he was in the mood to be dominant; make her cry one moment, kiss her tears away the next.' But perhaps men were different; their heads were often full of absurd illusions of freedom and independence. Woman was far more the practical down-to-earth creature; she knew just what she wanted. She knew that her life would never be complete until she got her man.

Mrs. Rainer had given up trying to help with the packing, taking the wrong things out of the drawers or the wrong dresses from the closet. She sank breathlessly on to the bed beside the suitcase Beth had almost finished packing.

'You've had quite an exciting week, haven't you, darling? Three nights you've been out dinner-dancing. So much more exciting than going back to that stuffy office, poring over ledgers and typing letters.'

'The office isn't at all stuffy, Mumsie. It's centrally heated and air-conditioned.' She laughed and added, 'Not that we need air-conditioning over here in the summer. But as you know, I'm working for an American firm and they think it necessary.'

'That seems a very nice young man, the one who called for you the other evening; Mr. Landour. He was talking to me while you finished dressing. He told me that his mother was English and that he had been up at Oxford. I wanted to ask him if he were married or engaged, but you came into the room just a moment too soon.'

Beth laughed. 'Chris isn't married, or engaged, as far as I've gathered. He describes himself as too slippery an eel to be caught by a woman.'

'I don't think that's a very nice way of putting it,' her mother said primly. 'It's cynical, to say the least of it. What sort of a young man is he?'

Beth thought about that for a few moments. She wasn't quite sure how to reply.

'I'm not sure he's really as cynical as at times he makes himself out to be,' she returned finally. 'I like him, anyhow. I enjoy being with him and he makes me laugh. I don't even mind his sudden probing questions. I admit they embarrassed me at first, but now I'm more used to them I just laugh them off. I certainly enjoyed myself with him the other evening.'

'What does Mr. Dillan think of him taking you out?' her mother asked.

A faint shadow fell over Beth's attractive, vivacious face. That, to her, had been the only fly in the ointment. Tom hadn't seemed to mind at all! The suggestion that Christopher should take her dancing that night had cropped up while the three of them were having lunch at the Caprice. Whenever they had had lunch together before, Tom and she had usually gone to a small unpretentious restaurant near his office.

Tom disliked ostentation and smart society restaurants. But Christopher thought differently.

'I like going to smart restaurants where everyone else wants to go,' he said. 'People aren't fools. If there wasn't something special about the place they wouldn't go there. We'll go to the Caprice; it's always crowded and it's fun. I like looking at stage and screen stars in their more relaxed moments.'

Chris had asked Tom over a deliciously cooked lunch what he was doing that evening, and Tom had said that he was dining with some old friends. Chris had turned towards Beth: 'Why don't we go out dancing together and take in some of the nightspots? O.K. with you, Tom?'

Tom gave a half-smile. 'Why ask me? Beth's a free agent. I'm sure if she's agreeable, she'd enjoy herself.'

'Then that's settled,' Christopher grinned. 'I'm not going to allow you to disappoint me, Beth.'

She had enjoyed herself; much more

so than she had imagined she could enjoy herself anywhere without Tom. They had dined at l'Escargot, in Soho, because Christopher said he had a passion for snails. Beth said the very thought of them made her shudder. But when Christopher had insisted — and he could be very insistent — that she try one of his, she had been surprised to find that the taste of the snail cooked in garlic and butter was distinctly appetising.

Christopher had crowed over her triumphantly. 'So you see, like most of the English you're prejudiced about certain types of food. You will have to get used to eating strange and exotic foods once you get to Japan; they love serving raw tuna and sea bream sliced thinly, fried honey bees and salted thrush hearts. There's one restaurant where the speciality is snakes.'

'Goodness gracious!' She shuddered slightly and laughed. 'I may have eaten a snail, but I swear you'd never get me to eat a snake. And what on earth makes you think that I'll ever go to Japan?'

He closed one eye in a prodigious wink. 'That's my secret,' he said, and immediately changed the conversation.

She decided he must have been joking. She was entitled to three weeks' holiday in the year, but even if she flew out to Japan, where would she get the money? It wouldn't be like going to the Continent, even as far south as the Riviera. Last year she hadn't even taken her vacation. They had been busy in the office. Besides, a holiday alone — even on the glamorous Riviera — isn't much fun. Most of the girls she knew who had taken such a holiday had done so hoping to pick up an attractive escort, preferably a rich young business executive. But usually the only men who seemed interested in them turned out to be gigolos, and they left the girls flat when they found out that they were merely office workers on vacation.

That night Christopher and she had gone the round of the smart night-clubs, places she had read about in the social columns but had never actually been to. She was thrilled by the infectious gaiety of the atmosphere, the lovely clothes of the women, the top flight jazz bands. She danced easily with Christopher now and enjoyed every moment they were on the floor together. She would gladly have stayed on at the first club they went to, but Christopher kept suggesting that they go on somewhere else. He was full of a nervous restless energy. She wondered if he ever relaxed. Was that typical of American men? Tom, too, was obsessed by a relentless driving force. He was impatient of any form of delay and considered the leisurely luncheon hours which most London business executives took a colossal waste of time.

It was after three in the morning when Christopher finally drove her home. Oddly she didn't feel in the least tired; she felt happy and exhilarated. Tom had lent Christopher his Bentley for the evening. When they drove up to the front of the house which led into the small garden that Mrs. Rainer so lovingly tended, he said half humorously, half seriously, 'I'd like to kiss you good night, Beth, but I don't suppose that's in our bargain.'

'What bargain are you talking about?'

'But I thought it was agreed we should be allies and that I should help further your romance with Tom. I thought the odd spot of jealousy wouldn't hurt him.'

'Is that why you took me out tonight — to see if we could make Tom jealous?' She felt a faint sense of let-down, of disappointment.

'I admit I had that idea in the beginning when I suggested we hit the nightspots. But now,' he gave a low chuckle, 'I'm damned if I care whether Tom is jealous or not. Now will you kiss me?'

She almost weakened. He had given her a lovely and exciting evening. Surely one kiss was little by way of repayment? But would it end with one kiss? Christopher was essentially male and demanding. And mightn't it spoil the sense of understanding companionship she had come suddenly to realise meant a great deal to her?

'No,' she said decisively, 'I'm not going to kiss you, Christopher. I'd like to keep our friendship just as it is.'

He didn't argue. Instead he asked, 'Do you mind if I ask you a question? Has Tom ever kissed you?'

She could feel her cheeks hot and was glad of the darkness. She felt angry, too; angry with him, with herself, but also with Tom.

'No, he hasn't,' she snapped. 'Tom wouldn't kiss a girl lightly.'

'Well, well, you surprise me. Tom certainly does need bringing out of his shell. It's a darned good thing that I flew over to take matters in hand,' he added, chuckling.

5

They had a late breakfast in an old oak-beamed inn in East Grinstead. There was a log fire burning in the inglenook fireplace to drive off the chill of the bright early spring morning.

Christopher, who had been driving, held his hands out to the blaze and looked about him with obvious satifaction.

'No breakfast in this world is as good as one in an old English hostelry,' he announced with satisfaction. 'The English cuisine may not be supreme in this world, but they do provide you with the best breakfasts. You can order exactly the same food in America, but somehow it doesn't taste half so good.'

Breakfast, when it came, lived up to all Christopher's expectations. There was porridge, then kippers and eggs and bacon, crisp hot buttered toast, and Oxford Marmalade, and aromatic coffee.

Christopher fell upon it eagerly, but Tom ate very little. All that week he had been preoccupied and withdrawn, and Beth knew what was upon his mind. It must be strange and bewildering for a man like Tom suddenly to discover that he had a teenage daughter, a daughter half of another race and brought up in a foreign land. Christopher's report on the attitude of the foster-parents, Mr. and Mrs. Ito, made the whole situation even more complicated. The girl Michiko had apparently refused to talk to Christopher because he was an American. She had, according to them, repudiated her father, looking upon him as her mother's seducer. But how impossible to think of Tom, with his decency and honesty, in the role of a seducer!

Beth wished she could talk to the girl and make her realise what a wonderful character her father was. It was through no fault of his that he had been prevented from marrying her mother. She wished Tom would talk to her about it. It hurt her not a little that since that night at the Savoy he had made no further effort to take her into his confidence. But perhaps during the weekend he would make an opportunity to talk the situation over with her. And yet she had no idea what advice she could give him. The girl had been brought up in her mother's country, apparently strictly, according to the old-fashioned Japanese tradition. Was she perfectly content with that life? Would it be kind or wise to try and uproot her?

They arrived at Alfriston, that quaint old Sussex village that had once been a smuggler's stronghold, in mid-morning. The vicarage with its oak-beamed façade and bluey tiled roof was on the edge of the village. It was a large rambling L-shaped structure, surrounded by an ill-kept garden in which, nevertheless, yellow daffodils made a glorious show of colour.

Christopher drove the car into the circular drive and tooted his horn vigorously. The door opened and an elderly man in a clerical collar, grey slacks and a sports coat, shambled out. He had a benign, rather vacant expression, and his grey hair was very thin on the top of his head.

Christopher sprang out of the car to meet him, and the Rev. Charles Tiswell, who was considerably shorter than his nephew, reached up and patted him affectionately on the shoulder. Beth heard him say, 'Well, it's nice to see you again, dear boy. How long ago is it since you last visited us? Two years, if I'm not mistaken.'

Christopher laughed. 'It's all that and three more, Uncle. How is Aunt Jessie?'

'Fine, fine,' his uncle said, running a hand over his thinning hair. 'A mite stouter, but then I think that's becoming in a woman of her age. I know dieting is all the rage these days, but I don't hold with it, especially when you're getting on in years. I tell that to my scraggy parishioners.' He chuckled, and Beth saw a glint of humour in the pale blue eyes.

Christopher introduced Beth and Tom.

He welcomed them in the same vague kindly manner with which he had welcomed Christopher.

'Jessica sends her apologies for not being here to meet you. She's at one of her blasted committee meetings — you wouldn't think they'd hold them on a Saturday morning, would you? But that's to trap the wealthy weekenders who abound in this district. She will meet you at lunch. Now let me take you up to your rooms.'

Beth had a large cheerful bedroom with chintz curtains, a four-poster double bed, and some really fine old pieces of Georgian furniture. The floor was polished oak with handmade hooked rugs, and from the lattice window you had a magnificent view of the surrounding countryside with the downs in the distance.

Beth washed in the large unmodern bathroom, which was apparently the only bathroom in the house, changed into a tweed skirt and an eau-de-nil short-sleeved lightweight wool sweater which her mother had knitted for her and, after she had run a comb through her hair, went down to the lounge where Tom and Christopher were chatting with their host.

Despite the bright sunshine outside it was chilly in the lounge. There was no fire, but instead there was an arrangement of assorted pot-plants in the fireplace. Christopher laughingly explained to her later that on the first of April all fires were discontinued in the vicarage and the pot-plants were moved in to the vacant fireplace.

'Boy, have I been cold here in April!' he said, and shuddered.

Mr. Tiswell said he had some visits to make.

'Perhaps you'd care to come with me, Christopher?' he suggested. 'Since you remind me that it's so long since you've been down here, I feel I have a great deal of ground to cover catching up with what you've been doing.'

'I'll be delighted to come with you, Uncle,' Christopher said readily, smiling down at the elder man.

'You don't mind driving in the old Austin?' Mr. Tiswell asked diffidently. 'It's badly in need of an overhaul, but I never seem to be able to spare it sufficiently long to send it in to the garage.'

'Perhaps this is an opportunity, while we're down here, to get your car overhauled,' Tom suggested. 'I'm sure Chris will be glad to drive you round in the Bentley.'

'Now that *is* kind of you,' Mr. Tiswell said gratefully. 'I'll phone through to the garage, and even though it's the weekend I'm sure they'll oblige me. I've only once driven in a Bentley,' he added rather wistfully. 'It was owned by one of my wealthy parishioners. Unfortunately she has since become a Roman Catholic and now takes the priest joy-riding in it.' He hurried out into the hall to telephone the garage and Tom turned towards Beth.

'Shall we go out for a walk? It will do us good to stretch our legs after the drive down.'

'I'll run upstairs, collect a cardigan and change my shoes.' She smiled. 'I'll be down in a jiffy.'

She felt excited at the prospect of this walk. All this week, since that night at the Savoy, she had been conscious of a faint sense of strain between them.

Beth and Tom went round the side of the house, through the walled vegetable garden and out the back gate. They started across the fields towards the foothills of the downs. The fields were lush and green and the atmosphere was sparkling clear. The young leaves on the trees looked polished in the sunshine, and the hedges which surrounded the fields were already thick with spring foliage.

'It struck me as very strange when I first came to this country to realise the downs were up,' Tom commented. 'In some places they're almost small mountains and so curiously free of trees and shrubs. But their very bareness contributes greatly to their picturesque charm.'

'I love the downs,' Beth said. 'I've always wanted to spend a holiday here. But I've usually gone to visit Mummy's relatives in Gloucestershire.' She gave a little rueful smile and added, 'So much of your life seems to be taken up in doing what you consider your duty. Wouldn't life be thrilling if we could only once get rid of our consciences and do what we really wanted to do?'

'A vast majority of the population would end up in the local jail,' Tom commented dryly.

She laughed. 'I never thought you were a cynic, Tom. Quite the reverse. I'd expect Christopher, not you, to make such a statement.'

'You think Christopher's a cynic?'

'I don't think he is,' she said thoughtfully. 'But I think he likes to imagine he is.'

'You seem to have come to know Christopher pretty well during the past week.' There was a distinct edge to his voice.

She glanced towards him quickly. It couldn't be that he was jealous; it was almost too much to hope for. Her heartbeat quickened.

'I wouldn't say that I know him. He isn't an easy man to understand. But you know him so well, Tom, you must understand him.'

'I like to think I do,' Tom agreed. 'But though he's my best friend and I would do anything in this world for him, and I know he'd do the same for me, I'm not altogether sure that I actually know him. I don't always understand his varying moods nor basically what makes him tick over. During our long years of friendship he has done so many things which have not only surprised but have completely bewildered me.'

She nodded. 'I can quite believe that. He *is* a surprising person. But you don't think he rather likes to play upon that fact?'

Tom grinned boyishly in the way she

loved to see. 'You may be right. I've often thought you were a little shrewdie when it came to summing up a person's character. That's why I always have you in the room when I'm interviewing new applicants for a job.'

She blushed with pleasure. 'I'm always flattered when you ask my opinion.' She laughed and added, 'A girl likes to feel she's important.'

He turned his well-shaped head towards her; his handsome, strong-featured face was very serious. 'You are an important person, Beth — very important to me, anyhow.'

Suddenly, with an abrupt movement, he took her hand and drew it through his arm. 'Did you know that? You're very important to me, my dear,' he added in a lowered voice.

She turned her own head and smiled at him with her clear amber-shaded eyes. 'Am I, Tom? You've become a very important person in my life too.'

His pressure on her arm tightened. 'I'm glad to hear you say that, Beth.

I've been thinking about things a great deal this past week.'

'Yes,' she breathed when he had paused. Was he going to say at last what she had been waiting for, praying to hear these past two years?

'I've decided to go to Japan, Beth,' he said finally, 'and I want you to come with me.'

She was so completely taken by surprise she could only stammer stupidly, 'You want me to go to Japan with you? You're going to Japan?'

'I've been turning over everything in my mind pretty thoroughly this past week. I've decided the best — the only thing I can do — is to fly out to Tokyo. We're fairly slack in the office at the moment. Carruthers can take care of everything. The firm owes me six weeks' vacation. I was talking the situation over with Christopher last night. He agrees that in the circumstances the best thing I could do would be to fly over. Michiko can't very well refuse to see *me*, her own father.'

Diffidently she voiced what she had been thinking only that morning: 'You don't think if she's happy and settled in her present mode of life it mightn't be best to leave her alone?'

He looked at her almost in horror. 'You suggest that, Beth? But I thought you were my friend.'

'Of course I'm your friend, Tom,' she cried, and she felt tears pricking the backs of her eyes. 'I was thinking of Michiko . . . Forgive me, Tom. I can understand how much it means to you to see her, to talk to her.'

'It means everything to me. I've been thinking of nothing else this past week.' He gave a sound that was half laugh, half sob. 'Of course I'll be scared stiff of meeting her in the flesh; my own little girl, Eiko's daughter and mine. I know at the moment she has said she doesn't want to see me, but I'm hoping when she realises I've flown out from England especially to see her, she will feel differently. I'm sure if you fly out with Chris and myself, you'll be of great help to me, Beth.'

'That's why you want me to come — to help you get into personal contact with Michiko?'

'That isn't the only reason, Beth. I've come to depend on you so much, I don't like the thought of your being out of my life even for a short space of time.'

'It's nice to hear you say that, Tom.' Her heart was throbbing almost painfully. 'I shouldn't like to be away from you for any length of time either.'

'There's a great deal I'd like to say to you, Beth,' he went on in the same low-pitched voice, 'but I feel that it must wait until the situation about Michiko has been clarified. Michiko is predominant in my thoughts at the moment . . . Please try to understand.'

She nodded slowly but her heart was rebellious. Why must everything depend, or at least be put aside, until he had or had not established some sort of relationship with his daughter? Was it fair to her, who had loved him for over two years, that she should be asked to step aside at least for the moment?

He seemed to read her mind. His voice was apologetic as he went on: 'You may not think I'm being fair to you, Beth, but honestly at the moment I feel in such an emotional and mental turmoil, it wouldn't be fair to you or to myself to ask you to make a definite decision at the moment about our future relationship. I hope . . . I beg you, Beth, to understand.'

She felt that he needed her in this great crisis of his life. Was it the only way she could prove her love for him — by complying with his request?

'I'll come if you think you really need me, Tom.'

'Bless you, Beth.' He pressed her arm firmly against his side. 'You're the best sport in this world. Some day soon I hope to be able to tell you just how much you mean to me.'

They had reached the stile which led them out on to one of the main roads which led up to the downs. He climbed over first, then he held out his hand to help her over. But in climbing over she caught her heel on one of the wooden bars and fell against him. He put his arms about her to break the fall and just for a moment, a fraction longer than was necessary, she lay against him, with his arms tight about her.

'Beth . . . ' His voice was muffled and hoarse.

'Yes,' It was a breath more than a whisper. Would he kiss her? Would he finally give in and tell her he loved her? Her whole body was tense, expectant, waiting. And then from the roadway came the insistent hooting of a motor horn.

His arms fell quickly to his sides. They both turned sharply; the Bentley had drawn up on the roadway a few yards from them. Chris was leaning out of the driver's seat, calling, 'Do you want a lift?' He added, laughing, 'You'd better accept the offer; it's almost lunchtime.'

Beth felt flustered and bitterly frustrated. What mightn't have happened if the Bentley hadn't been returning down the road after Mr. Tiswell had made a duty call on one of his parishioners? She could cheerfully have murdered Christopher. He must have seen Tom standing with his arms about her. Had he deliberately stopped and called to them?

She blushed inwardly, wondering what Mr. Tiswell might be thinking. But as they reached the car she saw that Chris's uncle was engrossed in some notes he had made for his Sunday sermon. She noticed a mischievous, almost malicious gleam in Christopher's eyes as she climbed into the back of the car. He seemed to be enjoying the situation and her anger against him mounted.

Tom was very silent during the short drive back to the vicarage. Was he, too, annoyed? Or — and the thought hurt her intolerably — was he secretly relieved?

6

They met Christopher's aunt, Jessica Tiswell, when they got back to the vicarage. She was certainly plump, but despite the extra pounds she had to carry she was brimful of energy. Beth thought that the popular theory that fat women in late middle age were inclined to be slothful and lacking in energy was certainly not borne out in Mrs. Tiswell's case. She kissed Christopher on both cheeks and welcomed Tom and Beth cordially.

'I'm afraid you'll have to fend for yourselves. Our domestic staff is practically non-existent. I have a dear old soul who comes in to clean when the mood takes her. But apart from that, what cleaning there is done, as well as the cooking, I do myself. But then few people these days can afford a resident staff; certainly not a poor country vicar.'

Her husband smiled at her with great affection, crinkling his kindly blue eyes. 'I hate servants hanging round anyhow. They're always dusting and moving my papers so that I can't find them.'

They all trooped into the kitchen while she finished preparing the lunch she had already started on, and all the while she was cooking she kept on asking Christopher questions, particularly about his father; his mother was dead; his uncle was Edward Landour. She wanted to know all about his job and his life in Tokyo. But she scarcely ever waited for him to give her a satisfactory answer before she plied him with another question.

'You're worse than the F.B.I., Auntie,' he said, laughing. 'I feel as though I'm up on a security or even a criminal charge.'

'Well, it's years since I've seen you and I want to know everything. I'm insatiably curious as you well know. Now where's that dratted uncle of yours? He always slips away to his study when there are chores to be done. But isn't that typical of a man? And I bet he actually believes that he's an immense help to me in the house.'

Lunch was a cheerful meal, which they ate in the breakfast room which adjoined the kitchen. The large dining room with the refectory table, she told them, was only used for special occasions. 'And those special occasions are as few as I can get away with,' she added grinning. 'The room's too large and too darned cold. No wonder most of our guests bring fur wraps and keep them on during dinner, even during the summer.'

She turned towards her nephew and asked, 'Are you still keen on riding, Christopher?'

He nodded. 'Of course,' and turned towards the others: 'How about you, Tom and Beth? Suppose we all go for a gallop tomorrow morning? We could hire horses from the stables. I suppose those stables in Alfriston are still functioning, Auntie?'

'Oh, everything in Alfriston is functioning the same this year as it has been for the past fifty years,' she replied with a half grin, half grimace.

'I'm afraid you'll have to count me out,' Tom said. 'I haven't ridden in donkey's years. If I did, I should have to take my breakfast off the mantelshelf for the rest of the week.'

'But you, Beth?' Christopher turned towards her. 'I'm sure you ride.'

'I do ride on Wimbledon Common at weekends,' she admitted. 'But I haven't brought any riding clothes down with me.'

'Don't worry about that, child,' Mrs. Tiswell said. 'Helen, my godchild, is often here of a weekend and leaves her jodhpurs down here. She's about your size; they should fit you nicely.'

'Then that's settled,' Chris said with obvious satisfaction. 'We'll go for a gallop over the downs in the morning, Beth.'

She looked towards Tom. He caught her glance and smiled. 'Why not, Beth?

You will enjoy it.'

Mrs. Tiswell, too, had caught the glance. She looked from one to the other of them, but unlike her usual self she made no comment. But she did remark afterwards to her husband: 'A pity. I thought Chris had found a nice girl at last with whom he could settle down. I admit I haven't seen much of her, but from what I've seen, I like the girl. She's not only pretty but she seems to be business-like and sensible. Besides, it's time Chris thought about settling down.'

Mr. Tiswell chuckled and there was a definite glint of humour in his pale blue eyes. 'I rather fancy Chris would agree with you, Jessie. Why else would he stop the car and make that awful din on the horn when he saw the girl slip off the stile and fall into Dillan's arms? Of course I said nothing; I was busy studying the notes for my Sunday sermon.'

The rest of the day passed pleasantly and uneventfully. Mrs. Tiswell had invited some old friends in to tea to remeet her nephew, and in the evening they went to a quite shocking performance of *The Mikado* in the local hall.

Tom made no effort to get Beth on her own. She was both relieved and disappointed. What he had said to her that morning, and especially the moment when she had fallen from the stile and he had caught her in his arms, had filled her with hope: yet at the same time she had a nagging sense of frustration. If he loved her, what did the situation about this unknown daughter really matter? As his wife, Beth would have welcomed the girl gladly.

She was awakened at six-thirty the following morning by a rat-tat-tat on the door of her bedroom.

'May I come in?' Christopher called.

She reached out and hastily seized a bed-jacket and wrapped it about her.

'Come in,' she called.

Chris was already dressed in jodhpurs, shirt and riding boots. He stood there very tall in the doorway, carrying a tray.

'I've brought you some tea and toast. You wouldn't want to go riding on an empty stomach. But get going, my poppet. I phoned through to the stables and the horses are ready. We don't want to miss too much of this glorious morning.'

'You've caught me without my make-up,' she accused him. 'I feel completely naked.'

He grinned as he placed the tray on the bedside table. 'I approve of make-up, but I must say you're one of the few women who look darned seductive without it.'

She flushed slightly. She had been paid many compliments but she had never been called seductive before. But Chris was nothing if not unconventional.

'Get on with you. I'll drink the tea and eat the toast while I'm dressing.'

'Don't be long. I'll be waiting for you on the front porch.'

She had tried on Helen's jodhpurs the night before. They fitted her perfectly, and the boots fitted too. She had brought a white shirt-blouse down with her and because the morning was cold she put on her cardigan.

Christopher had brought the Bentley round to the front door.

'I didn't ask Tom if I could borrow it, but I don't think he'll mind.'

'I wish he could have come along with us.'

'Of course you do — you're a loyal little soul. Or are you just pigheaded?' he said, and grinned.

There was a slight nip in the air but the sunshine sparkled on the country-side and on the distant downs. It took them less than ten minutes to reach the stables.

The horses were ready and saddled in the stableyard. Beth's horse was a ginger mare; Christopher's a large grey stallion.

'You can go round by the road,' the stableman told them, 'or you can cut across the fields, but you may have to hurdle a few hedges.'

'How do you feel about it, Beth?' Christopher asked.

'I have jumped, but I don't know how good I am at it. I'm quite game to try.'

'No,' Chris decided, 'we'll go round by the road. I don't want you to end up with a broken neck.'

Beth was secretly relieved. She hadn't had much experience in cross-country riding. She had an uneasy premonition that this would be very different from riding sedately on Wimbledon Common.

Ginger — that, she had been told, was her name — was a well-behaved horse. Jupiter, Christopher's mount, was far more sprightly and adventurous. But Christopher handled him expertly. Occasionally she glanced towards him; he sat very straight on his horse. She could see the strength of his muscles through the light shirt he wore. He wasn't wearing a jacket.

'Did you suggest to Tom that he ask

me to fly out to Tokyo with him?' she asked abruptly.

He didn't look at her. He looked down at the hand which held the reins. 'Why should you think that I suggested it, Beth?'

'You said something about my going to Tokyo the other night when we were out dining. I thought at the time it was nonsense; you were just spinning a fairytale, something you thought might please me.'

'Well, doesn't it please you? You're in love with Tom; you want to keep close to him, and on this occasion when he gets in touch — or tries to get in touch — with his long-lost daughter, I think is an occasion when you should keep close to him. He may need your help or your sympathy.'

'But *did* you suggest it, Chris?' she asked him directly.

He let the reins slacken and shrugged slightly. 'I may have. Does it matter? But directly the idea was put into his mind he seized on to it enthusiastically.'

He smiled slightly and added, 'He's such a straitlaced fellow; if I hadn't put it to him that it would be perfectly natural and beneficial for him to take his secretary along, he might have been squeamish. But directly I suggested it, he was all for it, as eager as a schoolboy.' He added soberly, 'You know, Beth, as far as adult emotional experiences are concerned, I think Tom reached a sort of maturity at twenty, but he's never gone further than that. He's been living all his life in a dream of the past, and that isn't good for any man. But you're coming, aren't you? The whole situation is going to be darned difficult, and I've a feeling you'll be able to help Tom considerably. In fact, if Michiko refuses to see him, I've already got a scheme in mind, and that closely concerns you.'

'Concerns me?' she echoed. 'But what do you want me to do, Chris?'

'You'll learn all in good time. For the moment I am going to say nothing further about it. Anyhow, the project I have in mind may not be necessary.'

She had to be content with that for he would say nothing further on the subject.

He urged his horse into a gallop and she followed suit. He was an excellent horseman. She felt in comparison that she made a very poor showing.

Presently they reached the bridle-path that led over the downs. They had to ride in single file; he took the lead and she followed. The air was sharper the higher they rose, but the atmosphere was crystal clear. The whole countryside stretched beneath them. It was as though they were looking down upon it out of a plane. She felt strangely exhilarated, the feeling you have before something very important is going to happen in your life. Was it the thought of going to Japan, a country she had always longed to see? But she knew that as far as that trip was concerned she had doubts and misgivings that ran alongside with her sense of pleasure. How would Tom feel once he was united with his daughter? Would his feelings change towards herself? Would he no longer feel the need for her companionship, even for her love? He had spoken yesterday of his need for her, but he hadn't asked her to marry him.

Yet the way he had held her arm closely pressed against the side of his body, the way his arms had closed around her when she had tripped climbing over the stile, all pointed to the fact that he loved her. They were little things for her to feed her own love upon, but she clung tenaciously to the thought of those few incidents. Tom, she knew, was extremely diffident and reserved when it came to showing his emotions. A gesture of love which might seem small, even trivial, where other men were concerned, meant much more when such a gesture came from him. Or was she fooling herself, making herself believe something because she wanted to believe it?

She tried to put these thoughts out of

her mind and give herself up wholly to the pleasure of the moment, of this brisk ride across the downs on that early spring morning, the wind teasing her hair, the sun hot on her face.

Presently the bridle-path led them back on to the road once more. Christopher hadn't spoken for some time.

'Did you enjoy that?'

She nodded, her eyes shining. 'It was wonderful. I felt as though I was riding on top of the world.'

She noticed that he was looking at her intently, and a faint flush rose to her cheeks. She had seen Chris look at her like that before and it never failed to embarrass her.

'You're flushing,' he commented. 'Don't you like my looking at you?' And then he added in a low voice as she didn't speak, 'Please don't mind, Beth, but you make quite a picture with the sun shining on your hair. It's almost more red than golden in this light; and the wind has played havoc with it; it looks like a small boy's tousled head. I may be losing my mind, but to me you look quite devastatingly pretty. Have you been told that before?'

She nodded slowly. 'Perhaps.'

'Of course. It wouldn't be my luck to be the first man to tell you the truth about yourself.' There was a half-mocking, half-serious note in his voice and he was still gazing at her intently.

Her feeling of embarrassment increased, but besides that, she was aware of a strange sense of exhilaration. She glanced down at her wristwatch. 'Goodness, we'll be shockingly late for breakfast.'

He glanced at his own watch. 'You're right. I'd no idea the time could pass so rapidly. If you're really good at jumping hedges we can take the shortcut back to the vicarage across the fields. We could tie the horses up at the vicarage and take them back to the stables after breakfast.'

She still had that same sense of exhilaration, even of recklessness. 'Why not? I haven't done much jumping, but

I'm sure I'll be all right.'

He looked a little doubtful. 'You wouldn't prefer to go round by the road?'

She shook her head decisively. 'No. I'll enjoy riding across the fields.'

She cleared the first hedge easily and the second, but at the third she may have felt over-confident or the horse may have stumbled, but suddenly she was conscious of floating over his head and that was all she remembered.

She didn't know how long she lay there unconscious, but as she came slowly out of her dazed condition she was dimly aware of a man bending over her. He was kissing her cheeks and her eyes and her lips.

'Beth! Beth darling, say something! Say something!' he was beseeching.

'Tom!' She didn't know whether she had said the name aloud. But it seemed to her in her semi-conscious state that it must have been Tom. Who else could have been kissing her, calling her darling?

A few moments later, when she opened her eyes and regained complete consciousness, she told herself she must have dreamt it all. Tom wasn't anywhere around, and Chris was kneeling beside her, looking anxious.

'You all right, Beth? I felt you over while you were unconscious; there don't seem to be any bones broken.'

'I'm sure I'll be all right,' she said faintly. 'Was I unconscious long?'

'I saw you fall and rode straight over. You gave me a shock, young woman. What happened?'

'I don't really know, but suddenly I seemed to be flying through the air. After that I didn't remember a thing. Was the horse hurt?'

'No. He galloped away with my horse, both heading for home, I take it. I suppose I should have tethered both the brutes to the stile, but I was too anxious about you. I'll carry you back to the vicarage; it's only a short distance.'

She smiled. 'That's a very gallant

thought, Christopher, but I'm sure I shall be perfectly able to walk.'

'What's wrong with me carrying you?'

'Nothing, but I don't think it will be necessary. Just help me to my feet.'

He drew her to her feet and supported her with an arm about her waist. She was a little unsteady on her feet at first, but presently she began walking in a perfectly normal manner. She didn't need his arm supporting her.

'I'm all right now.' She moved slightly away from him. 'Thanks for the help, Chris.'

Immediately his arm fell from her. 'That's quite all right,' he said in a casual manner. 'I admit I was a bit worried at first, but you don't seem to have suffered any actual injury.' His voice seemed to dismiss the whole incident. It made her more convinced than ever that what she had imagined was a hallucination.

She had read that people recovering consciousness after a fall or a blow upon the head were often subject to hallucinations. The very fact that she had imagined it was Tom bending over her, kissing her, calling her darling, strengthened her conviction.

'I'm sorry we couldn't wait breakfast for you,' Mrs. Tiswell apologised when they appeared in the doorway, 'But your uncle, Christopher, has to be at the church.'

'I'm sorry we're late.' Christopher explained briefly what had happened. He concluded by saying, 'But apparently the gal is all right. No bones broken, and she answers questions in a completely lucid manner. Now I must go and phone the stables to see if those darned horses have got back safely.'

'I've already put your breakfast in the oven to keep warm,' Mrs. Tiswell said. She added solicitously to Beth, 'Why don't you go and lie down, dear? You're probably badly shaken up. I'll bring something up to your room on a tray.'

'Yes, do that, Beth,' Tom said, with a note of authority. 'I'll help you upstairs.'

She didn't protest. She had to admit to herself she did feel rather shaken, though she didn't know whether it was through that strange half-dream she had had or the result of the fall. But she welcomed Tom's supporting arm as she climbed the old oak staircase. It was sheer heaven to relax against him, to let him help her down on to the bed and to pull off her riding boots. His good-looking face was heavy with anxiety. He kept asking her if she thought he should call a doctor.

She smiled. 'No, Tom. I really feel perfectly all right. But I'm a little tried after the ride.'

He said angrily, 'You should have come home by the road. I could murder Christopher for having allowed you to jump those hedges.'

She stretched out a hand to him. 'Don't worry, please, Tom. And it wasn't Chris's fault. I was sure I could manage them. It was my fault — conceit probably. The air was so lovely up on the downs; it must have intoxicated me. I was sure I was equal to anything.'

'I don't know what I should do if anything happened to you, Beth,' he said unsteadily. 'I rely upon you for so many things.'

Her smile deepened and was reflected in her amber-coloured eyes. 'I'm glad you do, Tom. It's a lovely feeling to believe you're wanted.'

He pressed her hand harder. 'It's the truth, Beth. I got such a shock when Chris first told us of the accident, and then I found myself wondering, if anything had happened to you, could I possibly get along without you?'

'You'd be all right, Tom. You'll always be able to get along under your own steam, but I'm glad you feel you need me.' There was a sudden mistiness in her eyes.

He leant farther over her. 'Beth . . . '

Mrs. Tiswell, panting from the ascent of the stairs, appeared with the breakfast tray. 'Here you are, my dear. Eat what you can, but don't be afraid of leaving anything you can't manage.

Christopher asked me to tell you that the horses returned to the stable safely. Now I'm going to shoo this young man out of your room; I think you need complete relaxation.'

Beth would have liked Tom to have stayed with her while she ate her breakfast. What had he been going to say when Mrs. Tiswell had interrupted them? Was it what she had been waiting for; that had given her that keen sense of expectancy all morning ever since Christopher and she had started out on the ride?

But Mrs. Tiswell was used to having her instructions obeyed. She literally marched Tom out of the room.

7

The modern magic carpet is undoubtedly the aeroplane. But this twentieth-century magic carpet is real, not a fantasy. Beth stood in an attractively furnished hotel room and wondered if she could be actually here in Japan. It seemed incredible. It was such a short while ago that they had left the London Airport in a jet-propelled plane. She felt completely exhausted, but at the same time tremendously excited. She had suffered no ill-effects from the fall, which was as well, for the ten days before they had embarked on the flight had been tremendously busy ones.

Christopher had been away most of the time on flying visits to various friends he had made while he had been up at Oxford. Many nights Tom and she had worked late at the office getting everything in readiness for his assistant to take over. They'd take half an hour or so off for dinner, but it was always a rushed meal in the small restaurant situated in a lane off Piccadilly which they usually patronised. The restaurant served typically well cooked English food, but the décor had no romantic trappings where you might be encouraged to linger over your food.

In the short time that intervened after they had returned from the weekend in Sussex and before they had set out on their flight, Tom had been preoccupied, not only with business, but, she guessed, with the prospect of arriving in Tokyo and confronting his daughter Michiko. In fact, during that period his behaviour was so impersonal towards her, she wondered if he regretted the things he had said to her walking in the fields behind the Sussex vicarage. There were times when her sense of unhappiness and frustration were so great that she had been inclined to tell him that she wouldn't go with them to Tokyo after all. But she never did tell him for she knew in her heart that she was longing to go.

And now she was here in a charmingly furnished room with an adjoining bathroom at the Imperial Hotel, the best hotel in Tokyo, and certainly, with its pagoda-like appearance, its gardens laid out in a typically traditional Japanese style, the most attractive to tourists. It had been a thrilling day from the moment their attention had been drawn by the airliner steward to the beautiful spectacle of snow-capped Mount Fujiyama, rising up in the low-lying clouds, to the time the plane had dropped height so that they could look down on the surrounding countryside; the green pine-timbered mountains, the terraced fields of rice, the green-brown waters of Tokyo Bay. She had found herself thinking of the popular song which Christopher and she had danced to that first night at the Savoy:

'*I stood in the moonlight and watched the lights flicker,*
Flickering on the water of Tokyo Bay;
Alone there I stood, for I was a stranger,
I came in a steamer that arrived that day.'

She had wondered if Christopher was thinking of that, too. He was just over the aisle from where she and Tom were sitting. He had insisted she sit with Tom, and though that was, of course, where she wanted to sit, Tom had talked very little. His preoccupation of the past two weeks had still been with him; in fact he had grown more preoccupied and silent as they had drawn nearer to Japan. She could see, too, by the way he had fidgeted, by his inability to concentrate on a book or a magazine, that he was nervous, quite desperately nervous, and she had never thought of Tom as a man who would give way to nerves.

She had wished he would talk to her about his worry; not that she could advise him; but talking to her of his coming meeting with his daughter might help to relieve some of the tension which she knew had been mounting in him ever since the jet-propelled plane had taken off from London.

Finally they had touched down at Haneda Airport. She was amazed at its size and extreme modernity.

Christopher had told them as they walked across the tarmac, carrying their hand luggage, that it was not only the largest and most modern in Asia, but that few airports in the world could rival it.

'Wait till you see the other modern buildings, especially those in the Marunouchi quarter, which is the trading centre,' he had told them. 'The new buildings in Tokyo are as spectacularly modern as in any city in the world.'

Beth had given a wry little smile.

'Somehow I've always thought of Japan as being quite different; quaint and olde worlde, full of cherry blossom and picturesque shrines.'

'There's all that, too,' Christopher had told her enthusiastically. 'It's full of the most beautiful temples and shrines and palaces thousands of years old. But despite its antiquities the commercial cities of Japan are amongst the most modern and prosperous in the world.' He had laughed that gay laugh she had come to associate with him. 'But I don't want to sound like a tourist guide. You'll be able to see it all for yourself. I cabled and booked you in at the Imperial Hotel. It's not only the best in Tokyo but the most Japanese of all the tourist hotels, except, of course, the real Japanese inn.'

They had no trouble with the Customs and Immigration Officials. Beth had found them exceedingly polite. Tom and she had 'Tourist' marked on their cards, and more than one official, bowing to them, had wished them a very happy stay in Japan.

'I must say some of our own Customs men might take a lesson from the Japanese,' Tom had commented with a rueful grin. 'Is their manner a pose or are they genuinely keen to welcome you?'

Christopher rubbed one finger down the side of his rather long nose. 'I've been here several years and even now I can't answer that question. Some are naturally friendly; but with a great number of them it is part of an age-old tradition. They are extremely formal and polite, not only in their dealings with foreigners but with each other. They find it almost impossible to understand our easy casual manners. You'll have to be very careful in dealing with them. I made one or two bad slips when I first came over here.'

The American limousine, which belonged to the firm and was driven by a Japanese chauffeur in smart livery, was waiting for them.

It was a fairly long drive into Tokyo

and Beth had found the outlying suburbs depressing. The buildings were small, impoverished and cramped together. Most of the shops were mere stalls opening out on to the streets, and the men and women she had expected to see in colourful Japanese kimonos mostly wore drab ill-fitting and shoddy European clothes. Occasionally you saw a man or woman in a kimono, but even these were drab garments.

They drove past the Imperial Palace where you had an occasional glimpse of green pines behind high walls. The Palace is encircled by a moat where the swans still manage to look white despite the soot of the commercialised city. They passed high office buildings and large stores. The pavements were crowded with hurrying men and women, all dressed in European spring clothes, and presently they had turned in the curved drive of the Imperial Hotel with its quaint pagoda-like structure, its flowering shrubs, and Beth had felt that she had at last seen a slice of the Japan she had always pictured.

They went up the stairs through the glass door into the reception lounge. Chris saw that they had their room reservations and then had excused himself, saying that he wanted to get back to the office to see what was cooking.

'I'll be back at five,' he had told them, 'and then we can have a drink. Afterwards I'll take you to a *suki-yaki* restaurant and then we can go out and see the sights of the town.'

'I didn't come here to see the sights of Tokyo,' Tom had said tersely, showing the state his nerves were in.

'I know,' Christopher said soothingly. 'But it mightn't be expedient to rush matters. I'll consult Mr. Oswara. He's one of the principals of the detective agency I employed — Oswara and Hajo. It was through them we were able to track down the aunt and subsequently get into touch with the Itos.'

'I'd like to meet Mr. Oswara,' Tom had said urgently.

'You shall,' Christopher had told him placatingly. 'I'll phone from the office and if he has anything fresh to report I'll telephone you immediately, Tom. And since you're anxious to meet him, Tom, Mr. Oswara might come round this evening and have a drink with us.'

'Now that I'm so close to her, I can scarcely wait to see Michiko.'

Christopher had looked at him almost pityingly and shook his head slowly. 'I know you have high hopes, Tom, but I shouldn't build too much on Michiko consenting to see you.'

'Then what the devil am I doing over here?' Tom had asked angrily.

'I don't think you could have stayed away and had any peace of mind,' Christopher had returned quietly. 'And it's quite on the cards that she may be persuaded to see you.'

'I'm sorry I spoke sharply, but this inaction gets me down,' Tom had rumbled.

Christopher had burst out laughing. 'But you've only just arrived, man.

While I'm trying to get some information for you, why don't you and Beth take a stroll down the Ginza? It's quite a sight — the next best thing to Broadway.'

But Tom had brushed the suggestion aside.

'I didn't come here as a darned tourist,' he had said shortly. 'I'll wait up in my room in case you should want to telephone me, Chris.'

Now Beth showered and changed. She had told Tom she would lie down. But she didn't feel tired. She glanced at her wristwatch. It was half past three, an hour and a half before the scheduled meeting.

She went down in the lift into the foyer, which is on two levels, the upper half being furnished as a lounge where tea and drinks are served. The doorman, who spoke perfect English, suggested a taxi. But she smiled and said she preferred to walk and asked the way to the Ginza.

He showed her the direction and she

started walking, excited and thrilled with everything she saw. The roads were crowded with cars and hooting taxi cabs. She had never seen anything like the speed at which the Japanese taxi man drove, honking his horn continually, dodging in and out of the traffic. She had read somewhere that Tokyo was the noisiest city in the world and she could well believe it.

The pavements were crowded with business men and women hurrying to and fro and with shoppers, many of whom were clustered round the windows of the big stores that rivalled anything she had seen in Europe, and the smaller shops where everything imaginable was offered for sale — printed silks of every design, beautifully embroidered satins and handsome brocades. She had never seen such glorious materials and she determined she would have some dresses made while she was out here. Chris, who knew Tokyo well, would advise her.

She had changed some money at the

airport and knew that a hundred yen was the equivalent of a two-shilling piece. None of the prices seemed excessive and the watches, fountain pens, binoculars and cameras she saw displayed seemed almost ridiculously cheap. There were numerous jewellery stores which displayed cultured pearls exquisitely set in necklets, ear-rings, brooches, bracelets and rings. Some were of white cultured pearls, others, expensive, a deep blue-grey colour.

'I wish I had a sizeable bank balance,' Beth thought with an inner twisted smile. 'Goodness, what fun you'd have shopping here!'

She passed many restaurants and studied the menus displayed outside. Most of the dishes meant little to her, but from what Chris had told her, she recognised the names — *suki-yaki* and *tempura*. They had lunched early on the plane and the sight of these exciting-sounding menus made her feel hungry.

She glanced at her wristwatch and

was shocked to find that she had been so thrilled by the sights on the Ginza that she had forgotten the time; it was after five. She was nervous about taking a taxi, but if she didn't she would be late in getting back to the hotel.

As though sensing her need a driver drew up by the kerb and beckoned invitingly: 'You want to go somewhere, lady?'

She breathed a sigh of relief when she heard him address her in English.

'Yes, I want to go back to the Imperial Hotel.'

'You step in, lady. A few minutes and we are at Imperial Hotel.'

It was a small cab, a little seventy-yen Renault, one she learned later, of the sixty to seventy-yen Renaults which had got themselves the name of *kamikaze*, meaning suicide cars, because of the way they hurtled themselves at a suicidal speed through the traffic.

She leant forward and gasped, 'Must we go so fast?'

He turned his head and his small

seal-brown eyes glinted mischievously. 'I not go fast, lady. But all tourists afraid of Japanese taxis.'

When she reached the Imperial she gave him a hundred-yen bill and he bowed his gratitude.

Tom was pacing up and down the foyer. He looked really agitated. 'Where the devil have you been, Beth? I've phoned your room repeatedly but there hasn't been any reply.'

'I didn't feel tired so I took a walk down the Ginza. You said you didn't want to go out, you wanted to stick by the telephone.'

'I know. But I didn't know you would go out alone. I've been nearly out of my mind with worry.'

'I'm sorry, Tom. I thought you were too wrapped up in your own affairs to worry what I did this afternoon.'

They walked up the stairs into the main lounge, beautifully furnished with Japanese antiques and with a glorious cherry blossom tree with pale pink blossoms growing from a huge pot.

'I'm sorry I'm late, but the shop windows along the Ginza are so fascinating.'

'But anything might have happened to you.'

She was touched by his concern. She felt a surge of happiness inside her and she laughed.

'Apart from the taxi cabs — and all the drivers should be arrested for dangerous driving — this is one of the politest and I'm sure most law-abiding cities I have ever been in. If anyone bumps into you, they stop and bow and apologise. At least,' she smiled slightly, 'I presume they're apologising.'

'If you'd really wanted to go, I'd have gone with you,' he persisted. 'I suppose you think I was selfish wanting to wait in by the phone.'

'Of course not, Tom. You're disturbed and anxious about your interview with Michiko. Has Chris telephoned?'

He nodded. 'He telephoned a short while ago, saying he would be a little late. He is bringing Mr. Oswara with him.'

'I'll slip up to my room and powder and meet you down here, Tom.'

Surprisingly, he caught hold of her hand. 'Don't be gone long. I had such a scare when I found you weren't in the hotel. I don't want to let you out of my sight again.'

'I'm sorry I worried you, Tom.' But she felt happy as she went up in the lift.

When she came down again into the lounge, Christopher and Mr. Oswara had joined Tom. Mr. Oswara was a shortish, slight man with black hair, dark brown eyes, a pale yellow skin and flat cheekbones. He wore a European suit, rather exaggerated in cut, which emphasised rather than concealed his taut, strong muscles. He wasn't good looking, but then Beth had decided from the short while she had been here that very few Japanese men could be described as good looking, whereas the women were not only dainty and petite but usually pretty and very often beautiful.

When she was introduced, Mr. Oswara

bowed to her several times, drawing in his breath with a peculiar hissing sound.

'Let's go into one of the alcoves in the passageway,' Chris suggested. 'We can order some drinks and can talk undisturbed.'

The corridor was wide, with small travel offices on one side and on the other alcoves where you could sit and talk and open the french windows which led out into the garden. They gave you a sense of privacy and a charming glimpse into a formal Japanese garden.

Christopher suggested to Tom and Beth that they might try sake, which was the chief Japanese drink, a colourless rice wine. 'I've developed quite a taste for it,' he said. 'But you needn't be scared; it isn't especially potent.'

Tom and Beth said they would be glad to try it and Mr. Oswara looked gratified. They talked trivialities while the waiter fetched the sake. The liquor was served to each person in a delightful white pottery container with saxe blue decorations. They drank it out of tiny pottery bowls. Beth was much more intrigued by the way it was served than by the wine itself. She thought it rather tasteless.

Tom had been showing signs of impatience while the sake was being served, and directly the waiter had gone, he drew his chair forward.

'Well, Mr. Oswara, what have you got to tell me?'

'I am afraid that the news I have for you is not good, Mr. Dillan,' Mr. Oswara said in his almost faultless English. But he spoke it with a slight American accent. 'As requested by Mr. Landour in his air-letter, I arranged another interview with Mr. and Mrs. Ito. It was not easy; they were very reluctant to grant the interview and told me over the telephone that nothing would come of it. But I was insistent and they finally gave way. They own a large home in the Azabu district, and take in foreign students as paying guests

— but not Americans; they are adamant on that point. Pardon, gentlemen, but I've already explained to Mr. Landour that Mr. and Mrs. Ito have a hatred of Americans.'

Mr. Oswara drew in a deep sucking breath and went on: 'They are not friendly or in any sense co-operative. They flatly refused to have me meet their foster daughter, Michiko-san. They insisted, as they had insisted before, that it was Michiko-san's own wish that she have nothing whatever to do with the man who had betrayed her mother. I even suggested that if they would co-operate with me it might be decidedly to their financial advantage. Perhaps I should not have said that. The Japanese are a very proud race and few of us will accept a bribe when our conscience dictates otherwise. They both rose to their feet and formally asked me to leave the house.' He shrugged and added, 'I could only go. I regret very much, Mr. Landour and Mr. Dillan, I have failed in my mission.

You will wish me to give up the case, and undoubtedly you will find some more worthy agent.' He looked very dejected. Obviously his professional pride had been hurt.

'Nonsense! We wouldn't hear of you dropping the case. You have accomplished so much.' And Chris looked towards Tom for agreement.

'I'm sure you've done the best you can, Mr. Oswara,' Tom said, and added angrily, 'All the same, I am determined to see Michiko, even if I have to force my way into the house. The Itos may be Michiko's foster parents, but it wasn't a legal adoption.'

'Michiko-san was entrusted to the Itos by her aunt after the death of her mother. She paid them regularly until her own death and settled a small sum of money on the girl. That, with what the young lady earns with her teaching, enables her to be independent.'

'Michiko is teaching?' Tom asked sharply.

Mr. Oswara nodded. 'She teaches in a neighbouring kindergarten.'

141

'But she is little more than a child herself,' Tom objected.

'Your daughter is seventeen,' the Japanese reminded him. 'I understand she is a very intelligent young lady.'

'Couldn't I go and see her at the kindergarten?' Tom suggested.

'It might cause trouble, even a scandal for the young lady. I have made inquiries and it is understood in the neighbourhood and also in the kindergarten that Michiko-san is of pure Japanese blood.'

'That may be so, but I'm not going placidly to accept the situation.' He still sounded angry.

'I quite understand, Mr. Dillan,' the detective said sympathetically. 'I hope in my humble capacity I can be of further help to you. I have thought that if someone could enter the Itos' household and gain Michiko-san's confidence, that might be of some help. She must not know, of course, that the person who enters the household has any connection with her father — humble apologies,

Mr. Dillan — whom she professes to despise. The Itos, who regard her as a daughter and wouldn't want her to leave their home, have undoubtedly guided and prejudiced her. But although she professes to hate the Americans, she may be disturbed in her mind and welcome a confidante.' He bowed to Tom. 'Merely a humble suggestion, Mr. Dillan.'

'I think it a damn' good suggestion,' Tom said thoughtfully. 'We badly need an ally in the enemy camp. But if someone was planted in the household, wouldn't the Itos smell a rat?'

Mr. Oswara raised his hand to his lips and chuckled behind it: 'You mean rat make bad smell, Mr. Dillan? Very funny. But it should not be too difficult. I have advertisement here in my pocket.' He reached for his wallet and took from it a small clipping from a newspaper. 'It says here that foreign students are welcome for board and lodging at the home of Minami and Maki Ito.'

'But if they're so damned prejudiced against Americans why should they welcome foreign students?' Christopher ejaculated.

'There are many foreign students besides Americans,' Mr. Oswara said. 'There are Germans and Russians, and many Eastern countries send their young men and women here to study at our universities and acquire our culture. I have a list here of the guests boarding at the Itos' residence: Wang Lee and John Chao, both Chinese gentlemen; Zontan Andrassi, a Hungarian; and Ivan Surkov, of Russian nationality.'

'A curious list of guests,' Chris commented thoughtfully. 'They sound like Commies to me, or at the best, fellow-travellers.'

'I believe you are right, Mr. Landour,' Mr. Oswara agreed seriously, 'though Mr. John Chao is a British subject and comes from Hong Kong. There is a Japanese also boarding in the house, a nephew of Mrs. Ito, Yaizu Seki. I understand a gentleman named Dr. Frank Rickard, who has a surgery with an adjoining flat nearby, takes most of his meals with the Itos.'

'Dr. Frank Rickard,' Tom put in. 'At least he sounds either English or American.'

Mr. Oswara smiled slightly, showing yellowish teeth. 'He is certainly not American or he would not be practically a member of the Itos' household. He, like your daughter, is of mixed parentage, Mr. Dillan. His father was English; his mother Japanese. I met him while I was making investigations in the neighbourhood. As a matter of fact, I called at his surgery on the pretext of stomach trouble. I wanted to see if I could find out anything further about the Itos' establishment.'

'And did you find out anything?' Christopher put in.

'Nothing of any importance to you gentlemen,' Mr. Oswara said. 'He is more English than Japanese in appearance, but I gather he, too, is prejudiced against his father's race. Though he graduated in England, he preferred to come back to this country and work for the poor of his mother's people.'

'It certainly sounds a very curious set-up,' Tom commented. 'And one I don't like my daughter being associated with. I should like to get her away from the influence of that household as soon as possible.'

'It will not be easy, Mr. Dillan,' Mr. Oswara observed thoughtfully. 'Ito-san and his wife are devoted to Michiko-san, and from what they say, she is equally attached to them. But that is, of course, what *they* say. But it would appear, anyhow, that they have great influence over the young lady. That is why I suggest that we might try to get someone besides yourself, Mr. Dillan, or Mr. Landour who is known to the Itos, to gain the young lady's friendship and persuade her that American gentlemen are both generous and kind, only trying to keep the peace in the world.' Again he gave that slight, half-ingratiating smile. 'Then she might be persuaded to meet her father and talk to him. I'm sure if she could be brought to do so and Mr. Dillan could tell her the truth about himself and his relationship with her mother, she might come to feel very differently. She might even wish to join her life with his.'

'Yes,' Tom said in a deep undertone. 'That's what I want. It's what I want most in the whole world — my daughter, Eiko's daughter, under my protection, in my own home.'

Beth respected the sincerity of his wish and she believed she understood it, but she wouldn't have been human if she hadn't felt slightly hurt. He had said that what he wanted most in the whole world was to be reconciled with his daughter. She told herself she understood, but the hurt remained in her heart. Because she felt ashamed of it; because she felt she must do something to help Tom — and why else had she come out here? — an idea suddenly occurred to her.

She spoke impulsively: 'Why shouldn't I go to the Itos' household as a paying guest? They don't know me. They have no reason to know that I have any connection with Michiko's father or with Christopher, or with you, Mr. Oswara. I could pretend to be studying the Japanese language. There must be some language institutes here where I could enrol.'

'But naturally,' Mr. Oswara was sitting forward on his chair, his seal-brown eyes snapping excitedly. 'That is a very worthwhile idea, Miss Rainer, and to have you under the same roof with Michiko-san might be most advantageous to Mr. Dillan's interests. I understand you are his secretary; then you are obviously someone he can trust.'

Tom was looking at her earnestly and with gratitude.

'You'd really do this for me, Beth?'

'Didn't I come out here to help you?' she asked rather sharply and added, turning towards Mr. Oswara: 'How old is that advertisement? Do you think the vacancies will be already filled?'

'It appeared only yesterday,' the Japanese detective said. 'I understand that

148

to stay at the Itos' is by way of being expensive. Not many poor students can afford the prices they charge. Certainly few Japanese students. I suppose that is why they advertise for foreign students. Mr. Ito is in business, but only in a small way.'

'At least I can try,' Beth said as though the matter were settled. 'Should I telephone them first?'

'I think not wise,' Mr. Oswara said. 'They might be suspicious of a mere voice on the phone. Besides, undoubtedly they will wish to ask you questions.'

It would certainly be an adventure, and although she had lived very quietly, she was of an adventurous nature.

The only objection came from Christopher, and that was sharp and vehement: 'I don't like it at all,' he said decisively. 'Beth may be exposing herself to danger. Supposing the Itos found out her connection with you, Tom?'

'Even so, what could they do but turn me out of the house?' Beth argued. She had made the suggestion on an impulse, but now she was passionately determined to carry it through.

'I still don't like the idea,' Christopher objected again. 'Possibly the Itos might not harm Beth, but she might be subjected to considerable unpleasantness.'

'I'm quite willing to risk that if it would help Tom in any way,' Beth said determinedly.

Tom had been enthusiastic at first but now he looked undecided. 'You might find yourself in an embarrassing situation, Beth. Chris may be right.'

She gave a small laugh and tilted her small pretty head at a defiant angle. 'I can put up with a little embarrassment, even unpleasantness, if need be. As I said, they couldn't possibly do me any physical harm. If the Itos took me in I could at least make contact with Michiko. Please don't argue any more; it's obviously the best plan we have. Otherwise we may sit around here for days, even weeks, accomplishing nothing. Just how do you think I should go about it, Mr. Oswara?'

'I can arrange to have you driven out to the Itos' residence in Azabu tomorrow morning. I shall also take the precaution of enrolling you at the International Language Centre here in Tokyo and of telephoning the Itos from there to make an appointment for you. That is in case the Itos decide to check up on you before they accept you under their roof.'

He turned towards Tom: 'I think it would also be wise if Miss Rainer went to stay at a much less pretentious hotel and preferably a Japanese hotel. If, as I said before, they do try to check up, it would make Miss Rainer seem a more serious student of the Japanese language and culture if she were staying in a Japanese inn. I know of such an inn, run by a friend of mine, in the Akasaka district. They would make you welcome and comfortable, Miss Rainer, but of course the inn is run in the Japanese style.'

'That sounds excellent.' She smiled at the doubtful expressions on the other two men's faces. 'Please don't worry about me; I'm sure I'm going to enjoy this adventure.'

Mr. Oswara glanced at his wristwatch. 'I think if Miss Rainer is going to register at the inn, it would be expedient for me to drive her out there now. Later, if you two gentlemen wish her to spend the evening with you, I can drive her back here. In the morning I shall send a car to the inn to drive her to the Itos' home. You do not mind sleeping Japanese style on the floor, Miss Rainer?'

Beth gave a wry smile. 'By the time I get to bed tonight I should say I would be able to sleep anywhere.'

'Good.' Mr. Oswara nodded approval. 'We can start now. But it will be necessary to take some luggage with you, Miss Rainer.'

Beth rose to her feet. 'I'll pack a suitcase. If I succeed in getting into the Itos' I can take some more of my luggage there tomorrow. Will you all excuse me? I won't be more than a few minutes.'

She had been tired previously, but now she felt full of energy and excitement. She slipped into an off-white wool coat and packed a few things for overnight into her smallest suitcase. The case wasn't heavy; she carried it downstairs herself and joined the others.

'My car is outside,' Mr. Oswara said. He took her suitcase from her and the four of them went through the lounge down the steps and into the foyer.

A group of American tourists had just arrived and were talking animatedly as they registered at the reception desk. Tom took hold of her arm and drew her a little behind the other two men.

'I can't tell you how grateful I am to you, Beth.' His voice was deep with emotion. 'I shall try in some way to repay you for what you're doing for me.'

'I don't need repayment from you, Tom.' She hadn't meant it to be, but her voice was edged.

'Even if you don't succeed, I shall be eternally grateful.'

153

But it wasn't gratitude she wanted from him. Couldn't he understand that? She felt suddenly tired and for some reason almost afraid of what she had undertaken. She tried to speak lightly: 'Please don't worry, Tom; I shall meet you for lunch tomorrow and report.'

'Bless you, my dear,' he muttered. His hand touched her arm; he gripped it tightly for a moment.

Her brief flare of anger towards him evaporated. 'I hope I'll have something successful to report, something you're wanting to hear, Tom.'

They had reached the drive. Chris was waiting and told them that Mr. Oswara had gone to fetch his car. It arrived a few minutes later with Mr. Oswara at the wheel.

Chris gave her his card with a number scribbled on the back of it: 'Here's my private number, if you should want me.' His long thin face slipped sideways in a grin, but his blue eyes were very tender. 'You're a game kid, Beth.'

8

The street where the Japanese inn was situated was in a suburb of timbered houses behind high fences, with a smattering of small open-fronted shops, many of which had already lit their hanging paper lanterns to offset the dusk of the coming evening. She noticed that many of the men as they clumped down the pavement on their wooden *getas* were wearing kimonos or happi-coats over European trousers; the women also mostly wore kimonos with the obi, a tight sash that has a bowlike effect at the back. Some of them had young babies strapped to their backs.

The inn was a timbered two-storied building, larger than the rest of the surrounding houses, set back from the road, with a small rock garden surrounding a goldfish pond on which a fountain sprayed. It was a charming setting and the inn itself was attractive, built in the popular pagoda-shaped style. Mr. Oswara, carrying Beth's suitcase, stepped up on to the porch and rang the front doorbell.

A few moments later a young Japanese woman opened the door. She was dressed in a sky-blue kimono with a deeper blue obi, and her hair was dressed high and lacquered in the traditional Japanese fashion. She bowed deeply several times to both of them and then Mr. Oswara addressed her rapidly in Japanese. She bowed again and smiled, and after they had removed their shoes and changed into house-slippers which were standing lined up on the porch, she led them into a small foyer rather dimly lit by a hanging Japanese lantern. There was a reception desk. She slid gracefully behind it and produced a register, which Beth signed. She noticed that all the other signatures were in Japanese characters. The girl, whom Mr. Oswara addressed as Tokuko-san, said '*Doozo*,' which Beth came to know meant please or thank you. She beckoned to Beth to follow her and led her up the stairs, along a corridor, and then slid back a paper-covered door, standing back for Beth to enter.

Beth took it that this was to be her bedroom, but it was unlike any bedroom she had ever seen in her life. The floor was covered with *tatami*, thick finely woven reed mats about six inches by three, wedged tightly together, creamy in colour and soft to walk upon. The three sides of the room were papered on thin woodwork. There was an alcove with a scroll of Japanese writing, a low shelf on which stood a delightful arrangement of bright pink cherry blossom and other spring flowers. The only furniture in the room was a table with a shaded lamp and some cushions. Beth wondered where she was supposed to sleep.

The woman bowed again and said 'Doozo,' and then slid back a screen door to reveal a large well-equipped cupboard. At one side there were drawers and hanging space, and in the other half was a mattress and bedding.

Beth smiled and nodded to show she was satisfied.

Again the woman led her out of the room along the corridor and down the stairs.

'Is everything to your pleasure, Miss Rainer?' Mr. Oswara said, bowing and drawing in his breath with that curious hissing sound.

'It's a delightful room.' Beth smiled and added, 'But from our point of view, it isn't furnished at all.'

'We Japanese do not like cluttered rooms. We like every room to give a suggestion of space.'

He said something in Japanese to the proprietress. She bowed and smiled as though he had been paying her a compliment. Then he turned back towards Beth.

'I have arranged for your dinner. It will be served in your room. I have ordered *tempura*, which is one of our main dishes, it is quite delicious, small pieces of a various assortment of fish, fried in batter; after which the maid will make up your bed and you may retire when you wish. I have already paid your bill as you may still find our currency difficult. The car to take you to the residence of Mr. and Mrs. Ito will call for you at nine in the morning.' He smiled and added, 'O yasumi nasai! — which means in your language, 'Good night and rest well,' Miss Rainer.'

She smiled in her warm friendly way. 'Thank you for everything, Mr. Oswara. Please say what you said again slowly. If I am supposed to be a Japanese student, I must try to learn a little of the language.'

He repeated the phrase slowly for her and she said it again after him while the small black-haired proprietress looked from one to the other of them, smiling.

She led Beth again to the bedroom. This time she produced a kimono from another paper-screened closet. 'Doozo,' she said, smiling and handing it to

Beth. Obviously in the evening you relaxed in a kimono while you ate your dinner.

Beth wished she knew the Japanese word meaning thank you and determined to find out the next day.

The proprietress said something in Japanese and after bowing deeply again, she slipped noiselessly out of the room.

'Well,' Beth thought, 'this is certainly proving an adventure.'

She hung her dress and coat in the closet and slipped into the kimono. It was a dark leaf-green, patterned with golden flowers. She looked at her reflection in the small hanging mirror and liked the look of herself. Some of the golden leaves stencilled on the kimono were almost the exact shade of her red-golden hair.

'I must buy a kimono to take back with me,' she decided.

A little kimonoed dark-haired maid knocked and came in. She at once fell down on her knees, the palms of her hands stretched on the floor, and bowed deeply to Beth. When she rose to her feet she opened one of the sliding doors in the wall and produced a large and a smaller bath towel, which she handed to Beth. Then she said, '*Doozo*,' and beckoned to the girl.

Beth, greatly mystified, followed her out of the room. The maid led her farther down the corridor, said a word which sounded like '*Benjo*' and pushed open a door. Inside was a washbasin and toilet. Beth nodded and they continued their way down the corridor. Right at the end she pushed open another door and led Beth into a spacious room with an immense round bath like a very small swimming pool sunk into the floor. She felt the water and smiled and invited Beth to do likewise.

Beth, by this time, was thoroughly intrigued as to what was expected of her.

The maid assisted Beth in taking off her kimono and indicated that she should take off her bra and pantie-girdle. Then she took her into a small recess, which was an enclosed shower room, turned on the shower, put Beth under it and thoroughly soaped her. Afterwards she led Beth back into the main room with the round shallow bath, handed her the small towel, which most inadequately covered her, and urged her into the enormous round shallow bath. She bowed twice and said, 'Arigatoo' and left Beth to luxuriate in the pleasant warmth of the water.

The water was delightfully relaxing. Beth lay there feeling contented, and some of the tension of the long day left her. She no longer worried about her coming interview with the Itos, nor Tom's preoccupation with his daughter, which was almost to the exclusion of herself. She remembered gratefully Chris's concern for her and fell into a comatose condition of half waking, half sleeping. She didn't even look round when she heard the door open, thinking it was the little maid come back to fetch her. But she did look up startled when she heard two male voices and one female voice speaking together in Japanese. She stared incredulously at the newcomers. She glanced up and saw to her horror that the newcomers were two Japanese men, one considerably younger than the other, and a short rather stout Japanese woman. They all bowed to her and said, 'Konban wa!' which she later learned to be 'good evening.'

They then proceeded to divest themselves of their kimonos and holding the small square towel about their middles, they proceeded into the shower room.

Beth had heard about Japanese mixed bathing, but she had never expected to experience it. She felt covered with embarrassment and confusion at her own state of nudeness. She grabbed her own small towel and while they were in the shower room she hastily dried herself with the larger towel, seized her underclothes and fled from the room. She half ran down the corridor and pushed open the door of her room. But what she saw there made her pause on the threshold and utter a small cry of astonishment.

Seated cross-legged on a cushion before the little round table which the maid was already laying for dinner, with a widespread grin on his thin attractive face, sat Christopher Landour!

9

'Hallo!' Chris said, springing lithely to his feet. 'I've just learned from the maid that you've been indulging in the communal bath. How did you enjoy your first experience of living in the Japanese way?'

She was still too astounded by his presence to do more than stammer, 'I didn't enjoy it at all. Directly those other people came in I hopped out and fled.'

Chris chuckled richly. 'It must have given you a shock when strangers trooped in on you in the semi-nude. What would your friends in Putney think?'

Her small pretty face flushed scarlet. 'Someone should have warned me.'

'I didn't think about it and I'm sure Mr. Oswara didn't think about it either. But then he wouldn't; to him, mixed bathing is a perfectly natural custom. The Japanese are completely unself-conscious about displaying their nudity while they are taking a communal bath. But I'm sorry if you were embarrassed. It's the heritage of your Puritan ancestors.' His voice was faintly mock-ing and he still had that abominable grin on his face.

'What are you doing here in my bedroom in any case?' she snapped back at him.

'It's your room, I admit, but it won't be considered as your bedroom until your mattress and bedclothes are laid down on the *tatami* for the night. This is a room not only in which you sleep but also in which you eat, and receive your visitors. I thought you might be lonely stuck out here in a Japanese inn on your first night in Tokyo. I decided I'd come out and keep you company over dinner. Mr. Oswara supplied me with the address while you were upstairs at the Imperial packing your suitcase. Don't tell me you're mad at me?'

'I am mad, good and proper,' she stormed. 'Please leave here at once.'

'Oh, come, Beth! You can't be so hard-hearted as to turn me out before we've enjoyed our dinner. I spoke to the proprietress and ordered a very special dinner — for two.'

'Mr. Oswara had already ordered my dinner.'

'I know, the proprietress told me. *Tempura*. I managed to persuade her to put on a few extra Japanese side dishes and to serve us with sake and champagne.'

The sake had already arrived. He indicated the ornamented porcelain jar on the table with the two small bowls standing beside it: 'Let's forget you're annoyed with me for coming out here and have a drink now.'

The little maid had been staring from one to the other of them as though fascinated by the foreign language, not a word of which she could understand. He said something to her in Japanese. She flushed slightly and bowed to both of them, said, 'Arigatoo,' and disappeared.

'What does 'arigatoo' mean?' Beth asked.

'It means 'thank you.' It's a word you'd better learn, especially as you intend to stay in a Japanese household.'

'Arigatoo, arigatoo,' she repeated after him.

He laughed. 'You're pronouncing it all wrong. But that doesn't matter; Japanese is one of the most difficult languages to learn and to pronounce. It's taken me two years to pick up the small smattering of Japanese I have.'

There was a pause while they looked at one another. She was very conscious that she had nothing on under the green kimono and that she was still clutching her underclothes in one of her hands. With the other she kept the kimono firmly drawn about her.

'You look very pretty in that kimono, Beth,' he said finally, his voice low and intent, his blue eyes no longer mocking. 'Prettier than I've ever seen you. I like

168

your hair like that, half wet and half tousled, and you're one of the few women I've ever met who doesn't need makeup.'

He moved quickly towards her, hugging her tightly. She struggled against him: the clothes she was holding fell to the floor; the kimono slipped slightly open, showing the rounded curve of her breasts. He bent his head and kissed her throat. 'God, you're lovely,' he said hoarsely. 'I'm crazy about you. Did you know that?' And then he kissed her on the throat and on the curve between her breasts, and afterwards, firmly and with passion, he kissed her lips as no man had yet kissed her, except in that half-dream she had had while she was recovering consciousness after the horse had thrown her jumping over the Sussex hedge. She knew now it hadn't been a dream; Christopher had kissed her as he was kissing her now.

'I love you! I love you, my darling,' he muttered. And that, too, was said in the same tone of voice she dimly remembered.

She felt momentarily limp. She had no longer the desire to struggle. Strange thoughts whirled in her head; she was conscious of new feelings within her, unexpected but peculiarly sweet.

It was some minutes before she took control, before she forced herself free. She felt angry and ashamed. She felt she almost hated him.

'What on earth do you think you're doing, Chris?' she demanded.

'Making love to you, of course.' The half-mocking grin showed again on his face. 'When I see you standing before me like this, looking so damnably lovely, I'd be only half a man if I didn't make love to you. Don't you agree?'

She was too angry and confused to reply to that.

'I wish you'd go,' she said shortly.

She half turned to move away from him, but he caught her hand. 'You're not really mad at me, Beth? You must have known I was in love with you. It isn't easy for me to hide my feelings, though I've tried — God damn it, I've tried. And please don't ask me to go. I might even take you at your word and you wouldn't like that.'

'But I do want you to go.' Her voice quavered a little and was uncertain. Suddenly she knew that if he did take her at her word she would feel desperately lonely. She couldn't describe the feeling logically; she only knew that in her heart she wanted him to stay.

'Will it help if I apologise, Beth?' he was saying humbly. 'I shouldn't have rushed you like that. Will you forget it for the present? I promise to be a good little boy while we're having supper; and afterwards I'll leave you to get to bed.'

His voice pleaded as she didn't answer: 'You wouldn't want to eat dinner alone — not the sumptuous repast I've ordered for us; a typical Japanese party meal with all the trimmings. I swear if you turned me out now we'd both be damned miserable.

Please, Beth, put it down, if you like, to an uncontrollable impulse. I swear I won't offend again.'

She weakened and was ashamed of herself because she wanted to weaken.

'If you promise to behave?'

He raised one hand. 'I solemnly swear it, Beth.'

She half smiled. 'It would be a pity if the dinner you ordered was wasted. I hate eating alone, anyhow.'

'You're a darling.' He gripped her arm tightly and his blue eyes looked smilingly down into her face. 'I've a good mind to kiss you again by way of saying 'thank you'.'

She drew away from him, laughing a little. 'I've had quite enough, thank you, for one evening.'

'Then you're no longer mad at me?'

'Of course I'm mad at you.' But her voice lacked conviction.

He shook her playfully. 'You're laughing — that's good. It's going to be a wonderful dinner. I'm going to enjoy every moment of it.'

She asked the question that had been in her mind ever since she had first come into the room and seen him sitting there: 'Why didn't Tom come along with you tonight?'

He looked faintly guilty. 'To tell you the truth, Beth, he doesn't know I was coming here. I came on a sudden impulse. Previously I had suggested to him that we go out and dine together and I'd show him the town, but he said he was too tired; he would go to bed and have a meal sent up to his room. I was on my way back to the flat in a taxi when I suddenly decided to come out and see how you were making out. I came purely on an impulse; I thought you might feel rather strange and lost. Of course,' he grinned down at her, 'I didn't know you were indulging in communal bathing. A communal bath when you've nothing to hide as it were from your fellow bathers, is a great way of making friends.'

'Especially if you don't speak the language,' she commented tartly. 'I can imagine what a cheerful conversation I could have carried on with those Japanese.'

They both laughed and for the time being the strain in the atmosphere vanished. They were friends again. Suddenly she knew that she wanted very much to keep him as a friend. She didn't love him — not as she loved Tom — but just for a moment she had responded to his kisses. That had been only a physical attraction. A modern girl understood these things. You must never let yourself be led astray by a purely physical attraction. You might give way to it momentarily, but it didn't mean anything. Love was something quite different; friendship was something different too. The kind of friendship she and Chris shared was very precious. She must be careful in future that nothing happened to spoil it. Chris had begged her to forget the incident and she would forget it and behave as though it hadn't happened. Having decided this in her mind she felt calmer and more sure of herself.

'Please go out of the room for a few minutes, Chris. I want to get dressed.'

'Need you?'

She nodded solemnly. 'Most certainly I need to.'

'Well, don't take off that kimono. You look stunning in it. Besides, it's just the right garment for a typically Japanese meal.'

She dried her hair and combed it through. The curls fell into place naturally. She was one of those lucky girls with naturally curly hair. She slipped into her underclothes, put on some light make-up, hesitated whether to put on a dress or the kimono, but decided on the kimono. She had to admit that she looked well in it. A kimono gives a woman a delightful air of ultra-femininity.

When he knocked tentatively on the door, she was ready for him. His long lean body filled the doorway; he stood there, smiling in at her.

'Very nice,' he said approvingly. 'I'm

glad you kept on the kimono. It shows you take some notice of what I say.'

'The dominant male,' she mocked him. 'Why do men always feel they want to impose their willpower on defenceless females?'

'Defenceless? I like that,' he said, with a short laugh. 'We men may strut about beating our chests in the Tarzan manner, but women merely smile and do what they damn' well please.'

They both laughed and almost immediately the little maid, whose name Beth learnt was Tamiko, came in with a tray bearing a large assortment of hors d'œuvre. There were raw wild vegetables, smoked oysters, sauté mushrooms, thin slices of raw tuna and salmon, chrysanthemum petals, which, much to her surprise, she found quite delicious, and sliced sausages, which Christopher told her were made of smoked duck and fresh ginger.

Tamiko served them kneeling beside the table, smiling and bowing each time she refilled their plates. Most of the tastes were strange to Beth, but she didn't find them unpalatable, though she had to be urged by Chris to eat the thin slices of raw fish. But once she'd overcome her aversion to the idea and tasted the slices, she found she liked them.

'Most of the natives in the South Sea Islands practically live on raw fish,' Chris commented. 'And they're supposed to be the healthiest people in this world.'

After Tamiko had cleared away the hors d'œuvre, she brought in the *tempura*, which consisted of assorted pieces of fried fish, including shellfish cooked in batter and still sizzling in a chafing-dish. After the copious hors d'œuvre Beth hadn't thought she could eat any more, but the *tempura* tasted delicious and she found she still had quite a healthy appetite. They had drunk a small cupful of sake first. Beth had made a wry face and said, 'I suppose I'll get used to sake, but I don't really like it.'

'I'll admit it's an acquired taste,' Chris agreed. 'Don't drink much of it. As I said, there's champagne to follow.'

Tamiko brought in the champagne, which was nicely iced, with two long-stemmed glasses. Chris drew the cork and filled their glasses while Tamiko, kneeling beside the table again, served them with the numerous side-dishes in pottery bowls that went with the *tempura*.

After the little Japanese maid had cleared away, she bowed deeply to both of them and withdrew.

Beth rose to her feet. 'I must stretch my legs. I'm not used to sitting for long in such a cramped attitude.'

'I admit I found it difficult at first,' Chris sympathised. 'My legs are so darned long, anyhow.' He laughed, rose to his feet and, refilling their glasses with champagne, handed one to Beth.

She hesitated before accepting it.

'I've already eaten and drunk more than I should have.'

'But this is a celebration,' he urged.

'Your first Japanese meal on Japanese soil. Anyhow,' he slanted a grin at her, 'the wine will make you sleep better — even if you do have to sleep on the floor.' He added seriously, 'Did you enjoy the meal, Beth?'

She nodded, 'Very much. I really liked the food once I got used to the taste of it. The little maid is sweet. I never imagined you could get such personal service anywhere in this world.'

'Service like that is all part of the Japanese tradition, but you won't find it in the Westernised hotels.'

'I wish Tom had come along. It might have helped take his mind off his worry about Michiko.'

'I ought to be a loyal friend to Tom and agree with you, shouldn't I?' His smile was slanted again. 'But I'm glad we've had this evening together. More glad than I can tell you.' His voice was low and intent.

She felt herself flushing. She evaded his eyes. 'Yes, it's been very pleasant, Chris.'

'Is that all you can say?'

She nodded slowly. 'It's all I *want* to say, Chris. And now, don't you think you'd better go?' she added quietly.

'I'm damned if I want to go, but if you insist, Beth — '

Suddenly he caught hold of her arm and said explosively, 'I don't like the idea of your going to board at the Itos. I hope to heaven they refuse to have you.'

She looked up at him, her amber eyes widening. 'But why, Chris? You said before I might be walking into danger but I don't see how that is possible. I'll be flying under false colours, but where would the danger come in?'

'I'll admit that on the surface Japan seems an ordinary modern prosperous country,' he said. 'But politically it is very much disturbed. There is a strong anti-American feeling, prompted not only by the Communist Party but by a great number of fanatical students. You must have read some time ago of the murder of the Socialist Party Chairman, Inejire Asanuma. There were riots afterwards in which a large group of

180

Zenjakuren students demonstrated outside parliament and the premier's, Mr. Hayato Ikedas's residence. Revolt has been smouldering ever since. There are rumours that another big anti-Government political demonstration is under way; there may be further political murders, even wholesale massacres. As you know, the Itos have strong anti-American prejudices. Mr. Oswara has told us they are fanatical on the subject. They may be in contact with the organisers of the simmering revolution. They may even be taking a leading part in it. The present paying guests in the Itos' home, of which Mr. Oswara told us, sound doubtful politically, to say the least of it. It is conceivable they might consider you were planted in the house as a spy, especially if they found out that you were working for Americans. I think it's a big risk you're taking, Beth. Won't you be guided by me and tell Tom and Mr. Oswara that you're not going on with the venture?'

He was so urgent in his plea that she hesitated for a moment. But finally she gave her head a small determined shake. 'No, Chris. It was my own idea and it's the only way I can see to help Tom to get into contact with his daughter. He would be bitterly disappointed if I backed out now. The thought of his daughter and getting to know her after all these years means so much to him.'

'It shouldn't mean more to him than the thought of your safety,' he said harshly.

'But Tom doesn't believe I shall be in danger. Nor does Mr. Oswara. I don't believe it either. I think you're only trying to scare me, Chris. I promised to go through with this and, whatever you say, I am determined to do so.'

He put both his hands on her shoulders and shook her a little. 'You're a game kid, Beth. I don't approve, but I admire you. And you have my private phone number. Promise me you will keep closely in touch with me. If you don't, I swear I'll come out to the Itos' house and carry you away forcibly.'

She gave a small rather shaken laugh. 'Then I'll have to keep in touch with you, Chris. Anyhow, I'll be seeing both you and Tom at lunch tomorrow to tell you whether or not I've had any success in getting myself into the Itos' household.'

'I'll be there, but I pray to God — and I mean this, Beth — that they refuse to take you in.'

'Good night, Chris,' she said firmly, 'and thanks for the dinner.'

His long thin face slipped again into that lopsided grin. 'I'm being kicked out on my ear, eh? Well, good night, Beth. I suppose you need your sleep. Thanks for everything — darling.'

For a moment she thought he was going to kiss her again, but instead he turned and went quickly out of the room without looking back at her. She gave a small sigh. She didn't know whether she was relieved or disappointed at his abrupt departure. She had to admit that she had enjoyed this evening, even those moments when he had taken her in his arms and kissed her. She was a little ashamed of herself for admitting this. She was in love with Tom, but she wondered uneasily whether it was possible to be in love with one man and feel a strong physical attraction towards another. But she was too tired to think about it tonight and the champagne had made her feel slightly dizzy.

She was glad when Tamiko came back into the room, took her bedding out of the cupboard and made up the bed on the floor. The bed seemed very hard at first, but finally she became more used to it and was able to relax. She sighed again and turned over on her side and a few minutes later she was fast asleep.

10

The Itos' house was a large old-fashioned frame structure which stood on the crest of a hill which gave a magnificent view of the city of Tokyo. Once it must have been the big house of the district in which some nobleman or *Samurai* lived. Large grounds must originally have surrounded it, but much of the land had fairly recently been cut up into allotments on which were red-roofed modern houses. But there was still a sizeable garden with cherry blossom trees in full bloom, their soft pale pink petals coating the earth beneath them. There was flowering shrubbery, and, near the porch, an ornamental Japanese garden with a rockery, stone paths and a fountain playing. Steps led up on to the porch on which were placed a row of house slippers so that the incoming guests could change their shoes for the slippers before entering the house.

The car which had brought Beth had been told to wait. Even if she was successful in acquiring accommodation at the Itos' guesthouse, she would have to go back to the Japanese inn and then to the Imperial to collect some luggage. Anyhow she had promised to meet Tom and Chris at the Imperial for lunch and tell them how she had fared.

Mr. Oswara had promised that Mrs. Ito would have been warned of her coming. But before ringing the doorbell she slipped off her shoes and put on one of the pairs of house slippers lined up on the porch.

When she rang the doorbell the door was opened almost immediately by a neatly kimonoed little Japanese maid who bowed to her low several times, sucking in her breath.

'Is Mrs. Ito in?' Beth asked.

The little maid nodded her head and beckoned.

Beth followed her across a wide front

hall to the door of a sitting room. The maid opened the door and said '*Doozo*,' indicating that she should enter. A rather stout Japanese woman in a patterned kimono of bright blue with pink chrysanthemums, her thick black hair piled high and lacquered, stood in front of the *tokonoma*, a recess which contained an engraved scroll and some beautifully arranged flowers. Mrs. Ito bowed very low to her and Beth bowed back.

'You are Miss Rainer, the young English girl the International Language Centre telephoned about?' Mrs. Ito asked.

'Yes, I am Beth Rainer,' Beth said, and smiled.

But Mrs. Ito didn't smile back. She had a hard rough-skinned face and she wore no make-up. Her seal-brown, slightly slanted eyes were looking Beth over and she was taking her time doing it. Beth had an uncomfortable feeling, as though she were practically naked under the elder woman's gaze.

Beth had been nervous all morning

over this coming interview and now her feeling of nervousness increased. She finally broke the silence, stammering slightly, 'I have heard that you give accommodation to foreign students, Mrs. Ito. I am studying Japanese and would very much like to stay in a Japanese household.'

'You speak some Japanese?' Mrs. Ito asked in almost faultless English.

Beth shook her head. 'I'm afraid I don't. I'm just starting my lessons and I find the language very difficult.'

'Why do you wish to learn Japanese?' Mrs. Ito asked abruptly.

'I am working for a firm in England which has business connections with Japan. It would be very useful if I could acquire some knowledge of the language. I heard that you had accommodation to offer foreign students.'

'That is so,' Mrs. Ito nodded. 'But in the last few days all my available accommodation has been taken.'

Beth felt a sharp sense of disappointment. She had promised to help Tom. It seemed at the outset she had failed in her mission. Her dismay must have shown on her face for quite surprisingly Mrs. Ito smiled.

'I have a suggestion to make to you, Miss Rainer, or else I would have told them when they telephoned from the centre that I had no accommodation left for students. Our daughter, Michiko, has a large room with space for extra matting. If you would care to share a room with her, something might be arranged.'

Beth could scarcely believe her good fortune. Sharing a room with Michiko would give her an opportunity of gaining the girl's confidence.

'I should be delighted to share a room with your daughter, Mrs. Ito.'

'Come this way and I will show you the room,' Mrs. Ito said.

She shuffled across the room in her slippers and Beth followed her. The Japanese woman led her up a wide staircase. The house was two-storied as had been the house at the Japanese inn.

They must both have been built about the same period, Beth thought.

At the end of the corridor Mrs. Ito opened the door of a large, almost pleasant, bare room which held a small dressing-table, another round table and Japanese cushions. One of the walls was opened and showed through a plate-glass window a view of the garden.

'It *is* nice,' Beth said. 'I should very much like to stay here, Mrs. Ito.'

'You may find it difficult to get accustomed to our household at first,' Mrs. Ito smiled back. 'Our house is run strictly on a Japanese pattern. We make no concession to Westernised ideas.'

'But that is what I want,' Beth said eagerly. 'I want to learn the Japanese way of life.'

The elder woman nodded and the faint smile that touched her hard lips showed her approval.

'We of old Japan are proud of our traditions; we do not want to be Westernised, especially we do not want our country Westernised in the American way of life. We had the Americans here during the Occupation and afterwards; we still have them, but we do not like them or their Westernised habits. We do not want them or their modern innovations. We want to keep to the old tradition of our Japanese behaviour and culture.' She spoke vehemently and with bitterness, and her face was drawn into hard, taut lines.

Beth found herself thinking that this woman could be a dangerous, even a ruthless enemy. She remembered Chris's urgent warning that by going into this household she would be stepping straight into danger. But even so she was doing it for Tom's sake, and being able to share a room with Michiko was unbelievable luck.

'I hope you don't dislike the English, Mrs. Ito?'

'I do not like or dislike the English,' Mrs. Ito said. 'At least they have sense enough to mind their own business. Dr. Rickard, a gentleman who eats with us, is half-English. He is a very good young man; he works selflessly and for very small pay for the poor in Japan. You will meet him at dinner — that is, if you decide to stay with us.' The Japanese woman added, 'We have not yet discussed terms.'

Beth waited. The slanted eyes were very shrewd now as they looked at the girl.

'Usually I charge one thousand seven hundred yen a day for accommodation, breakfast and dinner. I do not think the sum in any way excessive. Undoubtedly your firm back in England is paying your expenses.'

'That figure would be satisfactory,' Beth said, though after doing a rough calculation she considered that the sum asked was excessive. It would correspond to about thirty-four shillings a day.

Once again Mrs. Ito's hard, taut face relaxed in a smile. 'Since that is satisfactory to you, then everything is arranged.'

Beth had a feeling she was very pleased over the financial bargain she had made.

'You will wish to pick up your luggage. When may I expect you here?'

'I shall come in the late afternoon,' Beth said. 'Thank you very much for taking me in, Mrs. Ito.'

The elder woman bowed low and drew in a sucking breath. 'It is my pleasure, Miss Rainer.'

'I thank you, Mrs. Ito,' Beth said and bowed low, but she wondered how many of Mrs. Ito's boarders were asked to pay thirty-four shillings a day and, if they were, how they could afford it.

They were both in the front hall and Beth was on her way out when there was a sudden almost violent interruption. The door was pushed open and a young man stood there carrying the limp body of a girl in his arms.

Beth noticed fleetingly that he was tall, fair and good-looking, and yet there was something about the cast of his features that suggested the East. The unconscious girl had dark hair falling about her face and was very lovely. Beth thought her one of the most beautiful young girls she had ever seen. Despite the dark hair and eyebrows, her face was light complexioned, the features fine and delicately etched.

Beth noticed all this in a fleeting moment while they all stood motionless in the hall. Then Mrs. Ito screamed 'Michiko! What has happened, Dr. Frank?'

'They called my surgery from the school. They said there had been an accident; she had fallen in the garden; but I don't think that Michiko has been seriously hurt. I went over her immediately. She will be all right.'

'Please tell me everything!' Mrs. Ito's voice had a high-pitched hysterical note in it. She seemed suddenly a changed woman as she fluttered about the unconscious girl. She was no longer the hard-faced shrewd proprietress of the guesthouse but a woman desperately afraid for someone she loved deeply.

'She is in no danger, Maki-san,' the tall lean young doctor said. 'She has a slight case of concussion. If you will lay out the mattress I will take her upstairs.'

'Yes, of course,' the Japanese woman muttered, but she added hoarsely, 'You are sure it *is* nothing serious, Dr. Frank?'

'I don't know how it happened.' He spoke briskly. 'They told me at the school that Michiko had gone out for a walk in the garden during the mid-morning break. When she didn't come back to attend to her classes they went out to look for her. They found her in the garden, unconscious.'

Mrs. Ito wrung her hands. 'Michiko! Oh, Michiko, my darling!'

'Hurry, Maki-san,' Dr. Frank said impatiently, 'and get the room ready.'

'Of course. Of course.'

She scuttled up the stairs, paying no attention to Beth. She seemed to have forgotten about the girl's presence completely.

Beth looked at the unconscious girl and thought again how completely lovely she was. So this was Tom's daughter — a daughter any man might be proud of. This girl might one day be her stepdaughter. She felt a sudden surge of deep tenderness towards her.

'You think she's been badly hurt?' she said to the young doctor.

'No. I examined her thoroughly, but I do not think it was an accident. Undoubtedly Michiko will tell us the truth when she comes round. Who are you, by the way?'

'An English student who is coming to board here.'

He nodded. 'It will be nice to have an English girl in the house to talk to. I am half-English myself. I was educated in England and I took my medical degree there. I have not been back in this country long and am finding the Japanese language difficult. That is why Mrs. Ito and I speak together in English.'

The Japanese woman appeared on the stairs.

'Everything is ready, Dr. Frank.'

'Good.' He nodded to Beth and carried the unconscious girl up the stairs.

Beth thought it would be best to beat a hasty retreat. Mrs. Ito might use Michiko's accident as an excuse not to have her in the house. She wondered how the accident had occurred. Michiko must have slipped and fallen in the garden, maybe hitting her head upon a stone. But the young doctor, who had given her a feeling of confidence, had assured them all that it wasn't serious. She wondered how much of the incident she should relate to Tom; she didn't want to worry him and there was nothing he could do about it.

The car was still waiting for her. She went first to the Japanese inn to collect her small suitcase, after which she asked to be driven to the Imperial Hotel.

11

Tom was waiting for her. The moment she pushed her way through the glass doors she saw him standing on top of the stairs which led into the lounge, and as usual the sight of him after even a short absence made her heart leap and begin to pound madly. He looked arresting standing there, undeniably handsome with his strong regular features, his rough brown hair which was inclined to curl, and his dark grey eyes intent upon each newcomer into the foyer.

The moment he saw her he ran down the stairs and clasped hold of her hands. 'Beth! Beth!' His voice was full of warmth and eagerness. 'I've been waiting for you for the past hour.'

'I'm sorry but I got rather held up.' She indicated the page-boy who was following her with her suitcase. 'Will you please tell the boy to put the suitcase with my other luggage?'

He turned towards the boy and gave him the instructions in English. The boy bowed low and said '*Arigatoo*,' but he still waited.

Beth gave a faint smile. 'I think he's waiting for a tip.'

'I'm sorry, I forgot,' Tom mumbled, producing a coin. 'But I'm so darned keen to know what happened to you this morning.'

'You mean at the Itos'?'

'Of course I mean at the Itos'.'

She smiled again, a little wryly this time.

'Well, they've taken me in, though at a price. I bet very few of the other students can afford that rental.'

'It doesn't matter. They didn't suspect anything?'

'I only saw Mrs. Ito and I don't think she suspected anything or she wouldn't have suggested I share a room with Michiko.'

'You are actually going to share a

room with Michiko? That's splendid, simply splendid. How on earth did you manage it?'

'I didn't. It was she who suggested it. Apparently all the other rooms are taken. But Michiko has a large room, quite large enough for two, as Mrs. Ito explained.'

He grasped her hand fondly. 'I'll never cease being grateful to you, Beth.'

She looked at him and said steadily, 'You know I'd do a great deal for you, Tom. Couldn't we sit down somewhere? I'm rather tired.'

'I'm sorry, Beth, I should have thought of that before. I suppose I'm too darned anxious to find out everything I can about Michiko. Now that I'm actually here in Japan, I don't seem able to think of anything else but of her, when I can see her, when I can talk to her, when I can convince her that her thoughts of me have been all wrong. I loved her mother sincerely; I wanted to marry her as you know.'

Beth nodded slowly. She could

understand Tom's impatience and anxiety to get news of his daughter. But her heart felt faintly chilled. Her feet seemed to drag as she walked up the stairs into the lounge.

He hadn't yet asked her how she had spent the night; he didn't seem interested. But in a way she was glad he hadn't asked her. She didn't want to keep anything from him, but on the other hand she felt reluctant to tell him that Chris had visited her and that they had spent the evening together.

They sank on to a deep couch and Tom ordered two dry Martinis from the hovering waiter.

Beth wedged herself comfortably into a corner of the couch. 'This is wonderful after sitting on the hard floor on cushions,' she sighed.

'There were only cushions at the inn? Were you all right there, Beth?'

'I'll have to get used to sleeping comfortably on a mattress on a hard floor,' she said. 'I slept last night; I was so doggone tired.'

'I hate to put you to so much discomfort but you see how much this whole thing means to me? When will you see Michiko?'

The waiter had brought their cocktails, also some olives and nuts, had bowed and withdrawn.

'I have already seen Michiko,' she said quietly.

He stared at her. He had put out his hand to take up the stem of the cocktail glass, but suddenly he withdrew it. 'You have seen Michiko? Tell me about her. Tell me *all* about her, Beth.'

'She is very lovely. I don't know when I have ever seen a young girl quite so beautiful. Her hair is black, but her skin is almost white. Her features are finely shaped and delicate, and she is very slender.'

'What did she say to you?' Tom asked hoarsely.

Beth hesitated. 'We didn't speak, but since I am sharing a room with her, I shall have an opportunity of talking to her this evening.'

'Does she look at all like me?'

'I noticed a resemblance in the chin,' Beth smiled. 'It is a small chin but a determined one.'

Tom beckoned the waiter and asked him to bring two other Martinis. Beth shook her head and said, 'No, thank you, Tom.'

Tom grinned. 'You don't mind if I do? I feel so excited that you've actually seen Michiko. I'm so glad she is beautiful. Eiko was beautiful, but more in the Japanese way than you described Michiko. She was short and very petite, with a pale yellow skin and seal-brown slanting eyes. What colour are Michiko's eyes, Beth?'

'I only saw her briefly in the hall. I didn't notice.'

He nodded. 'Tomorrow you'll be able to tell me more about her. I can't get over the good luck that you're actually going to share a room with her. I never dreamt when I asked you to come out here with me that you would be able to do me such a good service.'

She felt slightly irritated and could only put it down to jealousy at his absorption in his daughter.

'I am glad I've been able to be of use, that I've been worth the expense you were put to in bringing me out here.'

He heard the dry note in her voice. He looked at her with concern: 'What's the matter, Beth? I brought you out here because I wanted you to be with me at this critical period in my life. I had no idea then of using you in any way.'

'I know, Tom.' She touched his hand briefly. She wondered why it was when you loved a man you were so prone to take offence.

'You mean so much to me, Beth. I should have hated the thought of coming without you,' he said with great sincerity.

She felt ashamed of the jealousy which had prompted her remark.

'I'm sure you didn't, Tom.'

There was a pause while she took an olive off the small earthenware plate and nibbled it. Then she said, and the remark was unexpected even to herself, 'Was it you who first suggested my coming out here or was it Christopher?'

She saw him start and a faint colour stained his handsome face. 'Why should you ask that, Beth?'

'I just wanted to know.'

'I don't see what difference it makes, but it might have been Chris. But the moment he did suggest it I was all for it. I saw . . . '

But she broke in angrily, 'You mean you saw that I might help you in getting in contact with Michiko!'

He stared at her aghast. 'What's the matter with you, Beth? I wasn't going to say anything of the sort; I was going to say that I saw I would be damned lonely and missing you like anything. You've come to be so much a part of me, Beth.'

She, too, flushed, and she felt the grittiness behind her eyes which suggested tears.

'I'm sorry, Tom. I shouldn't have said

that, but at times you do say things you don't really mean.'

'I guess you think I've been too absorbed in Michiko — to the exclusion of you, Beth,' he said quietly. 'It may have seemed like that, but that isn't the truth. I'm not only deeply grateful for what you are doing for me; that means a great deal to me and I think about it constantly; I feel for you not only a very warm affection but a great sense of companionship. Apart from Michiko, you are the only person of importance in my life.'

He hadn't said love; he had used the words 'warm affection.' But Tom would be reluctant to use the word love, even though he meant it. He was very reserved, almost inhibited. Chris had used the word love to her last night. But then he was of the type, she decided, that would use the word freely. He would tell a girl he loved her while he was kissing her, even though he should forget all about her a few minutes later. Tom would say he loved her in his own good time, and then she knew he would mean it.

'Let's go and have lunch,' he suggested. 'You must be hungry after all your adventures this morning. By the way, I changed some money for you; you'll need it to cover your expenses.'

He gave her a wad of thousand-yen notes and several which represented a pound each, and many one-hundred yen notes, the equivalent of two shillings.

'Thank you, Tom.' She took the notes and thrust them into her handbag. 'What about Chris? Isn't he coming to lunch with us?'

He shook his head. 'Apparently he has a luncheon date. He said he'd join us afterwards for coffee.'

It was curious that she should feel a faint sense of disappointment. Surely she welcomed this opportunity of lunching alone with Tom? She supposed she was disappointed because she had wanted to tell Chris about her adventures of the morning. If she had an opportunity she might even tell him of the way Dr. Frank Rickard had carried Michiko unconscious into the house and the young doctor's strange words. What had he meant by inferring that Michiko's fall mightn't have been an accident? But perhaps, she decided a few minutes later, as they went downstairs in the lift to the Westernised dining room, it might be better if she didn't tell Chris. Chris had been against her going to the Itos'; he had warned her that she might be stepping into danger. He had said so forcibly last night.

The dining room at the Imperial is a large room furnished in the Western manner. You can eat European or Japanese food and are served by waiters.

'The food's quite good. I ate down here last night,' Tom commented. 'I had a darned good steak, the best I've had since I left New York. Did you get anything decent to eat at that Japanese inn you went to, Beth?'

'Yes, it was quite wonderful, but it was wholly Japanese.'

'I used to eat Japanese food when I was over here before,' he said as the waiter seated them at a small side table. 'I can't say I had to pretend to like it for Eiko's sake, but raw fish is something I never could stomach.'

Beth smiled. 'I didn't think I could at first, but I found I rather liked it.'

'Little savage.' His dark grey eyes smiled humorously across at her. 'Did you have some raw fish last night at the Japanese inn? What else did you have?'

'Lots of Japanese hors d'œuvre and *tempura*.'

'You mean fish fried in batter? I rather liked that. You must have had quite a feast. A pity you had to eat it alone.'

She started to tell him that Chris had been with her but for some reason she didn't. She felt guilty she hadn't told him and after she had let the remark pass it was too late; it might make the incident seem too important. Chris had come on an impulse; what had happened between them afterwards had also been impulsive and, and . . . She sought for a word in her mind — unimportant. Yes, of course, what had happened between Chris and herself last night was completely unimportant.

'What do you feel like eating?' Tom asked. 'As I told you, the steak here is good. We could have some smoked salmon first and,' he laughed, 'no more of that sake; let's have some French wine.'

She said she didn't want anything to drink, but Tom insisted: 'Well, you don't mind if I have a glass of beer?'

'Of course not.'

The smoked salmon and steak were good, but no better, she thought, than you could get at any first-class hotel in England. It seemed a pity to have come all this way to Japan to eat what you could eat just as well at home.

The dining room was filling up. Most of the guests were obviously tourists and talked loudly in English. She noticed that those at the tables surrounding them also ate Westernised food.

'It's queer that people come all the way to Japan and then eat the same sort of food as they would eat at home,' Beth commented.

She saw a faint flush creep up to Tom's temples. 'I'm sorry, Beth. Is that meant as a dig at me? Would you have preferred to eat Japanese food?'

'Not now, but it does seem sad to think so many of these tourists will go away without ever having tasted real Japanese food. If you travel, the native food is so much a part of the country; just as much a part of it as cathedrals, temples, palaces and parks.'

'I guess the stomach doesn't take in foreign matter as easily as the eye,' Tom commented and grinned. It was the boyish grin she had always loved, which made him seem suddenly so much younger. When he grinned that way he didn't look old enough to be Michiko's father, that lovely young girl she had last seen lying unconscious in Dr. Frank's arms.

He kept questioning her about Michiko, just how she had looked and what she had worn. He wanted to know all about Mrs. Ito, too.

She described in detail the rather square middle-aged Japanese woman with the hard face and shrewd and knowledgeable eyes.

'I'm convinced it's the woman I'm really up against,' Tom said. 'It is she who has put all these thoughts of hatred for Americans — and especially towards me — into Michiko's mind. She must be a terrible woman.'

'I suppose in some ways she is,' Beth agreed, but she was remembering the change that had come over Mrs. Ito's face when she had seen Michiko lying unconscious in the doctor's arms. It had softened incredibly and the eyes were not embittered and hard, but full of love.

'We'll have coffee up in the lounge,'

Tom said. 'That's where we're going to meet Chris. But first I want you to come into the Imperial Arcade with me. It runs under this hotel. I have something to show you.'

'I didn't know there was a shopping arcade under this hotel.'

'I understand it's quite famous, and they certainly have lovely things displayed in the shops.'

They went down some stairs and found themselves in the middle of a curving arcade. It was full of tourists and small delightful shops of every variety — jewellers' shops which sold the famous Mikimoto cultured pearls, shops with lacquer ware, shops with delicate Japanese etchings, shops full of glorious brocades, silks and satins, shoe shops, shops which sold cameras of every sort and size.

Tom stopped outside one of the shops which displayed materials. 'I was inquiring in here this morning. They'll make up a suit or a dress in a few days. Later today why don't you go in there and order yourself a completely new outfit?'

Beth laughed. 'I couldn't afford a new outfit, not even here, where I must admit the prices are considerably cheaper than they are at home.'

'But it will be my gift to you, Beth,' he said earnestly but with diffidence.

She shook her head. 'All the same, I couldn't accept it, Tom.'

'But there is one thing I want you to accept from me. You can't refuse me this, Beth. I should be broken-hearted if you did.'

He led her across the narrow arcade to a jeweller's shop which sold the famous Mikimoto pearls made up in necklets, earrings, brooches, and rings.

'I've already picked out something for you this morning,' he said, smiling. 'Come along and see if you like it.'

He drew Beth up to one of the counters and immediately a small Japanese salesgirl was standing before him, smiling: 'You have come back with young lady, Mr. Dillan.' She not only spoke perfect English but she had remembered Tom's name.

'Yes. This is the young lady; Miss Rainer. I want her to look at the set I asked you to put aside for me this morning.'

The little Japanese salesgirl bowed low. 'With pleasure, Mr. Dillan.'

Beth felt a curious constriction in her throat and her heart was pounding. Just near them a couple of young Americans were standing looking over a selection of pearl rings set in diamonds. 'I like the look of this one,' the young man said. 'Slip it on to your finger, honey.' The girl held out her left hand and he slipped it on to her engagement finger.

The pounding of Beth's heart increased. Was Tom preparing some such surprise for her? Was he finally, in this rather unconventional way, going to ask her to marry him? And what should she say? She was a little surprised that the question crossed her mind; she had been in love with Tom so long; she had dreamt of little else but that eventually he would ask her to marry him.

She was so lost in this day-dreaming that she didn't notice the salesgirl had returned and that lying on a black velvet cloth was a lovely necklet of cultured pearls, with modern pearl clip earrings surrounded by a circle of diamonds. It was a beautiful set but momentarily her sense of disappointment was so great she felt tears pricking the backs of her eyes. She could have laid her head down on the counter and sobbed.

'What's the matter?' Tom was asking anxiously. 'Don't you like the set, Beth?'

'It's lovely, Tom,' she stammered. 'I scarcely know what to say.'

The smile came back to his face. He looked pleased and gratified. 'Try it on,' he suggested. 'If you don't like this set there are plenty more to choose from.'

The little salesgirl had come round from behind the desk. She put the lovely shining pearls about Beth's throat and clipped on the earrings, then saying, 'Please,' she adjusted a mirror on the counter and beckoned Beth to come and look at herself.

Certainly they suited her. The iridescence of the pearls seemed to make her pale skin glow; the pearls and diamonds glimmered on the lobes of her prettily shaped ears.

'They look grand on you, Beth.' There was a strong hint of emotion in his voice.

The Japanese salesgirl had moved tactfully away.

'Why are you giving me this lovely present, Tom?' she asked quietly.

'Why shouldn't I?' he countered. 'You've done so much for me, Beth, not only in the past years when you've been working in the office, but at the present moment when you are doing something for me for which I am unable to express my gratitude adequately in words.'

She turned half aside and bit her lower lip sharply. 'You're giving me this out of gratitude, Tom?'

He may have heard the quiver in her

voice for he asked sharply, 'What's the matter, Beth? Aren't you pleased? Have I said something to offend you? Don't you want me to be grateful to you?'

'Yes, of course.' But she blinked rapidly as she said it.

'Beth,' he went on in a lower voice, 'you know it isn't only gratitude I feel for you! You must know that. But just at the moment I don't want to say anything; I want to get this business of Michiko settled first. Please understand, my dear — my very dear. You will accept this small gift from me?'

'Of course, Tom.' She came towards him impulsively, not caring that he should see the tears in her eyes. 'I understand — at least I'm trying to understand. And you do know that I shall do everything in my power to help you.'

'Bless you,' he said, and added in a changed voice, almost boyishly, 'You do like the necklace and the earrings?'

'I like them, anyhow,' a laughing voice said from behind them.

They both swung sharply round. Christopher's long, lean figure was standing just behind them.

'Who's buying you pearls, Beth? Not the big boss himself? Fie! Fie! I hope you're not taking it out of your expense account, Tom? I'm glad I met you here for I want you to meet a very good friend of mine.'

Beth saw that a girl was standing at his elbow, a slight, very pretty blonde girl.

'We've been lunching round the corner at a Japanese restaurant. Sally wanted to make a few purchases, so I brought her in here before I met you for coffee. Beth, I'd like to have you meet Sally Hyman. This is Beth Rainer, Sally; and this is her boss, Tom Dillan. Sally and I have been good friends for a number of years. Her uncle is the Consul-General here and she's just flown over from New York to spend a holiday with them.'

'This sure is the cutest place,' Sally enthused. 'Chris has always been urging me to come over for a visit. I don't know why I delayed so long, especially since I have Chris to take me around.' She threw him a half-coquettish, half-admiring look from under her long lashes, which were several shades darker than her hair.

'I think she's a little in love with him,' Beth thought and wondered why she should feel disturbed at the knowledge. Chris was merely a good friend, and even if he had kissed her and she for a few moments might have kissed him back, he was no more and never would be any more than a friend.

'Chris always comes out to our place on Long Island and stays with us whenever he flies back to the States. He's told me so much about this country. I've been crazy to see it, but I had nowhere to stay until my uncle was recently appointed Consul-General. My, that's a swell pearl necklet and earrings. I envy you, Miss Rainer.' She laughed. She was friendly and uninhibited.

Beth felt ashamed that she couldn't

like her better. It might be because from an English point of view she was almost too uninhibited; she certainly made no secret of her liking for Chris.

'Won't you come up and join us for coffee?' Tom suggested to the American girl.

'I am coming,' Chris said, 'but this child has an appointment with a hairdresser in the arcade. Why whenever women arrive anywhere they have to rush for a beauty parlour, beats me?'

Beth had had her hair washed and set before she left London. She wondered uncomfortably if she needed a reset. It did look rather mussed, but in the brief time since she had arrived here she had had so much on her mind.

'Maybe I could have an appointment myself a little later this afternoon?'

Chris nodded. 'I'll see if I can fix it up when I take Sally back to the female torture chamber — for it must be sheer torture sitting under those hot driers with your hair all screwed up.'

Sally laughed. 'It isn't exactly my idea

of fun, but we poor gals have to put up with it. If we didn't, you stuck-up males would probably pass us by without a second glance. Come along, Chris, it's almost time for my appointment.'

'I'm coming.' He laughed, too, and added, 'Congratulations, Beth, on making that old miser, Dillan, part up with a really fine piece of jewellery. Is that all he's given you?' She noticed that he gave a quick glance at her left hand.

She felt herself flushing. 'It's more than enough. It's a beautiful set.'

'It sure is,' Sally said. 'Well, so long, folks; I hope I'll be seeing you again.'

'You certainly will,' Chris said. 'Now that we've got a foursome we must plan some outings. There are some grand shrines and parks and temples to visit. I want Sally to get to know not only the International Consular set with its numerous parties, but the real Japan.'

'O.K., Chris, I'm buying whatever you suggest,' Sally said, smiling.

'I'll meet you in the lounge in a few minutes,' Chris said to Tom and Beth.

Tom looked after them with both amusement and satisfaction in his humorous grey eyes. 'I wonder if Chris is about to be caught at last,' he commented. 'He's been dodging matrimony for a number of years. She's a sweet little thing, isn't she?'

'Yes, very,' Beth agreed. But she found she had to force her enthusiasm, and once again she felt ashamed of herself.

She was about to take off the earrings and necklet when Tom said quickly, 'Please wear them for me, Beth. You don't know what a kick I got out of choosing them for you.'

She was touched.

'It was sweet of you, Tom.'

He went towards the desk and paid out a stack of bills of high value. The little salesgirl bowed and thanked him profusely. Then she bowed low to Beth: 'I hope you get great pleasure and happiness wearing them, lady.'

'I am sure I shall,' Beth murmured. 'They are so beautiful.'

12

While they made their way up into the lounge for coffee Tom told her something of the history of cultured pearls, which he had been reading up in a guide book. There were apparently several farms for cultured pearls, the most famous being the Mikimoto Farms. The farms weren't far from Toba, in the north. At Toba off Sugashina Island, a short sail from the port, mostly women were used for pearl diving. These pearls were produced by introducing an irritant inside the shell of the oysters, causing them to secrete the nacre of which the pearls are formed. He added that it took about seven years for the pearls to develop fully.

She was interested in what he told her. She had always heard of Japanese cultured pearls but had had no idea just how they were cultivated.

They had reached the passage with the travel agency offices, which led into the main lounge. Chris was there waiting for them. He said he had already ordered coffee and asked if they would like brandy or liqueurs. Beth declined, but Tom and Chris both ordered brandy.

'You are a sly dog,' Tom said, laughing across at Chris. 'I thought when you told me you couldn't join us for lunch it was a business appointment.'

'So it was in a way. Sally's uncle and aunt were going off to an official luncheon. They asked me to look after the child. I'd be a liar if I said I was loath to take on the chore. Sally and I have been good friends for a number of years, and as she said, I've often stayed at her parents' home in Long Island. We all ought to have some grand excursions together. We might even manage a weekend at the Fujiya Hotel. It's a beautiful spot, especially lovely at this time of the year when all the cherry blossoms are out.'

'I'm afraid I've got too much on my mind at the moment for pleasure excursions,' Tom said. 'But I don't think you and Miss Hyman will miss Beth and myself.' His eyes twinkled humorously.

'But we shall,' Chris said quietly. 'At least *I* shall miss you.' He hesitated slightly, 'and Beth.' He turned and looked at her, his blue eyes smiling into hers. It was an intimate glance and it also seemed to be asking her to understand something, not to judge by appearances; at least to give him a chance to explain. And as yet he hadn't asked her what luck she had had at the Itos'. It was as though the arrival of Sally Hyman had momentarily put the other matter out of his mind.

Tom introduced the subject: 'Beth was in luck. Mrs. Ito apparently took to her and she's to stay at their home as a paying guest. But there's more to it than that. She is actually to share a bedroom with Michiko. That's grand news, isn't it?'

But Chris looked doubtful; his lean face had darkened, his lips were set tightly. 'I'm not so sure,' he said quietly. 'If the two girls become too friendly, Mrs. Ito may become suspicious.'

He turned towards Beth: 'Did Mrs. Ito seem in any way suspicious? Did she check up on your credentials?'

Beth shook her head. 'As far as I know, she didn't. But she did say that someone had telephoned about me from the International Language Centre. She seemed satisfied with that.'

'Did she ask about the Japanese inn where you had spent the night?' Tom asked.

Beth shook her head. 'No, she didn't.'

'Then you could just as easily have spent the night here,' Tom said, 'and I'm sure much more comfortably.'

Beth hadn't meant to meet Christopher's eyes at that moment, but somehow she did. One of his eyelids lowered in the suggestion of a wink. She felt suddenly guilty, but it was too late now to tell Tom that he had been out there last night. Tom would wonder why she hadn't told him at once, and after all, there had been nothing to it — well not much, anyhow.

'I don't know,' Chris answered. 'I'm sure it was a good experience for Beth staying at a Japanese inn. This hotel is too Westernised, to my view, for those who want to get to know the real Japan.'

'But a darned sight more comfortable, I'll wager,' Tom said again. 'When I was young and out here I stayed at several Japanese inns. I can't say I ever really liked them.'

'I'm glad I did stay there last night,' Beth said, and was surprised at the feeling in her voice. 'Anyhow, it started me getting accustomed to the Japanese way of life. I won't feel so green about their customs on my first night at the Itos'. But I do wish,' she added with a wry grimace, 'that there were chairs instead of mats to sit on. After sitting for a short while in that cramped position, my legs ache intolerably.'

The coffee arrived, with a liqueur brandy for each of the men.

'By the way, I've made you a hair appointment for three o'clock,' Chris said. 'I'll take you down when you've finished your coffee. Sally should be through about then. I've promised to take her sightseeing on the Ginza, which apparently to women means shopping. Her aunt and uncle are going on after the luncheon to a tea ceremony.' He laughed and added, 'Heavens, they can be tedious, though they are greatly favoured in polite Japanese society. The tea ceremony is almost a religion out here in the art of graceful living. One sits cross-legged or crouched on a mat, talks a little to one's neighbour or merely sits and contemplates while they serve a green tea that is delicately aromatic, but in my opinion horrid. It is supposed to have many highly-prized virtues such as relieving fatigue, delighting the soul and strengthening the will. But you certainly should go to a tea ceremony once. I must see that you and Tom get invitations while you are here, Beth.'

'I certainly want to see as much of Japan as I can while I am over here,' Beth said warmly. 'Not only the countryside but its people and its customs.'

Chris grinned. 'Well, you made a good start at the Japanese inn last night.'

She flushed slightly and didn't comment.

'And since the Itos are so violently nationalistic, you'll probably come across a lot of old-world Japanese customs at their house.'

A few minutes later Mr. Oswara joined them, bowing to them all profusely, sucking in his breath and apologising for being late. He rubbed his hands together with gratification when they told him the news, nodding his head several times.

'That is good, very good. You, Miss

Rainer, will have an opportunity of really getting to know Michiko-san. I am sure you will be able to influence her in her father's favour — not at first, of course, but by degrees.' He rose to his feet. 'I've come to take you to the International Language Centre. Are you ready, Miss Rainer?'

'But I can't come now — I've just made a hair appointment,' Beth gasped. 'And afterwards I think I should be getting out to the Itos.'

He bowed and said, 'As you wish, but I thought it advisable you should go today. They may ask you questions.'

'Mrs. Ito didn't ask me any questions when she accepted me. Will it be all right if I go with you tomorrow, Mr. Oswara?'

He bowed again, smiled toothily and said, 'As you wish. I understand the hair arrangement for young ladies is very important.'

Chris laughed. 'You're right there, Mr. Oswara. I've just left one young lady in the beauty parlour below and now I have to escort another one down.'

'I will get in touch with you here tomorrow, Miss Rainer,' Mr. Oswara said.

'I'll be here,' Beth promised. She added, 'There's no point in my hanging round the Itos' house during the day when Michiko is away teaching at the kindergarten.'

Chris glanced at his wristwatch. 'Are you ready, Beth?'

'Perhaps you will stay a few moments, Mr. Oswara,' Tom suggested. 'There are several matters I would like to talk over with you.'

Mr. Oswara bowed again and sat down. 'With pleasure, Mr. Dillan.'

13

Beth was glad of the opportunity to talk to Chris alone for a few moments. Directly they had started down the stairs towards the arcade, she said, 'Is there anywhere where we can talk for a few minutes undisturbed, Chris?'

He hesitated, thinking. 'Let's go into the bar. It's bound to be pretty deserted at this hour.'

She nodded and followed him.

The bar was a large pleasant room in a semi-basement, with high stools standing around the bar and small tables scattered about the room. They seated themselves at a table in a far corner. Beth asked for a lemon squash and he ordered a brandy for himself.

'Shoot,' he said, smiling across at her. 'What's on your mind? Nothing to do with last night, eh? I've gathered from our conversation you haven't told Tom about my calling upon you at the inn.'

'No, I didn't. I thought he might have been hurt that he hadn't been included.' She flushed slightly again.

'You mean it might have made him jealous,' Chris countered. 'But perhaps a little healthy honest-to-God jealousy is just what he needs, Beth.'

'Why do you say that, Chris?'

He looked at her quizzically. 'You do still want to marry him, Beth? Or,' he hesitated, 'have you changed your mind?'

She turned her head aside. She could feel his blue eyes looking intently down at her. 'I — I suppose I do, Chris.'

'You only suppose you do?' he caught her up sharply. 'You seemed much more definite about it when I talked to you in London.' He added after another pause, 'Has anything happened to make you change your mind, Beth?'

'No, of course not. I'm not the sort of person who changes her mind,' she said sharply, even angrily.

He reached across the table and took

one of her hands, holding it tightly in his own. 'Don't be mad, Beth, and we should all be able to have second thoughts. To change your mind according to the circumstances isn't a sign of weakness but one of strength. Only weak, stubborn fools persist in clinging to an idea despite changed circumstances.'

'You think I'm a weak, stubborn fool, Chris?'

He shook his head. 'Far from it, darling.' The 'darling.' seemed to slip out.

She caught her breath sharply and was suddenly conscious of a dizzy feeling of happiness she couldn't understand.

'I love you, anyhow, whether or not you're a weak, stubborn fool,' he added with a slight mocking grin.

'You seem to be able to love lots of girls, Chris. Do you love Sally Hyman, too?' But that was the last thing she had intended to say; and why should she throw the pretty blonde American girl at him almost as though she was accusing him of something? She had no right to accuse him of anything, no reason for it.

'Of course I love her. Sally's a dear, sweet kid. She and I have been friends for a number of years. Didn't you like her, Beth?'

'I liked her very much,' Beth lied.

He still had that half-ironical, half-mocking grin on his face. 'Is that what you want to talk about — Sally and myself?'

'Of course not,' she snapped. 'I don't know how we got into this discussion. I wanted to tell you about Michiko.'

'What about her? You haven't seen her yet?'

She remembered then that he hadn't been present when she had told Tom about Michiko.

She nodded. 'I have, but in such strange circumstances,' and she told him exactly what had happened that morning just before she had left the Itos' house.

He listened intently without interrupting, but when she told him that Dr. Rickard had hinted it mightn't have been an accident, he gave a low, startled exclamation.

'Do you think that young doctor meant that, Beth? Or did he just say it under the emotional stress of the moment?'

'I don't know, but he looked pretty grim as he said it. But he *was* obviously upset. He seems very fond of Michiko.'

'Do you think he's in love with her?'

She shook her head. 'I wouldn't know.'

'What you've said, Beth, has made me wish more than ever that you weren't mixed up in all this,' he said finally. 'My dear one,' he gripped her hand tighter, 'couldn't you draw out now? Tell Tom you don't want to go through with this, and send a wire to the Itos.'

She shook her head, then drew her hand out of his. 'I couldn't possibly, Chris. Tom is setting such store on my getting to know his daughter and maybe managing to influence her; and this present arrangement, sharing a room with her, is a heaven-sent chance.'

'Be careful, Beth,' he urged, his voice low and hoarse. 'I don't think the Itos' is a very healthy household.'

'I'll be able to tell you more about it tomorrow. Shall I be seeing you, Chris?'

'Why the hell shouldn't you be seeing me?'

'I don't know.' She hesitated. 'I thought you might be otherwise engaged.'

He grinned wickedly. 'Even if the girl doesn't want you herself, she's darned well going to see that no other girl gets you.'

'You're quite insufferable.' She got to her feet. 'We'd better be going; I shall be late for my hair appointment.'

'How are you going to get out to the Itos' house tonight? I'd offer to drive you but . . . '

'But you'll be busy,' she cut in on him. And again she was surprised at the sharpness in her voice.

He laughed outright, maddeningly. 'I

wasn't going to say that at all. I was going to say that I think it wiser you arrive in a taxi. It would cause less suspicion, especially since mine is an American car.'

'I must go for my hair appointment.'

But as she turned away from the table he caught her hands again: 'Will you lunch with me tomorrow, Beth?'

'You mean with Tom? We should all lunch together?'

'I didn't mean with Tom; I meant with me — one man, one girl; that's enough, isn't it?'

She demurred: 'But Tom will be expecting me to lunch with him.'

'Both of you, if you like; Sally will join us. We could all drive out to Ueno Park, which is wonderful at this time of year when the cherry blossom is in full bloom. There's quite a good Japanese restaurant nearby where we could lunch.'

'I'd like that.' But she did wonder if from now on all their parties would be a foursome.

She supposed she was horribly selfish but she had enjoyed having Tom and Chris to herself.

The beauty salon in the Imperial Arcade was evidently the same as all beauty salons and ladies' hairdressers all over the world. The girl at the reception desk bowed low to her and asked her if she would take a seat for a few minutes; they weren't quite ready for her.

The basement room was attractively decorated with flower arrangements and had all the latest modern equipment. Most of the young hairdressers spoke English, but with a faintly American intonation.

'Hallo! Is that you, Miss Rainer?' a girl's voice called. 'Do come and talk to me while you're waiting. I'm just finishing having a manicure.'

She turned and saw Sally Hyman in a far corner of the room facing a pretty Japanese girl manicurist over a small glass table.

'Come and help choose for me what

colour I'm going to have on my nails,'
Sally called.

Beth walked over to her. Sally had
looked very pretty before; she looked
quite lovely with the new hairdo. It was
a work of art and made her look much
more sophisticated.

Sally smiled up at her brightly. 'What
do you think of the hairdo?'

'It's certainly something,' Beth smiled.
'It's extremely attractive.'

Sally turned her small head from one
side to the other and looked at herself
in the mirror facing her with frank
admiration. 'It's quite somethin' as you
say. Better than anything I've had in
New York. And here was I by way of
thinking that this was a hick town. Wait
till they start on you, Miss Rainer. You
won't know yourself.'

Beth laughed. 'Does my hairdo look
as bad as all that?'

'A bit unsmart, if you don't mind my
saying so. Where do you get your hair
done in London?'

Beth had to admit that she went to a

small hairdresser's in Putney on a Saturday morning, as it was the only time she could spare.

'A special hairdo gives a girl a lift and confidence,' Sally said. She looked at herself again in the mirror, turning her pretty head from side to side. 'Hmmm, hmmm, not bad. I hope Chris will like it.'

Beth said, trying to make her remark sound like good-humoured teasing, 'It will mean something to you whether Chris likes it or not?'

'You bet,' Sally said, grinning impishly. 'Chris is my mentor on dress, hairdos, conversation and morals. The oracle speaks; I sit at his feet, approve and worship.'

Beth felt suddenly cold and for some reason intensely unhappy.

'I can see that you and Chris are great friends.'

'And how!' Sally said. She nodded and chuckled. It was a gay, infectious chuckle. 'Chris is big brother and all that and something besides. We've known each other practically all our lives. His parents had a house on Long Island Sound next to our own place. Have you known Chris long, Beth? I may call you Beth, mayn't I? And you call me Sally. Chris said that you and I and your boss, Mr. Dillan, are going to see an awful lot of each other. My, that was a lovely necklet and earrings he bought you this morning. Are you engaged to him?'

'No, we're not engaged.'

'But I'm sure you must be romantic about him,' Sally prattled on. 'He's old, of course, but as far as looks go, he's certainly a stunner — such strong, handsome features and that adorable cleft in his chin; the sort of boss all young secretaries fall for, and then usually marry one of the young clerks.'

'Tom isn't old.' Beth felt flustered and irritated.

'Well, he must be getting on towards forty, and surely *that's* old? At least it seems so to me.'

'But then you're very young,' Beth said.

'I'm nineteen,' Sally said, almost indignantly. 'How old are you, Beth?'

'Twenty-three.'

'You look it sometimes,' Sally said, cocking her head slightly to one side, 'when you're frowning and mad. You're mad at me now because I said that about Mr. Dillan being old. Well I think he is old, too old for you, Beth. Wait till you've had your hair done and bought yourself some exotic clothes from those lovely materials I see in the windows. You won't look a day over twenty, I swear.'

'Is that an advantage?' Beth asked. There was a slightly caustic note in her voice. But the shaft went right over Sally's head.

'Of course it's an advantage. Today the accent is upon youth. You'd be quite stunning, Beth, if you took a little more trouble over yourself and,' she grinned again impishly, 'forgot for once that you were Mr. Dillan's secretary.'

One of the attendants in a neat starched overall came up to Beth:

'We're ready to shampoo you now, Miss Rainer.'

Beth rose quickly to her feet. For the moment she was glad of the excuse to escape from this precocious young teenager.

'I'll be seeing you soon,' she said to Sally.

'You bet.' Sally nodded and waved a hand on which the bright coral nail varnish was drying. 'Chris tells me he's going to plan some stupendous outings. I can't wait to get to grips with this country. Be seeing you!'

14

While she waited for the assistant to bring the shampoo and towels, she bent forward closer to the mirror and for the first time in months she took a good look at herself. Had she been too wrapped up in her emotions concerning Tom, too busy with her work in the office to take proper stock of herself? Sally had advised her laughingly to glamorise herself, to stop looking like someone's secretary. Did she look like that? She had to admit that compared with Sally's new hairdo, her own red-brown naturally curling hair looked slightly mussed and wayward. Perhaps she should touch up her eyebrows and lashes so that they looked dark instead of a reddish brown. She might, she considered, pay more attention to her make-up. Usually, her make-up was a very slapdash affair, put on in a few moments while her mother was calling downstairs that breakfast was ready. She hadn't re-made her face since early that morning when she had got up at the Japanese inn. Her skin was lovely; her cheeks naturally rose tinted; but she suddenly realised there was a great deal she could do to improve her appearance. Why wait until a prattling young girl showed her how far she had been slipping?

'Could I have a facial after my manicure and hairdo?' she asked.

'With pleasure,' the manageress of the establishment said, bowing to her. 'We will do the facial before we have combed out your hair.'

'To hell with the cost,' Beth thought. 'I've been a fool. A girl should spend money on her appearance.'

She had just had her hair done up in curlers, a moment when a woman looks her very worst, and was waiting to go under the drier, when a laughing voice said behind her, 'Beth, my angel, you look like a space-woman.'

Chris couldn't have caught her at a worse moment and she was furious. The shampoo had taken all the make-up off her face and her hair was done up on plastic rollers. Undoubtedly she did look like a space-woman — someone dropped down out of Mars.

'You've no right to come in here, Chris. This is strictly a woman's domain.'

'The manageress made no objection,' he said, still laughing. 'It was worth it, anyhow, to catch you for once off your guard, Beth. That's the second time I've done it within the last few days.'

She flushed violently, remembering how he had caught her coming out of the communal bathroom, her hair half wet, with the silken kimono clinging to her naked body.

'Don't get all hot and bothered, my sweet.' He leant over her slightly, lowering his voice. 'You looked very lovely last night — as lovely as I have ever seen you, and that's saying

248

something. I can't quite say the same thing about you now, but it's a pity I won't be around when they turn you out the finished article. But I'll be seeing you tomorrow. So long for the moment.' He added in a much lower voice, 'I would love to kiss you, even with those awful contraptions on your head.'

She had to smile.

'I know I look an awful sight.'

'I'm ready, Chris!' Sally stood by them.

Chris's deep blue eyes obviously admired her. 'You're a sight for sore eyes, Sally — pretty but smart and sophisticated as well.'

She dropped him a little curtsy. 'I'm glad you like it, kind sir. Now let's get going. There's so much in this town I want to see.'

Beth envied her light-hearted gaiety, her supreme confidence in herself. She wished she could act and feel as carefree as the blonde-haired girl. But when an hour and a half later they turned her out of the beauty shop, even she had to admit that they had done a good job on her. The front of her red-golden hair was swathed across her forehead; the back was piled high in minute curls. Her skin didn't show an excessive amount of make-up; it looked fresh and lovely. The eyebrows were shaded to a deep brown; the high cheekbones faintly touched with rouge, the lips an attractive shade of coral. The pearl necklace looked lovely on her throat, and the diamonds in the earrings sparkled.

Tom was waiting in the lounge. He stood up and almost gaped at her. 'What on earth have you been doing to yourself, Beth?'

She smiled. 'It's what they've been doing to me down in the beauty shop. Do you like it, Tom?'

'I don't know. You look different.' He smiled and added, 'I don't know whether I like you to look different or not, Beth. I liked you well enough as you used to be — any way you are, you're beautiful to me.'

He had said it in all sincerity. She smiled at him affectionately. 'Thank you, Tom. It isn't often that you say such nice things to me.'

'Don't I?' He sounded surprised. 'I've been very remiss then. I think nice thoughts about you, Beth, all the time.'

She gave him both her hands impulsively. 'I'm glad, Tom.'

They stood there for a moment amongst the crowd of tourists hurrying to and fro, looking at each other.

'Beth . . . ' His voice had subtly altered, but he paused again.

'Yes, Tom?'

He looked embarrassed and then gave a short laugh. 'I don't want to hurry you off, Beth, but isn't it about time you should be making tracks for the Itos'?'

'I suppose it is.' Her voice had suddenly become listless. 'Will you arrange to have some of my luggage sent down for me, Tom? And get the porter to call a taxi.'

When she had approached the Itos' home that morning it had been bathed in sunshine; it had looked cheerful, even hospitable; but now as she walked up the front pathway the sun had set and the house was engulfed in early evening shadows. In that light the old-fashioned building had a much less friendly appearance. It looked grim and forbidding and Beth was conscious of a curious sense of apprehension. She shivered. She told herself there was nothing whatever to be afraid of. Even if they should find out that she was working for Michiko's father, she was committing no crime.

She asked the taxi driver to help her inside with her luggage. She did it mainly by gestures for the man spoke very little English, but she was faintly amused to see that before he stepped into the house he took off his shoes and changed into one of the pairs of slippers that were standing waiting on the veranda. She supposed she had better do likewise since it was the custom.

The little maid, whose name was Hanako, meaning Flower-child, opened the door to them. She spoke to the taxi driver in Japanese and he deposited Beth's luggage in the hall. Then she said, '*Doozo*' and beckoned to Beth and led her into the lounge room with its screen doors, its heavy *tatami* matting and the *tokonoma*, with its customary scroll of Japanese writing and a magnificent flower arrangement.

'The flower arrangement is very beautiful, Mrs. Ito,' Beth commented.

The elder woman nodded. 'It is Michiko's work. The child is very good at flower arrangements.'

'How is Michiko-san, Mrs. Ito?' Beth asked quickly.

'She is much better,' the woman said. 'In fact she has quite recovered. Apparently she slipped on a mossy stone in the kindergarten garden when she went out in her recess hour. She struck her head on the same stone when she fell. I have told her she is to have a roommate. She is pleased.'

'I am glad she is pleased,' Beth murmured.

'We serve dinner at seven in the dining room across the hall. Hanako will have taken your luggage upstairs. Would you like to go up now and unpack?'

'Thank you very much, Mrs. Ito,' Beth said, bowing. If you had told her a few days ago that it would come natural to her to bow when she met anyone or made a request, she would have laughed. But in this atmosphere it seemed quite natural.

'Come with me,' Mrs. Ito said, and led the way from the bare lounge room up the stairs, along the corridor, where she opened one of the doors slightly and called, 'I am bringing Miss Rainer now, Michiko. Is it convenient?'

'Quite convenient,' a girl's voice called back in English.

Michiko was standing before the mirror arranging her hair. It was sleek very dark hair, cut in the Western manner and it cupped her face delightfully, with two rounded ends going out on to her cheeks.

'This is Miss Rainer, Michiko,' Mrs. Ito said. 'She is studying Japanese. Perhaps you will be able to help her in her studies.'

'*Konnichi wa!*' Michiko said, bowing low.

Beth bowed too. 'I am very glad to meet you.'

A humorous look came into Michiko's large beautifully shaped grey eyes. 'You have not progressed very far with your studies, Miss Rainer.'

Beth flushed. 'I'm afraid I haven't. I've only just begun taking lessons.'

'We must all help you to learn Japanese quickly and correctly, eh, Mamma-san?'

'We will do our best, Michiko,' Mrs. Ito said. 'But of all foreigners the English seem the stupidest and laziest at picking up languages.'

The remark may not have been

255

intended as rudely as it sounded.

'The English are not stupid, Mamma-san,' Michiko said quietly. 'But it is true they have little aptitude for languages. In that respect they are like the Americans.'

'The Americans, bah!' the elder woman said. She drew in a breath and let it out with a hissing sound of disapproval.

Michiko smiled and Beth thought that she was quite lovely when she smiled. Her light-complexioned face lit up charmingly, her eyes danced. They were very dark grey eyes, more the colour of a European's eyes than the customary dark seal-brown eyes of the Japanese. Beth found herself thinking they were very like Tom's, and they had that same slightly humorous look in them.

'The English and Americans do not need to learn languages,' the girl said. 'Their language is fast becoming a universal one and other countries must learn it in order to do business and make friendships with them.'

'At least they might pay us the compliment of *trying* to learn our language,' Mrs. Ito snorted. 'As I said, I do not mind so much the English, but I detest the Americans.' As though to give vent to her feelings she went out of the room slamming the door after her.

Michiko laughed. It was a most attractive laugh, a low, sweet-sounding little gurgle. 'Mamma-san is a dear person but she is very outspoken. She was here all through the American Occupation and she has hated them ever since. I suppose it is pride that we should have been occupied by any foreign country. We Japanese are a very proud race.'

'I can understand that no nation likes an army of occupation,' Beth agreed. 'The same was true on the Continent of Europe when the Germans occupied their countries. Perhaps that is why we English are now more tolerant towards the Germans — we were never occupied. But,' Beth went on, 'just because you hate a nation that doesn't mean you should hate individuals of that nation. My mother had before the war, and has had since, very good German friends of whom she is fond. Do you hate the Americans in the same way as Mrs. Ito does, Michiko-san?'

The girl hesitated. She half turned away from Beth and glanced once more in the mirror. 'Perhaps I do not hate them so much,' she said presently. 'I was very young at the time of the Occupation, and since then although there are many Americans in this country, I have not met any of them.'

Then, as though to change the subject she went on: 'Mamma-san is very businesslike; sometimes too much so. I hope you are not paying her too much, Miss Rainer? This is a very humble household.' There was a faint look of concern on her pretty face.

When Beth mentioned the sum she was paying, Michiko looked shocked. She put one hand across her mouth with a small gasping sound. 'But — but that is so much, especially for a student to pay. Can you well afford it, Miss Rainer?'

'Yes, I can afford it.' Beth smiled back at her reassuringly, touched by the girl's concern. 'But please don't call me Miss Rainer; call me Beth.'

'Beth. Beth-san,' Michiko repeated. 'It is a very pretty name but unusual for us.'

'It's short for Elizabeth,' Beth told her.

'I like that name better — Elizabeth. May I call you Elizabeth, please?'

'Yes, do,' Beth said. 'My father always used to call me Elizabeth.'

'Your father.' Michiko said the word slowly, and a curious look which Beth couldn't define came over her face. 'You speak of your father as though he was dead, Elizabeth-san.'

'He is dead,' Beth said.

'You loved your father very, very much?'

Beth nodded slowly. 'Very, very

much. All girls should love their fathers; and their mothers,' she added.

'Sometimes it is not easy to love one's father,' the girl said with a faint sigh. 'It is not only difficult, it is impossible. I have no love for my father, only for my mother, and she died in a tornado shortly after I was born.'

Beth said with seeming innocence, 'Then Mr. and Mrs. Ito are not your mother and father?'

The girl shook her pretty dark head. 'No. But they have looked after me since I was a baby, and they are like my mother and father. They have been very kind to me; they have loved me. I know they still love me, but I must act as they want me to act; I must think as they want me to think. They are good Japanese people of the old-fashioned, traditional kind.'

'But you do not share all their views?' Beth put in quickly.

The girl shook her head. 'I am modern Japan. For one thing, I earn my own living, which would never have been tolerated when they were young. I would have spent my entire days in learning flower arrangement, practising the tea ceremony, making embroideries and learning to play on the samisen. Instead, even when I was young, I insisted I had a good education. Mamma-san and Pappa-san did not like it. They wanted me to be a traditional young Japanese girl, learn all the arts and later help Mamma-san in the house. But since they were not my parents I wanted to feel independent. It isn't that I don't love them.' Her voice softened. 'But today the young girl of Japan wants to be independent. Are you independent, Elizabeth-san?'

Beth smiled. 'Of course. I've been earning my own living since I was seventeen.'

'You are earning your own living?' Again the girl gave a small shocked gasp behind her hand. 'But how is it you can pay Mamma-san the large price she has asked you?'

'My firm is paying for me to learn

Japanese,' Beth said. It was the only explanation she could have given; but for some reason she hated having to lie to this girl. She was not only attractive and essentially likeable, but Beth sensed she was honest.

'That is all right then,' Michiko said. 'Would you like me to help you unpack?' She slid aside one of the paper-backed doors. 'Here is your closet. There is hanging space and drawers on the other side. Can you find room in this closet for everything? In Japan we do not leave clothes around the room as I have seen girls do in American and English movies.'

'Mrs. Ito allows you to go to American movies?' Beth asked.

'But of course.' The girl opened her dark grey eyes wide. 'I am a working girl; I do as I like. My aunt, my mother's elder sister, used to pay Mamma-san for my board and lodging when I was very young, but when my poor aunt died, it was then I decided to work for myself. I stopped my courses in flower arrangement, tea ceremony and samisen playing, though I sometimes go to evening classes in these subjects. They are all so very interesting. But during the daytime I studied and now I am kindergarten teacher.'

'Your father and mother would have been very proud of you had they been living,' Beth said. 'You did tell me that they were both dead, didn't you?'

'Only my mother is dead. I do not talk about my father,' Michiko said in a voice which closed the conversation.

Beth thought it unwise to pursue the subject at the moment; it might arouse the girl's suspicions.

Michiko, who had been dressed in Western clothes when Dr. Frank had carried her up to the house in his arms that morning, was now wearing a lovely kimono of a deep rich blue with a scarlet obi or long sash about her waist. Beth commented on how beautiful the traditional Japanese costume was.

'At home in the evenings we all dress in Japanese fashion,' Michiko said. 'You would look lovely, Elizabeth-san, in a kimono. You have one perhaps in your suitcase?'

Beth shook her head. 'I'm afraid I haven't, but I'm going to buy one.'

'Please let me lend you kimono for tonight.' The girl smiled prettily. 'I have many kimonos and I would love to dress you as young Japanese girl.'

Beth laughed. 'All right.'

It would be fun; she had never lost the love of dressing up she had had in her childhood.

'I lend you my best kimono,' Michiko said.

'Please, no. Any of your ordinary kimonos,' Beth begged.

But Michiko merely laughed and clapped her hands. 'No, you shall have my best — my very best.'

It was a glorious hand-embroidered dark green kimono with a long golden sash, which Michiko told her was made from hand-woven Nishijin brocade. She dressed Beth's red-gold hair in a way that made her look more Japanese; not that Beth could really look Japanese; there was too much gold in her hair; her skin was too fair.

'You look like geisha,' Michiko said, clapping her hands. 'Very beautiful geisha.' She added seriously, 'You must not be offended by being called geisha. Geishas are highly thought of in Japan. They are entertainers and undergo long years of training. They are not bad women as some Europeans seem to think. I have often wished to be geisha. They have more freedom; they go to theatres and nightclubs.'

'But surely you go to theatres and nightclubs?' Beth exclaimed in surprise.

Michiko shook her head. 'No. Mamma-san and Pappa-san will not allow. Not even when Dr. Frank ask me will they allow. I must be chaperoned, they say, and I know no other girl who could chaperon me — not one of whom Mamma-san and Pappa-san would approve. They are very strict.'

Beth saw an opportunity and seized upon it. 'Do you think they would allow you to come out with me and a friend?'

Michiko's eyes flashed eagerly; her lips curved in a smile. 'They might. Forgive me, but you pay them so well,' and again she gave that delightful gurgle of laughter, holding her hand up before her mouth. 'You have relatives here who might take us out?'

'I have a cousin,' Beth said, and again she hated herself for lying to this girl.

Michiko nodded eagerly. 'Yes, Mamma-san might approve. We go out with your cousin? We go to the Kabuki Theatre, perhaps, and then on to the Queen Bee. Such places I have always longed to see. Dr. Frank suggested taking me there, but Mamma-san would not approve.'

'But why?' Beth asked. 'Dr. Rickard — or Dr Frank, as you call him — seemed an exceptionally nice man.'

'You have met him?' Michiko asked.

'Briefly at noon today. I was leaving the house when he carried you into the house.'

'Ah, yes, after I have fall,' the girl said, and suddenly the expression on her pretty face changed. It had been gay and laughing a moment previously; now it was suddenly expressionless, and Beth saw — or thought she saw — a definite fear lurking in the dark grey eyes. The girl suddenly seemed smaller than ever, more childlike, more vulnerable.

Beth suddenly stretched out her hand and touched her. 'What is the matter, Michiko-san?' she asked.

The girl drew away. She shook her head fiercely, 'Nothing, nothing, Elizabeth-san, but strange fancies. But it is nothing, I assure you.'

Beth said, to change the conversation, 'Why doesn't Mrs. Ito allow you to go out with Dr. Frank? Surely with him you wouldn't need a chaperon?'

Michiko smiled again, but this time a little wistfully. 'She think Dr. Frank in love with me. She does not approve.'

Beth had already guessed as much.

'But why?' she asked.

'Dr. Frank not a rich man. He gives all his time to making the poor well.

Mamma-san would like me to marry rich Japanese man. She has already begun to make arrangements through a *nakado* or go-between. But I say no, no, I will not marry rich Japanese man.'

'But Mrs. Ito can't force you to marry anyone you don't want to,' Beth insisted. 'She isn't your mother.'

'No, but when Aunt died she left me in Mamma-san's care until I reach twenty-one. She cannot force me to marry but she can prevent me marrying a man of whom she disapproves.'

'Michiko-san, are you in love with Dr. Frank?' Beth asked quietly.

A warmly radiant smile played over the girl's pretty features. 'I love,' she said. 'Yes, I love Dr. Frank.' She added impulsively, 'But you will not tell?'

'I promise not to tell,' Beth said, and then they heard the gong sound for dinner.

15

The dining room was a large square room. The rich merchant who must originally have built this house on the crest of a hill looking down on to Tokyo, must have had a large family. The dining table was round; there were cushioned mats for the diners to sit on and each place was laid with a china bowl and chopsticks.

Before they sat down on their mats, Beth was introduced by Mrs. Ito to her fellow houseguests. She met Wang Lee, a Chinese student of medicine from Canton. He was tall for a Chinese and very thin. His face was a deep yellow colour and his expression was very intent. By his brown, slanting eyes one might guess that he had Mongolian blood in his veins. With him was another Chinese from Hong Kong, John Chao, shorter, plumper, but with the same seal-brown slanting eyes which gleamed behind thick-lensed glasses. His expression was kindlier; he looked less of a fanatic; as she was introduced to the Chinese students they bowed to her and she bowed back to them.

Zontan Andrassi, who was introduced to her as a Hungarian student, was reddish-blond. He was good-looking and fairly tall. He seemed disposed to be friendly and shook her warmly by the hand.

Ivan Surkov, whom she gathered to be Russian, was less effusive in his greeting. She felt that from the first he regarded her with obvious suspicion. He was blond and squarely built and there was the same almost fanatical hardness about his expression as she had seen in the Chinese Wang Lee's face.

The only other full-blooded Japanese besides the Itos was a Japanese student, Yaizu Seki. He was fairly tall, with dark hair, dark eyes and finely drawn features. His lips were thin and he kept them pressed tightly together. Although young he talked and acted as though he was used to taking command. Beth wasn't surprised to learn later that he was head of one of the most energetic and fanatical student organisations at the Tokyo University. When Mrs. Ito performed the introduction, he bowed low to Beth and she bowed back.

'Welcome to our humble lodgings, Rainer-san,' he said. He spoke as though he were the head of the household. Mr. Ito, a short plump man in a dark grey kimono, seemed undistinguished, almost like a guest in his own home.

Beth was surprised. She had always believed that the Japanese male dominated his women folk and ruled the household. But apparently with the Itos this was not the case; Mrs. Ito was obviously the dominant party. And she was to learn that Yaizu Seki, her elder sister's son, ruled the household in place of her husband.

They had all sat down on their mats, Beth in the place of honour beside Mr. Ito, and Hanako was already serving the soup, which was deliciously flavoured with fish and spices, kneeling beside each place as she served, when Dr. Rickard burst into the room. That was the way Beth described it to herself; he had so much energy and vitality she felt it would have been impossible for him to make a normal entrance into any room. He bowed to Mrs. Ito: 'I am sorry to be late, Maki-san,' he said. 'But just as I was leaving my surgery a patient arrived.'

'A poor non-paying patient, I'll wager,' Mrs. Ito said with a touch of irascibility.

He grinned delightedly. 'How did you guess, Maki-san?'

'It is always the same with you,' she grumbled. 'You work and get no money for it. You will end up a poor old man in an attic, and your friends will laugh at you and mock you.'

'Why should they mock him?' Michiko

broke in, her young voice hard and angry. 'If he has done good all his life for little or no money they will revere him.'

'Bah!' Mrs. Ito said. 'Take your place, Frank-san. You are lucky that there is any soup left in the bowl.'

His blue eyes twinkled as he sat crouched on his mat in the Japanese manner beside Michiko.

'You are better, Michiko-san?' His blue eyes had softened; there was a tender, almost caressing note in his voice.

'Yes, thank you, Dr. Frank, I am much better.'

Dining is a ceremony in Japan not to be taken lightly. During the commencement of the meal there was very little conversation. The soup was cleared away; the dish which followed was a vegetarian one, traditional to the old city of Kyoko, Mrs. Ito informed Beth. It was prepared in the same way as though it were fish or fowl. Certainly Beth agreed with her that it tasted delicious. Mrs. Ito told her that she herself was from Kyoko, where the people consider themselves true gourmets, and the housewives pride themselves on being the best cooks in Japan.

The traditional dish, *suki-yaki*, followed, which Hanako prepared in a huge chafing-dish over a low-burning flame. As well as the thin slices of steak there were mushrooms and other vegetables and many ingredients. The students seemed to enjoy it thoroughly and the Chinese students showed their appreciation by belching delicately.

Some of the conversation was carried on in Japanese. Occasionally, for Beth's benefit, they spoke English, a language which most of the students seemed to speak a little and understand even more. Dr. Frank, of course, spoke English fluently, as did John Chao, who had been brought up in Hong Kong. Wang Lee spoke English with difficulty. The Russian and the Hungarian were fairly fluent in the language though they spoke with a distinct foreign accent. Yaizu Seki spoke English quite well too.

Beth found it difficult both to keep up with the conversation and manage her chopsticks. Sometimes the food reached her mouth, at other times it didn't. She felt that some of the students must be secretly laughing at her inexperience with the chopsticks. She didn't like to ask for a knife and fork but struggled bravely on. 'At this rate, living in this household, I'll grow much thinner,' she thought with a wry inward smile.

A salad followed, made attractive by the petals of pale pink chrysanthemum flowers. As they ate it John Chao remarked, 'I understand that you are a student at the International Language Centre, Miss Rainer. I, too, am a student there. I am studying Japanese and Russian. It is curious that I have not seen you about the building.'

Suddenly Beth was very conscious that all of their eyes were upon her; some were interested, some were merely curious, but in others she read a definite suspicion. Wang Lee's eyes were hard with suspicion and so were Mrs. Ito's.

Michiko's eyes showed dismay. She rushed to her new friend's help. 'But there are so many students at the language centre, John-san. Surely it is not possible to know everyone there.'

'Oh, it's not such a big place as all that,' John answered easily. 'And,' he chuckled slightly, 'we lads usually keep an eye out for the new girl students.'

'But you *are* enrolled at the Language Centre?' the elder Japanese woman rapped out sharply. 'At least that is what you told me.'

'Yes, of course, but I only enrolled today,' Beth did her best to make it sound quite casual.

'I understood from what you said that you had already been studying there. I must have been mistaken,' Mrs. Ito commented. But her tone implied that she hadn't been mistaken. A swift look passed between herself and her nephew.

Beth felt embarrassed at being the

centre of so much attention. She felt apprehensive too. There had been too much made of the incident as though somehow it had become a matter of major importance. Even if they did find out that she was in the employ of Michiko's father, that wasn't a criminal offence; but she didn't believe that that was what they suspected her of. In the minds of most of them had been some other thought. Of what did they suspect her? She felt extremely uneasy during the remainder of the meal, and afterwards, when they drank Japanese tea served in thin china bowls.

Presently Mrs. Ito bowed low to them all, her head almost touching the table, and they bowed back to her, a sign apparently that the meal was over and that they might disperse. Beth had never been so glad in all her life to get to her feet. Her legs were aching from sitting so long in the crouched position.

She noticed that as they left the room Yaizu Seki said something in a low undertone to the other men who nodded and followed him down the corridor. Beth was left in the company of Mr. and Mrs. Ito, Dr. Frank and Michiko. They all went into the lounge. Here, too, there was nothing but mats to sit upon.

Beth looked towards Mrs. Ito with agonised appeal. 'I suppose it wouldn't be possible for me to have a chair to sit upon?' she asked humbly.

Mrs. Ito pursed her lips together as though in disapproval. 'I'm afraid we do not have a Western chair in the house.'

Dr. Frank laughed. It was a healthy cheerful laugh. 'Come, Maki-san, you must not be cruel to our young English guest. When I first came back to Japan, having lived for years in England, my legs used to ache too. You can't imagine, unless you're used to it, what torture it is sitting for hours in a crouched position.'

'I always forget you are more English than Japanese, Dr. Frank. I understood Miss Rainer wished to come to this country to learn not only the Japanese language but our way of life.'

'Even so,' he was still laughing, 'you don't want to make the poor girl's life a burden to her. There's a stool in the kitchen; let me fetch it for Miss Rainer.'

'You will do no such thing! And please remember that it is I who give the orders in this house, Dr. Frank. I forbid you to interfere in any concern of mine.' Her voice was not only sharp but Beth felt there was hatred in it. She glared at the good-looking fair young doctor, who might have been wholly English but for the suggestion of the East about his eyes. Did Mrs. Ito hate him because he obviously worshipped Michiko and she had other plans for her foster-daughter? But the good-looking young doctor and the charming half-Japanese girl would be an ideal couple.

Beth was more than ever determined to get Michiko away from Mrs. Ito's domination.

'Please, Mamma-san, let me fetch the stool for Elizabeth-san?' Michiko said with charming pleading. 'If we make her sit as we sit all night she will not be able to stand up tomorrow.'

The face of the Japanese woman softened. 'Very well, Michiko, since you wish it, fetch the stool for Miss Rainer.'

Michiko bowed low. 'Thank you, Mamma-san,' she said humbly.

It was the sort of kitchen stool which by a little manipulation could be used as a step-ladder. Probably that was why it had its place in such a very Japanese household.

Beth sank down on to it gratefully, although she felt very much out of place sitting so high up while the others sat on their cushions.

'Possibly you have work to attend to tonight,' Mrs. Ito said to Dr. Frank rather pointedly.

He shook his head, smiling. 'No, Maki-san, I haven't any surgery tonight. It is one of my free nights. I wondered if you'd allow me to walk with Michiko-san?' He said it diffidently and yet urgently.

Beth glanced at the girl and saw that

her eyes, too, were bright with eagerness.

'I am sorry, but no,' Mrs. Ito said positively. 'You have lived too long in England, Dr. Frank. Our young girls do not go out with young men unchaperoned.'

'Oh, nonsense, Maki-san.' The young doctor gave a short laugh to cover his disappointment. 'Young men and young girls — even in Japan — are much more modern these days; they go about quite freely together.'

'Not in a good *Japanese* household,' Mrs. Ito said angrily. 'I will not have you putting your Western ideas into my daughter's head. Michiko will play the samisen and sing for us this evening. A little later, if he comes back into the room, Yaizu will accompany her on the *taiko*.' And when he did arrive she told her nephew just what she had proposed.

Beth had no idea what a *taiko* was but she found that it was a very diminutive drum-stand. Yaizu tapped out the rhythm with thick drumsticks while Michiko played on the samisen, a strange-looking banjo, and sang in a curiously high-pitched soprano. Beth was not only fascinated by the performance but she was very aware of the love and devotion in the young doctor's eyes as he gazed at Michiko.

The other students did not put in an appearance and after Michiko and Yaizu had played several numbers, Mrs. Ito said that it was time for the two girls to go to bed.

Beth was amused. Mrs. Ito certainly took a great deal upon herself. It was more like being in a boarding-school than living in a guesthouse. But she was glad of a further opportunity to talk with Michiko.

Dr. Frank looked his disappointment that the evening had ended so abruptly and Beth gathered that he had only two free evenings each week from his work at the hospital.

The two girls went up to their bedroom, where Hanako, who seemed to do everything in the household, including cooking, washing, house cleaning and serving them at table, had already taken the mattresses from one of the cupboards and laid them out on the floor, making the mattresses up as beds.

Michiko gave Beth a little mocking smile. 'I hope you enjoyed your first evening with us and were not made too uncomfortable sitting crouched on a cushion during the meal?'

'It was kind of you to intercede for me and bring me the stool.'

'Mamma-san can be very naughty,' Michiko said. 'Sometimes I think she enjoys making other people feel uncomfortable. I could wish she were not like that.' She sighed a little. 'I wish she could feel differently about . . . ' she hesitated, 'other people.'

Beth knew she was thinking about Dr. Frank. She nodded in sympathy but remained silent.

'Sometimes it is difficult when your heart pulls one way and your loyalty another,' the girl went on quietly.

'But the Itos are not your real parents,' Beth insisted.

'No, but they have been very good to me. My aunt did not want me living with her because of the disgrace. My mother was never married to my father; he deserted her before I was born.'

'He didn't desert her, Michiko,' Beth broke in passionately. 'He was under-age and in the army. Before he was old enough to marry your mother, he was sent back by the army to America. Afterwards he came back to find her, but she was dead and he could find no trace of what had become of you. Your aunt told him that you had died in the same tornado which killed your mother.'

Michiko was staring at her, white faced and trembling.

'How do you know these things, Elizabeth-san?' she asked hoarsely. 'Do you know my father?'

Beth bit her lower lip. She had given herself away hopelessly.

'Yes, I know him, Michiko-san,' she

said in a low voice.

'And is that why you have come here?'

Beth nodded. 'Yes.'

'I understand,' Michiko said. 'But you should go away, Elizabeth-san, at once. It is not safe for you to stay here.'

'You mean because I know your father and Mrs. Ito might suspect?'

The girl shook her head. 'If it is true what you tell me about my father, I am glad. All my life I had thought hard things of him. I have hated all Americans because of him. Hated them — like Mamma-san and Yaizu hate them; only I do not want to kill . . . ' She broke off sharply. She looked momentarily distressed, even terrified.

Beth came up towards her and laid a hand upon her arm. 'What is all this about, Michiko? What are you afraid of? You *are* afraid, aren't you? I can see it in your eyes, and this morning Dr. Frank said something . . . something that made me suspect your fall might not have been an accident.'

Michiko's voice was low and urgent. She laid a hand across Beth's lips. 'You must not say that . . . You must not think that.'

Beth took the girl's hand away from her mouth. 'But I must say it for your own safety, Michiko. You see, in a way I feel responsible for you.'

'Because you know my father?' Michiko asked. Beth nodded slowly. 'Yes, because I know your father. He is a very good man, Michiko. You should be proud to have a father like Tom Dillan.'

'Is that my father's name?' Michiko asked. She hesitated. It was with a great effort that she finally asked, 'Tell me about my father, Elizabeth-san?'

How could she describe Tom to Michiko so that she could make him truly sympathetic in the girl's eyes?

'He is a very fine man,' she said slowly. 'A good man, Michiko. He is the manager in London of a big American business house that has branches both in London and Tokyo. All his life he has been trying to find you. But it was only recently through a private inquiry agent that he had any success. Your aunt would give him no information whatever — at least not until she was on the point of death. And then it was not to him she spoke but to the agent. She may have felt guilty about withholding the information from him so long.'

'If this is true what you tell me, Elizabeth-san,' the girl's voice quivered and then broke. But suddenly she pushed Beth away from her. 'But I do *not* believe you. My father is a very wicked man. Mamma-san and Pappa-san would not lie to me.'

'But your aunt was paying them to prevent them from telling the truth,' Beth insisted.

'I will not believe that they are bad.' Michiko's voice trembled. 'They have loved me; they would not lie to me. You have come into this house as a spy, Elizabeth-san. The others believe you are a spy; I heard them talking in Japanese between themselves. They do not believe you are a student at the International Language Centre. They think you have been sent into this house to spy upon them.' She said it so vehemently that Beth was taken aback.

'You mean to spy upon them because you are Tom Dillan's daughter?' Beth asked, bewildered.

The girl shook her head. 'No, not that.' Her voice was choked with emotion. 'They would not care about my father other than that he is an American and they are sworn to hate all Americans; they think you have come to spy upon them because of the students' organisation of which they are all members, an organisation which seeks not only to overthrow but to murder those who are in power at present. And not only those who are in power.' She was speaking rapidly, breathlessly. 'But to massacre all foreigners who have not Japanese blood in their veins. It is a secret fanatical organisation whose members do not hesitate to murder those whom they suspect of betraying them, even those who will not go along with them. I have hated the Americans all my life because Mamma-san has taught me they are bad, wicked people and that my father had betrayed my mother, but now I do not know what to think.' Her voice finally broke.

She flung herself down upon the mattress and burst into a flood of tears. Her small body quivered and shook convulsively.

Beth dropped down on to her knees beside the girl, smoothing her hair, trying to comfort her. But Michiko's soul was in torment; for the moment any comfort offered was of no avail. She lay there, prone upon the mattress, her face wedged into the pillow, sobbing her young heart out.

'Michiko! Michiko!' Beth called softly to her. 'I can see you're in trouble. Won't you let me help you? Are you upset about your father because you don't know whether or not you want to see him? Even though he has never met you, Michiko, he loves you. He loves you very dearly.'

But the girl continued her almost hysterical sobbing.

'What is it, Michiko? There is something else besides, isn't there? You are afraid of something. I saw it in your eyes tonight. Is it something connected with Dr. Frank?'

'Oh, no,' the girl murmured through her sobbing. 'He is my good friend, my very good friend. I love him.'

'You are worried because Mrs. Ito might not approve? But would that matter, Michiko? If you rejoined your father, I'm sure that he would approve of Dr. Frank. I am confident that the doctor is a very fine young man.'

But the girl continued her anguished hysterical sobbing.

Beth put both her hands upon her shoulders and shook the girl. 'Stop, Michiko, please stop. You'll only make yourself ill. If I am to help you — and I want so much to help you — you must tell me what you are afraid of. I was in the hall when Dr. Frank carried you in this morning after you had slipped and hit your head upon a stone. He was half-demented with concern for you and he said something . . . something about not believing it had been an accident. Do you know what he meant, Michiko? And had it anything to do with what is frightening you?'

Michiko didn't reply but she nodded slowly.

'Tell me, Michiko. Please let me help you,' Beth begged urgently.

'I can say nothing,' Michiko whispered finally. 'It might mean my death — even your death — if they should know that I had told you. They might be listening even now. They listen all the time to everything that is said in this household.'

Beth shook her again, sharply this time. 'Who is listening? Whom are you talking about, Michiko?'

'Hush!' Michiko said urgently. There was no sound in the room, and yet in that deep silence Beth thought she heard a faint noise. It might have been footsteps, someone stealing away from the door, but that, she told herself a moment later, must have been solely due to her imagination.

'Did you hear that, Elizabeth-san?' Michiko mouthed the words.

'I — I don't know.' Beth's own voice was shaken. 'I thought for a moment I heard something; the sound of foot-steps; but then I thought it was impossible.'

'I may have imagined it too,' Michiko whispered. 'I've had so many queer fancies lately — like I had in the kindergarten today that someone had sprung out from behind a bush and hit me on the head. You see, they had threatened to do it.'

'They? Who are they? And what did they threaten?' Beth's voice showed her complete bewilderment.

But Michiko shook her head stubbornly. 'I cannot tell even you, Elizabeth-san, whom I have begun to love.'

'But if you think they attacked you,

Michiko; if you think they tried to kill you?'

Michiko's hysterical sobbing had ceased. Now she gave a faint wan smile. 'I do not think they meant to kill me, otherwise I would now be quite dead,' she said simply. She added, lowering her voice, 'I think they meant to warn me that if I did not enter whole-heartedly into the organisation, I would be killed. They would have no mercy. All that matters to them is the success of the coming revolution.'

'But what revolution?' Beth asked again in extreme bewilderment.

'What I told you about before; the death of all the present leaders, the death of all foreigners in this country, the establishment of a new régime. Don't ask me to talk about it, Elizabeth-san. But because I will not agree to all this killing they have come to regard me as dangerous.'

'And that's why they are threatening your life?'

Michiko nodded.

'It all sounds too horrible,' Beth said and shook her head and added, 'Since you think you are in danger, Michiko, won't you come away with me? Let me take you to your father.'

'No.' The girl drew away from her abruptly. 'I cannot desert my people, the family who have brought me up. Besides, it would be of little use.' She gave a faint twisted smile and brushed the tears out of her eyes with the backs of her hands. 'Wherever I went they would follow me. They would kill me. I know too much. They might think I had confided in my father; they would kill him too.'

'Does Dr. Frank know about all this?' Beth questioned.

'Not all — a little. At first they tried to make him go in with them; the party needs young doctors, and for my sake, because he knew I was involved, for a time he agreed to do so. But now I do not think they trust him any more than they trust me. I'm more frightened for him than for myself. I would die if anything happened to Dr. Frank.' She said that with a childlike simplicity that was strangely moving.

She laid a pleading hand upon Beth's arm: 'Please do not talk about it any more tonight, Elizabeth-san. I am so tired and my head is spinning. Besides, as I said, there is nothing to be done; I cannot leave here. They would not let me leave. Besides, I do not want to leave here because of Dr. Frank. You had better go to sleep, Elizabeth-san. If they should hear us talking they might become suspicious.'

Beth thought it better to leave it at that for tonight. The little half-Japanese girl looked completely exhausted. But although Beth had slept well last night on the hard mattress on the floor, tonight she slept little; too much was troubling her. She must see Tom the first thing in the morning and tell him what had happened. She must also visit the Language Centre since John Chao would undoubtedly be looking out for her.

And Chris? But it seemed scarcely likely that she would see him that day. He had mentioned lunch but they had made no definite appointment. He would be fully occupied with Sally Hyman. She was amazed that she should feel suddenly almost bitterly resentful of the slight pretty blonde American girl. It wasn't as though she were in love with Chris — she was in love with Tom. But she knew as she tossed and turned trying to woo sleep that tomorrow would be rather a bleak day unless she did see Chris. She supposed it was because he could make her laugh. She felt sadly in need of laughter.

16

Eventually she slept and was sound asleep the following morning when Hanako, looking bright and cheerful despite all the work she had to do in that household, brought in the breakfast for the girls on a tray. There was Japanese tea served in small china bowls, and rice. Hanako knelt on the floor between the two beds and served them.

Michiko was very silent as she ate her breakfast. She answered any remarks Beth made to her in monosyllables. She avoided the other's glance. She seemed strangely withdrawn and at the same time embarrassed. Beth did her best to put her at her ease but there was little she could say while Hanako was in the room. But when the maid had taken away the breakfast tray and left them, she said impulsively, 'Don't be upset over anything you may have said to me last night, Michiko.'

'But I want to hear about my father. Is he actually here in Japan?' The words were low-pitched and tremulous.

Beth hesitated. 'Yes, he is here, Michiko. He has flown out from England to try and get in touch with you. Won't you see him, please? Just to see you and talk to you would make him so happy.'

But the girl shook her head and a stubborn line set her lips. 'No, Elizabeth-san. I've thought about it during the night — long into the night. I do not wish to see my father. My life is here in Japan. He might wish to take me away with him and I would not want to go.'

'I'm sure he wouldn't do that.'

'He is my father; he might insist. I do not know what rights he has over me, but I do not want to go back to England with him.'

'Because of Dr. Frank?' Beth asked gently.

The girl's pretty oval-shaped face

flooded with colour. 'Please do not talk to me about him either. I said too much to you last night. I was,' she hesitated, 'distressed.' She added more sharply, 'Please forget everything I said to you last night. I ask you; I beg it of you, Elizabeth-san.'

Beth said nothing and was glad that the girl had not asked her to give a definite promise.

Michiko had slipped into a house kimono, taken a towel and wash-cloth from the closet. 'It is time for my bath,' she said. 'Would you care to come with me, Elizabeth-san?'

But Beth, remembering her previous experience of bathing in a Japanese household, said she would wait a little until the others were through with their bathing. She decided it might be safer if she were to wait until she reached the Imperial Hotel, where Tom had kept her room on for her, and take a bath there.

There was a wash-basin in the toilet at the end of the corridor. She had washed there and dressed by the time Michiko reappeared.

Michiko looked at her in surprise. 'You have not bathed?'

Beth laughed, then told the other girl of her experience at the Japanese inn the night before. The other girl looked at her in surprise. 'You were self-conscious? But we think nothing of it here in Japan; we are not ashamed to show our bodies. Why are you ashamed to show yours, Elizabeth-san? I could understand it if you were humped-backed or even old and wrinkled. But you have a lovely body; I do not know why you are ashamed that others should know it.'

Beth smiled. 'I suppose it's the way you are brought up. It seems strange to a Westerner that you are not ashamed to bath in the nude and yet Mrs. Ito will not let you walk out with Dr. Frank unchaperoned.'

Michiko considered this.

'I suppose it must seem strange. I had not thought about it.'

She dressed quickly in the neat navy blue suit of heavy silk that Beth had seen her wearing when Dr. Frank had carried her in his arms into the house. She looked most attractive but certainly not as glamorous as she had looked in the lighter blue kimono with the scarlet sash. Certainly a kimono did something for women; Beth decided to buy one that very day. She would wear it tonight at dinner and would not need to borrow one from Michiko.

Mrs. Ito, who greeted her most affably that morning and seemed for the moment to have overlooked the matter of the stool, gave her directions for getting into Tokyo by bus. Beth thought it more fitting that she should travel by bus in her role of language student than call a taxi as Tom had suggested she do.

It was close on ten when she finally arrived at the Imperial. She asked at the reception desk for Tom only to learn that he had gone out and would be back at noon. She collected her key from the reception desk but on an impulse she asked the clerk if he knew of a place where she could buy a Japanese kimono.

'Oh, yes, certainly, Miss Rainer. There is a very nice little shop which specialises in Japanese kimonos down in the arcade.'

Even at this early hour the arcade in the basement was full of tourists, but most of them were in the camera and binocular shops. She was the only customer in the small slip of a shop where they sold Japanese kimonos and happi-coats. She passed over all the cheaper kimonos she should have bought and which she could easily have afforded and chose instead a very elaborate kimono of a glorious shade of golden-brown, with hand-embroidered flowers and a jade-green obi. She felt reckless and bought a happi-coat as well. It was emerald green patterned with pink chrysanthemums and reached to her knees. She felt wickedly extravagant, but for once she didn't care. She hadn't sufficient money with her but asked them to charge it to her room. Tom could deduct the price of the garments from her salary.

She bathed and changed her underwear and was preening herself before the mirror in her new kimono when there was a knock on the door. She thought it must be Tom, but when she opened the door Chris was standing in the corridor.

'Hallo,' he said. 'My, don't you look gorgeous?' His blue eyes, which were so surprising with his dark hair, smiled at her admiringly. 'This is the second time I've seen you in a kimono. Have you gone all Japanese on me?'

She laughed. 'No, but all the boarders at Mrs. Ito's change into a kimono for the evening meal. Even the men wear dark grey kimonos — except Dr. Frank.'

'And who is Dr. Frank?' he asked, grinning down at her. 'It sounds an English name. Have I got a rival?'

She laughed. 'Dr. Frank wouldn't

look at me; he has eyes only for Michiko.' She added seriously, 'He is a very nice young man, half-English, half-Japanese. He went through Oxford University and then was an internee at Guy's Hospital.'

'But he practises out here,' Chris suggested.

She nodded. 'He feels it his duty to help the Japanese people, especially the impoverished ones. He has a clinic. I gather he makes very little money.'

He frowned slightly. 'Tom may be disturbed. I think he has been hoping that he would have Michiko completely to himself. He may be jealous that there is another man upon the scene.'

Beth felt slightly shocked and also disturbed.

'Oh, surely not. I'm sure he would approve of Dr. Frank.'

'I believe it isn't easy for a father to approve of a daughter's suitor. But I wouldn't know.' He grinned again and added, 'I've never had a daughter.'

There was a slight pause and then he

said, 'May I come in?'

'I don't know . . . ' she began.

But he cut her short, laughing, 'Come, come, be your generation — Don't forget I've been in your bedroom before.'

'But that was different.'

'How different?' he demanded.

'I suppose because there was no bed in the room, only a mattress in the closet. It was like a sitting room.'

He laughed down at her affectionately. 'Little prude. What about the Itos' household? Do they embarrass you with their mixed bathing?'

Beth flushed and then she, too, grinned. 'I don't know. I didn't dare take a bath. I waited until I got here to the Imperial.'

'I'm coming in, anyhow,' he said. 'You could scream, of course, but I don't think you will.'

She felt it would have been difficult to refuse him. After all they were both adult. There would be no possible harm in their talking in her room at this hour of the morning, and she had a great deal to tell him.

'You look bewitching in that kimono. The colour is perfect with the brownish tint in your golden-brown hair. And the sash, jade green, is definitely one of the colours you should cultivate. I'd like to see you in a jade green brocaded ball-gown, Beth. I've a good mind to go down into the arcade and order one for you. Why not? Let's go now before the others catch up on us.'

'I couldn't possibly accept a dress from you.'

'Why not?' His long thin face twisted slightly in a lopsided grin. 'You'd let me buy you flowers and sweets; you might even let me make you a present of a piece of jewellery. So why not a gown?' He caught hold of her hands and held them tightly. 'Just for friendship's sake, Beth.'

She had a way of weakening when he looked at her like that, held her just like that.

'I suppose it does sound silly, but it's

just something that isn't done.'

'My sainted Victorian grandmother talking,' he said, and laughed again.

'All right, maybe I am in some ways Victorian.' She held her head at a defiant angle. 'Perhaps in some way all girls — even the most modern of them — are. I admit you could buy me enough flowers and chocolates to fill this room; all the same I won't accept a dress from you.'

'I still think you're a little prude, but quite a darling little prude.' Suddenly he had drawn her into his arms and was kissing her lips. Kissing them fiercely and with passion as he had kissed them the other night.

She should have drawn away — she could have drawn away — but for some reason she didn't; the feeling of his mouth against hers was very sweet. His hard lean hands as they caressed her body did something strange and unexpected to her. As on that other night, she found to her horror she was kissing him back. How low could a girl sink?

she thought in bitter self-reproach, and yet she went on kissing him.

'You mustn't, Chris! You mustn't!' she cried at last, when his hands had become too bold.

Surprisingly he let her go. His release of her was so sudden and, she had to admit, unexpected, that she stumbled back and almost fell.

He laughed at her softly with both a caressing and mocking note in his laughter. 'That's the result of seeing you in a kimono. Remind me always to kiss you when you're wearing a Japanese kimono. I'm glad you've bought one for yourself.'

So that was all it meant to him — it was by way of being a joke because for the second time in their fairly brief acquaintanceship he had seen her wearing a kimono.

'You beast!' She stamped her foot and flushed angrily. 'I've a good mind to return the kimono to the store.'

'You wouldn't want to do that,' he said. 'Besides, you know you enjoyed my kissing you as much as I did, Beth.' And once again his voice was both mocking and tender at the same time.

'Tell me about Michiko,' he went on in the pause. 'She's charming, you say?'

She nodded solemnly. 'She's not only extremely pretty but sweet and unaffected. She has a sense of humour, too.'

'Tom should be very proud to have Michiko for a daughter, and you should be equally proud to have her as a stepdaughter,' he said, grinning.

Suddenly she stood very still. She knew he had said something which was of vital importance. It was odd that up till now she had only once fleetingly thought of herself as being Michiko's stepmother.

'I'm — I'm sure any woman would be proud to have Michiko as a stepdaughter.' But her voice trembled slightly. She liked Michiko; almost she loved her. But it seemed ridiculous to think of the girl as being her stepdaughter. It would make her feel so old.

Old, she thought, suddenly rebellious, before she had grown old, before she had really known the heartbreak and ecstasy that a young love can bring you. She had worshipped Tom ever since she had started to work for him; he was the only man who had counted in her life. Because of him she had turned her back on all the other young men who had come after her. Surely that was love? But it was something very different from what she had felt during those moments the other night and again today when she had been held closely in Chris's arms, when she had accepted his kisses and given them back to him. That, she supposed, was sex, and then she felt a deep sense of shame.

'Please leave me, Chris; I must get dressed.' She tried to say it easily and nicely but to her own ears her voice sounded stiff.

'I'll only leave you if you'll promise to let me buy you a jade green brocade gown,' he said determinedly.

She capitulated suddenly and laughed, and suddenly she found it pleasant, even exciting, to give way to Chris. 'All right,' she grinned, 'but when I wear it I'll feel like a fallen woman.'

'You needn't tell Tom I gave it to you,' he said. 'That's all that matters, isn't it?'

He bent and kissed her lightly on the forehead. 'I like fallen women and I think you're the purest fallen woman I've ever met. We needn't tell Tom about the gown. Let it be our secret. I'll leave you now. I'll wait for you down in the lounge. By the way, you and Tom are lunching with Sally and me,' he added.

She felt strangely flat after he had left the room, though she had no idea why she should. It was perfectly natural that the four of them should lunch together. He had said he would be looking after Sally Hyman during her stay at the American Consulate. And afterwards? Would he be looking after Sally Hyman for the rest of his life? Her mind closed down upon the thought, and once again she felt that extraordinary sense of flatness.

She gave herself an angry shake and wondered what on earth was the matter with her. She had succeeded in winning Michiko's friendship, even though at the moment she had no idea how she could deal with the many problems with which the girl seemed confronted. But Tom and Mr. Oswara might be able to think out some solution. The main thing was that she had partially gained Michiko's confidence.

She hoped Tom would be pleased with her.

She slipped back into her blue linen suit, the one in which she had left the Itos' house that day, for it was important she should return wearing the same clothes in which she had set out that morning. It was also important, she knew, that she make an appearance at the International Language Centre; she had an idea that John Chao would be watching out for her.

Beth never dreamt it would be so thrilling to allow a man to choose a gown for you, to select not only the material but the design. It was like dabbling in something which was both wicked and at the same time exciting, almost indecently exciting. She had never suspected that a man like Chris with all his virile masculinity could be as knowledgeable about materials and choose exactly from a number of designs the one he wanted her to wear and which would obviously suit her best. The smiling shopkeeper unwound roll after roll of exquisite exotic material, the beauty of which made Beth catch her breath in an amazed gasp. She had never dreamt of herself wearing materials such as these. She felt as though the small shop had been transformed into an Aladdin's cave of lavish and gorgeous silks and satins. And after the material had finally been selected, the shopkeeper brought numerous sketches of evening gowns for Chris to glance through, which he did with an expert eye, throwing most of them aside until he had finally selected two which he inspected critically.

'This one,' he said finally, handing the sketch over to the smiling, bowing salesman. 'And how soon can the gown be ready? The day after tomorrow?'

'Oh, sir, that is giving us very little time,' the shopkeeper protested mildly.

'Time enough,' Chris broke in upon him. 'The lady will come in for a fitting tomorrow afternoon, otherwise,' he added curtly, 'we don't want the dress.'

'Yes, sir, of course, sir.' The shop-keeper bowed several times, drawing his breath in with a hissing sound. 'The gown will be ready for the young lady to fit tomorrow afternoon. Yes, sir; yes, sir.' He bowed again.

Beth laughed happily once they had stepped out into the arcade. 'You are a brute and a bully, Chris. Besides, I never suspected that any man could know or care so much about a woman's clothes.'

He laughed too and raised one dark

eyebrow. 'You suspect my masculinity. Supposing we step upstairs and you put on the kimono once again?'

She shook her head, still laughing, 'I shouldn't dare. But I never knew that choosing a dress could be such fun.'

'Life can be fun. That is, with the right person,' he amended, and now his long thin face grew suddenly serious. 'I want you to do something for me, Beth. I want you to help me choose a ring.'

She was startled.

'A ring?'

He nodded. 'A ring suitable for an engagement. Will you help me?'

Suddenly to her horror she was tremendously dismayed. A vision of Sally Hyman's pretty laughing face surrounded by blonde curls, rose up before her mind's eye.

But why not, she was asking herself a moment later; they not only came from the same country but they had been friends most of their lives. She had been well aware the other day that the girl was devoted to Chris. The fact that he had made ardent love to Beth on two occasions obviously meant little to him, or that he had bent over her when she had been thrown from her horse in the field behind the vicarage in Sussex and had called her 'darling.' Some men called every woman darling. She remembered one had told her he called every woman darling because he could never remember their christian names. And probably with a man like Chris, kissing a girl meant very little. She had been a fool even for a moment to think he might mean it.

She forced a smile and hoped it looked genuine. 'Of course I'd love to help you choose a ring. Who is it for, Chris?'

He laughed. 'That's asking questions. Let's say it's for a lady. A very pretty little lady, name undisclosed.'

'But wouldn't it be better if this very pretty little lady, name undisclosed, should help you to choose the ring herself? After all, she has to wear it.'

'That's where you're so very wrong,'

he said, wagging a finger at her playfully. 'I want this to be a surprise, and if she helped me choose the ring, where would the surprise be?'

'But you don't know her finger measurement,' Beth demurred.

'I can guess it,' he said. 'That doesn't really matter. We can have the ring altered after I have given it to her. But I'm sure you have good taste, Beth; that is why I want your help.'

They went across the arcade, into the same jeweller's shop where Tom had taken her to show her the necklet and earrings he had chosen for her, the shop which specialised in Mikimoto cultured pearls.

But Chris apparently did not want a pearl ring for Sally. He said he wanted a carved jade ring set in fine diamonds.

'We have a few such rings, but not a very large selection,' the salesgirl admitted.

'That's all right,' Chris said. 'Show me what you have.'

The jade rings were lovely, such delicate, exquisite carvings set in diamonds that winked and glistened under the electric light in the shop. One especially intrigued Beth. It was the carving of a minute Buddha set in diamonds.

'It's wonderful,' she said in a small awed voice. 'The carving is so delicate, the setting so exotic. It's the most fascinating and unusual ring I've ever seen.'

He cast an eye at her. 'You think the girl I have in mind would like that ring?'

'She'd be a dumbcluck if she didn't.'

He laughed. 'She'd have to take me along with the ring, of course. Do you think she'd be a dumbcluck, as you put it, if she didn't take me as well as the ring?'

Suddenly she felt herself flushing furiously. She knew it and was mad at herself.

'If the girl liked you, Chris, and had known you a long time, there's no reason why she shouldn't take you along with the ring.'

'You think it necessary for her to have known me for a long while?' he countered. 'I didn't think love was a matter of time. In fact I'm quite convinced you can fall in love with someone in a matter of minutes.'

'That's nonsense, Chris.' There was a small uncertain note in her voice. 'I'm sure you couldn't fall in love with anyone in a matter of minutes. You might be attracted to them, I admit; you might even,' she flushed again, 'want to have them kiss you. But love . . . ' She was stammering badly. 'Love is something quite different; I'm sure of that. It must be the outcome of long years of companionship, of mutual understanding, of deep affection.'

Chris was looking down at her curiously. 'I think you've got a father complex,' he said finally. 'It's a very dangerous thing to have.'

He turned back towards the girl

behind the desk and asked the price of the jade and diamond ring. In yen the price sounded colossal; it sounded colossal, too, when Beth had worked it out in her mind in pounds. But Chris said he'd have the ring, and asked the salesgirl to put it aside for him; he'd call round for it later.

They went up the stairs back into the lounge without speaking to each other. Beth was more annoyed with him than she cared to admit for having suggested she had a father fixation. The fact that she had lost a father whom she'd adored when she was young had nothing whatever to do with her love for Tom. He was considerably older, she admitted, but she didn't regard him in any way as a father. It was mean and horrid of Chris even to suggest such a thing. Why should he try to make her feel unhappy, especially now when he was on the point of becoming engaged to Sally?

Suddenly she found she was almost on the point of tears. She murmured to Chris, 'I must go upstairs and powder.'

'All right. We'll meet in the lounge at twelve-thirty for lunch. In the meantime you will be able to tell Tom all about Michiko.'

17

It was quite stupid and uncalled for, but the moment she got into her bedroom she threw herself down on the bed and burst out crying. She had no real idea what she was crying about either. Even if Chris had accused her of having a father fixation in her love for Tom, did it matter? She had always admitted to herself that Tom was everything she would have wanted her father to have been, honest, and upright, a man who was attractive to women though he didn't go out of his way to make himself attractive; a man who didn't make love to a woman lightly. In all the years that she had known him, he had never made love even to her. He had hinted at a deep affection, but he had never made love to her in the way that Chris had, a love to which she knew guiltily she had shamelessly responded. Was that what was the matter with her now — a guilt complex? She wondered what Sally would say if she knew that Chris had been making love to her; would she be furiously jealous? Or would she merely open her blue eyes wider and say 'Why not? He's a man — very much a man, and you're an extremely pretty girl, Beth. What did you expect him to do; pat you on the head?'

Presently she ceased her sobbing. She could have kicked herself for being such a fool in giving way to tears over something which didn't really matter. She looked in the mirror at her swollen eyes and was even more angry with herself.

It was almost twelve and they had told her at the desk that Tom would be back by twelve. He would be eager to hear all about Michiko. She was surprised that he had gone out at all that morning.

She went into the bathroom and bathed her face, pressing a wet cold towel against her aching eyes. Then very carefully she redid her make-up and felt more satisfied with her appearance. By the time Tom finally knocked on her door she was more herself.

She opened the door for Tom.

'I'm sorry if you've been waiting for me,' he apologised, 'but I went to see a firm of American lawyers over here. I wanted to know exactly how I stood legally with regard to Michiko. Luckily I have Eiko's letters, telling me of the baby's birth. They assure me that I can get my claim to Michiko officially recognised. Have you talked to Michiko?' His voice was almost pathetically eager.

She nodded. 'Yes, Tom, and I've a great deal to tell you. Won't you come in?'

'Wouldn't it be better if we went down into the lounge?' he suggested diffidently. 'We can talk there.'

'Of course. I'll come down with you now.'

He wouldn't come barging into her room as Chris had done. He respected her too much. She liked him for it, even if she did think in her secret heart his diffidence slightly old-fashioned in this day and age. She was sure it was what her father would have done in like circumstances. She pulled herself up short. What on earth was she doing comparing Tom with her father? She didn't remember a great deal of her father but she was sure that he and Tom weren't in the least alike. She cursed Chris silently for ever having put the idea into her mind.

The lounge was fairly deserted at this hour. It wasn't difficult to find a secluded corner.

'And now tell me everything — but everything — about Michiko,' Tom said with boyish eagerness. 'You've talked to her? But you must have talked with her since you told me you were going to share a room with her. Is she,' he hesitated, his voice broke a little, 'very wonderful? But she must be. Eiko was so lovely as I remember her.'

'She *is* lovely, Tom,' she said with whole-hearted enthusiasm. 'Beautiful, as I told you yesterday, like a delicate flower, and charming to talk to. She is kind and generous' — she was remembering the incident of the stool and the loan of the kimono — 'and she has a sense of humour.' She added gently, 'She has your eyes, too, Tom, large grey eyes and the loveliest creamy skin.'

'What did you talk about? Did you,' he hesitated and went on with an effort, 'mention me?'

'Yes, we spoke of you, Tom; not at first but after I had got to know her better.'

'Does she hate me? Does she really believe I betrayed her mother?' There was that same nervous tremor in his voice.

'She did believe it, Tom. You see, all her life she had been told that you had betrayed her mother and had left her to bear her, Michiko, alone. She didn't know that you had tried desperately to marry her mother but were prevented from doing so by army regulations and the fact that you were still a minor.'

'But you told her, Beth? She doesn't believe that any longer?'

'I hope she believed me,' Beth said slowly. 'But once an idea has been put into your mind as a child and has grown with you, it's hard to cast it aside in a minute. But she did want to hear about you.'

'Did she? Did she? That must mean she's not indifferent to me.'

'No, I don't think she's indifferent,' Beth agreed. 'She hated you. At least I think she made herself hate you. But in her heart I believe that she has always hoped that she was wrong, that what she had been made to believe wasn't true. I think if you can make her believe how much you loved her mother and that all you wanted in this world was to marry her, she would feel quite differently; she would come to love you.'

'You have done a great deal for me, Beth,' he said unsteadily. 'I don't know how I shall ever be able to thank you.'

'I don't want thanks, Tom,' she said stiffly.

'No? What is it you do want from me?' he asked simply. 'You know I'd give you anything in this world I could.'

'Yes.'

She found herself thinking, strangely, he would give me everything in this world he could — except that ardent young love he had once given Eiko. The Japanese girl had been his first love, his only love. Possibly he loved her, Beth, but he had no longer the passion of youth that had spent itself in the great love of his life. She would have to understand that if she married him, and not be jealous of the overwhelming love he had had for another woman. It might be a small sacrifice, but surely if she loved him enough she would be glad to make it?

A waiter had been hovering hopefully for several minutes. Tom seemed suddenly to become aware of his presence. 'Will you have a cocktail, Beth? Or would you like some of that Japanese rice wine, sake?'

She smiled. 'I'll have a cocktail, Tom;

a dry Martini. I like Japanese food, but I can't even pretend that I like the taste of sake. Besides,' she smiled faintly, 'I feel I need something to buck me up.' She gave a small laugh and added, 'It's been quite a morning.'

He looked at her curiously and with concern. 'Has anything happened to upset you, Beth? Now I come to think of it, you do look rather tired. Almost,' he hesitated diffidently, 'as though you had been crying. You wouldn't have been crying, Beth?'

She smiled. 'What would I have to cry over, Tom?'

'I don't know,' he said uncertainly, and added, 'It isn't anything about Michiko? You've told me everything? She is well and happy?'

'She seemed well enough last night, but I think she is afraid, Tom, and unhappy.'

'But why should she be unhappy? Aren't the Itos kind to her? If they're not kind to her, damn it all, I'll go straight out there now! I won't wait for any legal proceedings; I'll make them give me back my daughter.'

'Michiko's in love, Tom,' she said quietly. 'And the Itos do not approve of the man of her choice.'

'Michiko in love?' he repeated, startled. 'But that's impossible. Why, she's only a child.'

'She's seventeen, nearly eighteen,' she reminded him. 'Her mother must have been about the same age when she fell in love with you.'

'But — but,' he broke off, stammering.

She realised with a sharp stab of dismay that the news was unwelcome to him. Although he had never seen his daughter, was he jealous of the man she loved?

His voice was brusque, almost angry. 'Some Japanese man, I suppose? I hoped that Michiko, if she ever married, would marry an American.'

'She is in love with a young doctor,' Beth told him. 'His father was English, his mother Japanese. His name is Dr.

Frank Rickard, and I understand he is doing a very fine job out here running a clinic for the poorer people. The Itos do not approve because he is poor; they want her to marry a wealthy Japanese merchant. But Michiko really loves Dr. Frank, as they call him. I liked him very much. I'm sure you would like him, too, Tom.'

But he still looked angry, perhaps more hurt than angry. 'I hoped when I found Michiko that she and I could be together. I had never thought that she might have fallen in love. I still insist she is too young to know her own mind.'

'She is young, of course, but in some ways she is very mature. And I think she knows her own mind, especially about Dr. Frank. Perhaps I could arrange to have you meet him, Tom.'

He hesitated. 'If you think I should, I shall see him, Beth. But I warn you, he'll have to prove himself a very fine man before I allow him to marry Michiko.'

Beth smiled faintly, a little sadly. She supposed it was only natural he should resent this man who had won his daughter's love, especially when he had been looking forward to having her entirely to himself. But was that what he had been looking forward to? And where did she, Beth, come into his mental picture? It was a question she couldn't answer; or perhaps she didn't want to answer.

It was almost with relief that she saw Chris and Sally coming up the stairs into the lounge. The girl looked beautiful and radiant that morning. She wore a dress of cornflower blue linen with a wide-brimmed straw hat. She looked as though she had just stepped off the cover of a magazine.

Beth envied her; she had always wanted to look just like that and felt she had never wholly succeeded. Was the girl especially radiant because Chris had already asked her if she would accept the ring which Beth and he had chosen for her? Would they make an announcement over lunch? It would be an exciting occasion. Beth wondered why she felt peculiarly flat.

Tom, too, didn't seem as pleased as he might have been to see them. He had that same half-hurt, half-angry look on his face which he had worn when she had told him about Dr. Frank. For the first time in the three years that she had known him, Beth felt out of patience with him. What on earth was the matter with her today? She supposed she hadn't slept enough last night. Besides, everything seemed crowding in upon her; her talk with Michiko, not only about Dr. Frank but about the student terrorist organisation in which some, if not all, the members of the Itos' household, were involved. Michiko had hinted it had been formed to plan the assassination of some of the leading statesmen and to form a completely new régime that would have no truck with any foreign government; all foreigners in the country were either to be banished or assassinated. The whole thing sounded to Beth like a bad, unreal dream, and yet she knew that in Japan there had been several recent political assassinations.

Michiko was involved because she was a member of the Itos' household, Mrs. Ito's foster daughter, and obviously the short fat determined woman was very active in the organisation. Yaizu Seki, her nephew, was probably involved too. She suspected the two Chinese students, Wang Lee and John Chao, were also concerned.

She had not told Tom of the danger to herself which Michiko had hinted at. She had felt it would not only distress and upset him, but that he would be quite capable of rushing out to the Itos and trying to remove his daughter by main force. She was sure that nothing could be accomplished by such an action. It might definitely antagonise not only the Itos but Michiko herself. It might kill any friendly feelings the girl had begun to have towards her father. It was but natural that until she got to know her father and love him for himself she would side with the Itos. They had brought her up and obviously adored her.

It was with an effort that Tom brought himself to act as host, to order drinks for Chris and Sally and another round for Beth and himself.

Sally and Chris did most of the talking during cocktails and over lunch. The girl seemed to be enjoying every minute of her visit to Japan. She talked of the lovely party Chris had taken her to the previous evening at the British Consulate. 'And this afternoon he is taking me driving out to Ueno Park,' she prattled on. 'And tonight — what are we doing tonight, Chris?' She turned towards him and touched his arm with an affectionate impulsive gesture.

'We're going to the Noh drama. It's olde worlde, frightfully stylised, but very much in the Japanese tradition. No actresses appear on the stage; all the female parts are taken by men. The costumes are magnificent. I'm sure you'll be frightfully bored, Sally.'

She wrinkled her small attractively snub nose at him. 'Shush! Don't you know I had a Vassar education, Chris? I learned all about tradition.' She added almost defiantly, 'I'm all for it, anyway. That's the only thing I've been disappointed at in Japan; everything seems too darned modern.'

'I can see I shall have to take you to Kyoko and Nara to show you that the old Japan really exists, that it is as alive today as it ever was.'

'Then what's stopping you taking me, Chris?' she laughed back at him playfully. 'Any time you say. My host and hostess are such busy people they won't even notice that I'm not in the house.'

Kyoko, the old capital of Japan, about which Beth had read and heard so much since she had come over here; and Nara with all its shrines and temples, places she longed to see.

'I've read so much about Kyoko and

Nara,' she said impulsively. 'I'd love to go there.'

'Why not?' Chris said. 'We could make it a foursome. We could fly down to Kyoko and hire a car and chauffeur. Why shouldn't we all go down there next weekend?'

'Lovely, lovely!' Sally cried and clapped her hands in childish pleasure.

Chris grinned his pleasure at the American girl's enthusiasm. Then he looked across the table: 'What do you say, Beth?'

'I think it would be wonderful,' she said breathlessly.

He looked at Tom and raised one dark eyebrow; 'You agree, Tom?'

Tom shook his head. 'I wouldn't want to leave Tokyo at the moment. Not with things as undecided as they are with regard to Michiko,' he said with quiet determination. 'After all, it is because of Michiko and her future that I am over here.' He looked towards Beth. 'You understand, Beth?'

She nodded though she felt sick with

disappointment. 'Of course I understand, Tom.'

'Then it seems it will have to be a twosome after all, Chris,' Sally said and laughed her light gurgling laugh again, seemingly well satisfied.

Tom glanced at his wristwatch. 'I think we should be getting back into the lounge. Mr. Oswara telephoned early this morning he wanted to see me. Incidentally, you too, Beth. I suppose he's eager to know what you found out at the Itos' house.'

'I want Mr. Oswara to take me to the language centre this afternoon,' Beth said. 'One of Mrs. Ito's boarders is studying there, a Chinese, John Chao, from Hong Kong. He, too, is studying Japanese and mentioned the fact that he hadn't seen me at any of the classes. I said I had just enrolled; but it might be awkward if I didn't put in an appearance today.'

'Why should it be awkward?' Tom asked.

'Well,' she hesitated, 'they might think I was not a *bona fide* student.'

'Even so,' Tom insisted, 'I don't see what that has to do with them.'

'They might think I had been sent to the house to spy upon them.' But the moment she had said it she could have bitten out her tongue. She hadn't meant to give so much away — not at this present juncture. She knew so little really about the supposed terrorist organisation. She still couldn't believe it was as serious as Michiko had intimated. She had come from a law-abiding, organised country where such things as assassination and massacres were unknown. She still couldn't believe in the reality of such things.

But now she was forced to explain something at least.

'I believe that some of the young men in the house belong to a students' organisation. They are violently against the government. They might think I had been planted in the house to get information about them.' She tried to speak lightly, passing it off as though it were a joke.

'Oh, is that all it is; some foolhardy students' nonsense?' Tom said, dismissing the subject with a slight shrug.

But Chris was frowning.

'I don't think you should dismiss it like that, Tom,' he interjected, his fingers beating a nervous tattoo on the table. 'These students' organisations can be damnably dangerous. They have been known to overthrow governments, as they did some time back in Korea. The same sort of fanatical body of students has recently been responsible for some political assassinations here. Some years back, if you remember, a fanatical section which hates all foreigners, especially Americans, were able to stir up the public to such a pitch that the President of the United States thought it wisest not to visit the country. If they suspected that Beth was spying upon them, her life might be in danger. I don't like it. I don't like it at all. I think she should give up this pretence of being a language student and leave the Itos' house.'

340

'But then she would lose all contact with Michiko.' Tom stared across the table at him angrily. 'Already she has told me she has made great progress. If she left the Itos' house now, I might have to give up all hope of getting in close contact with my daughter.'

'I should think you'd be the last person to want Beth to step into danger,' Chris said quietly.

'Of course I don't want her to do anything that might be dangerous to herself,' Tom was still angry. 'But I can't believe in all this nonsense of a fanatical students' organisation and I can't see why they should suspect Beth or even want to hurt her.'

'You don't know the East as I know it, Tom,' Chris reminded him.

'But damn it all, man, this is the twentieth century.'

Chris gave a grim twisted smile. 'Yes, as you say, it is the twentieth century and yet worse things have happened already during this century than in any age known to man. I don't believe that basically any nation, or any one of us, if you like, is any more civilised than they or we were thousands of years ago. Governments are spending fortunes on hideous weapons of destruction; bodies of men — and they are not all adolescents or students — are organising with one thought in their minds: death and destruction to those who share other views from their own. For my part, I should wish Beth never to go back to the Itos' household.'

Tom shrugged. 'Some of what you say is right, of course, but all the same I'm convinced in my own mind that Beth is in no danger. Of course it's up to her. But it seems to me that if she left the Itos' house now, everything we have planned would be ruined. But as I said before, it's entirely up to Beth.'

She had seen the intense disappointment in Tom's face when Chris had suggested she shouldn't go back to the Itos' house, and she felt if she didn't go back she would not only be letting him down, she would be letting herself down, too. She had come to feel a very genuine affection for Michiko and she knew that the girl was badly in need of help. She was confident that she could give her that help.

'Of course I'm going back,' she said, with a faint quiet smile. 'It's nice of you to be concerned for my safety, Chris, but honestly I don't think I'm in any physical danger. I think the next few days are going to be very important in Michiko's life, and since I've formed a genuine affection for Tom's daughter, I want to be there to help her through them.'

Tom pressed her hand under the table. 'Thank you, Beth.'

'I see I'm overruled,' Chris said, 'but I still don't approve. You'll keep constantly in touch with either Tom or me, Beth. You have my private phone number?'

She nodded. 'I'll keep in touch,' she promised. 'And if I think there's any real danger I'll walk straight out of the house. But,' she smiled at Tom, 'I'll try and bring Michiko with me.'

18

Mr. Oswara was already waiting for them in the lounge where a fairly large cherry tree blossomed. He shook hands and bowed to them all several times by way of greeting.

Chris looked towards Sally: 'Well, if we're going to Ueno Park we'd better get cracking.'

Beth asked Sally if she'd care to come up to her room to wash and tidy before she started on the outing.

'I'll come,' Sally said with alacrity. 'I'd like to see the bedrooms in this hotel anyhow. Mom and Pop and I have travelled so much in the States and in Europe that we collect hotel bedrooms. We usually take a flashlight camera photograph of every bedroom we've slept in.'

'That certainly is a new one for a collector's hobby,' Tom said, smiling.

'I'll give these two men coffee and liqueurs while you two girls are upstairs.'

The girls went up in the lift and along the corridor to Beth's room.

'It was a sumptuous lunch, wasn't it?' Sally chattered happily. 'I love the hors d'œuvre here, so many more exciting things than those we have back home in the States and so attractively arranged. But then the Japanese are famed for their arrangements, aren't they? Not only their flower arrangement — gee! haven't we gone crazy about the Japanese flower arrangements in the States? — but the appetising arrangements of their food with such exciting things on the menu as thin wedges of raw fish. Golly, I never knew I would be able to eat raw fish and like it. They also eat the petals of chrysanthemum flowers, and they eat the leaves fried. They even eat fried honey bees, salted thrush hearts and assorted fried songbirds. It sounds awfully cruel, doesn't it, to eat a lovely song-bird? But someone at the Embassy party last night was telling me that they are even more cruel in China.' She shuddered prettily. 'Isn't it all too terrible? You always imagine the East as full of romance and poetry, but apparently the most terrible and frighteningly barbarous customs still go on. You heard what Chris was saying at lunch, didn't you?'

Beth nodded.

They had reached her room. She inserted the key in the lock and drew Sally inside.

'My, this is an attractive room,' Sally said, looking around her, and then went on resuming her previous conversation: 'Chris is very knowledgeable about the East. He's not only fairly fluent in the language but he knows all the strange customs. It's like going about with a guide — but a super guide and a most attractive one, don't you agree, Beth?' and she giggled.

Beth didn't say anything. She opened the bathroom door for Sally to pass inside. But Sally didn't go in immediately; she said instead, 'What do you honestly think of Chris, Beth? Do you think he's a nice guy?'

'I think he's a very nice guy,' Beth returned, forcing a smile. 'But you're surely not asking for my approval, Sally?'

'Oh, no. I'm all for Chris. I have been for years. He's almost a part of our family. I was just curious to know how you reacted towards him, and don't just ward me off by saying that he's a nice guy. I want to know what you really think of him.'

Beth found herself taken aback. She felt the hot colour creep up her cheeks. 'Does it really matter what I think of him, Sally?'

'Well, yes, in a way. It's always nice to have an outsider's opinion,' and once again she gave that small gurgling chuckle of laughter.

'Speaking as an outsider,' Beth said, 'I like him enormously. He's kind and considerate and,' she sought wildly in her mind and suddenly had a mental picture of them choosing the material for her gown and the design, 'he's such fun to be with.' But once again she felt herself blushing furiously. She was all too aware that Sally's inquiring blue eyes were registering the fact.

'Sure Chris is fun to be with — he always has been,' Sally said, and passed on into the bathroom.

Beth bit her lip. Had she said too much, sounded too enthusiastic? There had been a curious little smile on Sally's small pretty face as though she knew . . . But knew what?

Beth went quickly to the dressing table to repair her make-up, not that she thought you needed much make-up to go to the International Language Centre. She hoped there would be a Japanese lecture that afternoon. She would have to sit through it grimly and try and pick up something. She might be questioned about what she had learnt when she got back to the Itos' home. She thought of the prospect of her own afternoon and that of Sally's driving out in the spring afternoon to the Ueno Park, where this year it was said that the cherry blossoms made an especially grand spectacle. She would love to have driven out in the sunshine.

'You little fool,' she said between tightly clenched teeth. 'What's the matter with you, indulging in this wild orgy of self-pity?'

Directly the two girls returned to the lounge, Chris took Sally's hand and said that they would be pushing off.

'Shall we meet here for tea or cocktails?' he suggested.

Beth shook her head. 'I think directly I finish at the language institute I'd better go back to the Itos' house.'

'What's the rush to get back there?' Chris asked.

'I don't know,' Beth said slowly. But already she had an uneasy feeling; she didn't know why, or what had caused it, but suddenly she felt that all was not well at the Itos' house. Perhaps she should go back at once. On the other hand she felt that to put in at least an appearance at the language centre was important.

Mr. Oswara, who seemed to know everything, said that he had learned there was a Japanese lesson for beginners at the language centre at four o'clock that afternoon, which would last for one hour. He had already enrolled her. All she would have to do was to go there and attend the class. There was another class at three on Japanese flower arrangement.

'I'd like to attend that, too,' Beth said. 'While I'm out here I want to learn everything I can about Japan, and their flower arrangements are so fashionable and exquisite.'

Mr. Oswara bowed low to her and drew in his breath with a hissing sound. 'Miss Rainer is very intelligent young lady,' he commented.

'You bet she is,' Tom said, and laughed. 'She wouldn't have been my secretary all these years if she hadn't been. I'm very proud of her.'

But was he proud of her as a woman or as a secretary? Beth asked herself and hated herself for such a question. What *was* the matter with her today?

The language centre was situated in an old building in the Marunouchi District. A Japanese clerk in an outer office took her fee from Mr. Oswara and said that Beth had been enrolled the previous day. Beth said she would take courses in Japanese flower arrangement and also in the Japanese language.

'We have a class this afternoon in both subjects,' the little Japanese clerk smiled. 'You wish to buy books, exercise books, books on the Japanese language and one on flower arrangement?'

'Yes, please,' Beth said. It would look better, she thought, if she arrived back at the Itos' household with the books. It would look as though she intended to take her studies seriously. Besides, she was very interested in both subjects.

Mr. Oswara took leave of her in the hall and said that he would see her the following day around noon at the Imperial Hotel in case she had anything to report to him.

She followed the little clerk down the corridor and was shown into a classroom where the lecture on flower arrangement had already begun. Luckily it was a class for beginners given in English, so Beth was able to follow it easily. She found the lecture particularly fascinating. She discovered that the fundamental principles guiding the arrangement of flowers in a formal style followed three distinct patterns; the Leading Principle, which indicated Heaven; the Subordinate Principle, which represented Earth; and the Reconciling Principle, which was meant to represent Man; all formal flower arrangements must embody these principles. If a single plant or branch is used, the main part shooting upwards represents Heaven; a twig bent sideways in the shape of a V denotes Man, and the lowest twig or branch on the left, the end slightly bent so as to point upwards, signifies Earth. Three separate plants or branches, not necessarily of the same kind, are often used to represent these elements.

The lecturer emphasised that another important point consisted in treating the flowers from three different aspects according to the nature of the flower, the place in which it is to be put, and the shape of the vase. In decorating an alcove, called a *tokonoma*, with flowers they must be arranged so as not to hide the hanging scroll. For wedding feasts the flowers are arranged to look as natural as possible. The main flowers used for such an occasion are the pine, the bamboo and the Japanese apricot, representing constancy, prosperity and purity.

Since they were all beginners that afternoon they learnt how to arrange the *haran*, a long leafed variety of orchid. Beth was quite sorry when the class was over and looked forward to pursuing her studies the following day. She had only a few minutes to go to another classroom where the lesson in the Japanese language was being held. The class was for beginners, but she was aware that most of the students knew something about the language already. She found it somewhat difficult to follow, although she assiduously wrote down in her notebook certain expressions which she felt might come in useful: *O hayô!* which meant good morning; *Konnichi wa!* which meant good day, and *Konban wa!* good evening. There were other longer phrases which the lecturer wrote down on a blackboard and which she copied, such as *Jo koso, oid no sai ma shita*, which meant 'you are very welcome.'

But it was all very difficult and she felt that without a long period of study she never would get a grasp of the Japanese language. She wondered how Chris had become so proficient in it and her feeling of admiration for him increased. But she was glad she had gone if only for the fact that she noticed John Chao in the room, and more than once she saw his eyes through the rather thick-lensed spectacles fixed upon her.

As she left the room he came over to her, greeted her politely and fell into step beside her as they walked down the long corridor.

'You enjoyed the classes?'

'Very much.'

'But you were not here at the morning classes.'

'No,' she agreed. 'I'm afraid I'm not a very serious student, Mr. Chao. I only want to learn enough Japanese to learn to understand the people better. I was busy this morning, having a fitting.'

'Ah, so.' But she felt he was looking at her curiously and speculatively. 'Might I have a few words with you in private, Miss Rainer?' he said finally.

Her heart gave a slight lurch and once again she was conscious of that strange sense of fear and apprehension she had had ever since she had entered the Itos' household. But she forced herself to smile.

'But of course, Mr. Chao. Where shall we go?'

'The lectures are over for the day. We could go into one of the classrooms.' As he spoke he pushed open one of the doors and led her into a deserted classroom.

He glanced sharply about him. 'There's no one here. We can talk undisturbed.'

Her feeling of apprehension increased.

'What was it you wanted to say to me, Mr. Chao?'

'You are British, as I am, Miss Rainer,' he said finally. 'I thought it my duty to warn you.'

Her feeling of apprehension increased.

'To warn me — about what?'

'About living in Mr. and Mrs. Ito's house. It is not a healthy household for a young girl like you, Miss Rainer.'

'Why should you say that, Mr. Chao?' She was stammering slightly.

'I cannot tell you, but the others ask questions about you. They ask why you have come to the Itos' house; they do not believe that you are a serious student. It was stupid of me yesterday to say at the dinner table that I had not seen you at any of the classes. I apologise. I knew that afterwards I had done you a great harm. It was not only stupid but it aroused their suspicions.'

'But why do they think I am staying here?'

'To find out what you can about the student organisation to which they belong. They think you have been put into the house to spy for the powerful American industrialists who they believe would like to control Japan and her foreign policy.'

'But — but that's nonsense!' Beth gasped.

'Is it, Miss Rainer?' John was looking at her even more intently through his thick-lensed glasses. 'I, too, do not believe you are a genuine student. And I do not believe either that you came to the Itos' house by mere chance or in answer to an advertisement. That advertisement is put into the paper for a definite purpose, worded in a way that only those initiated in the organisation will understand and know where to come; the Itos' house is their headquarters. But as I said, I have a friendly feeling towards you, Miss Rainer, since we are both British, although politically we may have different ideas. I suggest very seriously that you do not go back to the Itos' household, that you never set foot in the house again . . . '

'But I must go,' Beth said, stammering, seeking in her mind for some excuse. 'I have left all my luggage there. Besides, if I didn't turn up again they'd believe their suspicions to be justified, that I had taken fright and fled.'

'There is that, of course,' John Chao nodded solemnly. 'They might suspect you had found out what you came into the house to find out. They might follow you, wherever you were; they might even kill you.' He said it quietly and undramatically, but Beth felt a shiver go down her spine.

'For my own information would you

kindly tell me why you did come to the Itos' house, Miss Rainer?' he asked presently.

She looked at him, wondering how much she should tell him, how far she could trust him.

He smiled a little grimly. 'I see you do not trust me, Miss Rainer, and yet if I didn't want to help you, would I have troubled to warn you? You can safely confide in me, Miss Rainer.'

'I came to get into contact with Michiko,' Beth said. 'Her father is an American. I am a friend of his.'

He nodded slowly, as though satisfied with Beth's explanation. 'Thank you. I believe you, Miss Rainer. But if you are a friend of Michiko's father, I think you should advise Michiko; I think you should persuade her to leave the Itos' house with you. The girl, I understand, is not sympathetic with the extreme plans of the organisation. It is as dangerous for her live in the Itos' house as it is for you, Miss Rainer. You should persuade her to leave with you at once.'

Beth nodded slowly. 'I'll do so if I can.' She looked up and asked suddenly, 'Mr. Chao, was that attack on Michiko in the garden of the kindergarten yesterday deliberate?'

'I think the attack was intended as a warning. I do not think they wished to kill her.' He shrugged and added, 'I have done all I can to persuade you not to go back to the Itos' house, but since you are determined, I beg you to be careful about what you do and what you say.'

'I'll remember,' Beth promised him. 'And thank you very much for your warning, Mr. Chao.' She added impulsively, 'I'm going to be rash and take a taxi back to the Itos' house; I feel too tired today to cope with the intricate bus system in this city. Can I give you a lift, Mr. Chao?'

But he shook his head violently. 'No, thank you, Miss Rainer.' He added with a slight grim smile, 'It would be as much as my life is worth if I were seen arriving at the house with you.'

Again a chill ran down Beth's spine, but she determined to conquer her fear. She was very anxious to re-meet Michiko and see if she couldn't persuade the girl to see her father.

It was the rush hour and she had some difficulty in getting a taxi cab, but finally she managed to attract the attention of a hundred-yen taxi, one of the larger variety, and asked him to drive her out to the Itos' house in the suburb of Azabu.

The front door was open to the soft spring night. She entered and ran up the stairs to the room she shared with Michiko. She hoped the girl would be home. She wanted, if possible, to have another long talk with her before dinner. But there was no one in the bedroom. She had brought the new kimono and the happi-coat in a box with her. She decided to wash and change and by that time Michiko would probably be back.

As she surveyed herself in the hanging mirror inside one of the cupboards she was more than ever pleased with her purchase of the kimono; the brown-golden tint complemented her hair; the chrysanthemums were the pale pink of her cheeks; the jade green obi or sash was perfect with the costume. In admiring the jade green sash she was suddenly reminded of the jade ring with the delicate carving which she had helped Chris purchase that morning. She didn't know why she should think of that ring with a vague stab of pain. Had Chris, she wondered, already given it to Sally among the pale pink cherry blossom trees and the pagodas at Ueno Park?

She knew suddenly she was envious of Sally, but since she herself was in love with Tom, wasn't her attitude selfish and completely indefensible? Sally and Chris would be flying down to the old capital of Kyoko at the weekend, a lovely, lovely trip. She wished like anything that she was going. But it was only natural that Tom wouldn't want to leave Tokyo, where

Michiko was. It was only natural that Tom should put Michiko first. After all, it was because of the girl he had flown out to Japan and brought her with him. She couldn't blame Tom; she mustn't blame him for putting Michiko first. She assured herself that she didn't even feel faintly resentful. But was it always to be like this? Would he always put Michiko's welfare, because she was his daughter by the woman he had loved in his youth, before her and her happiness?

A moment later she was disgusted with herself because the thought had even crossed her mind. If she married Tom she knew she would love Michiko as much as he loved her, although he had never met her. If she married Tom . . .

Ever since that weekend at the vicarage in Sussex she had been expecting him to ask her to marry him; and she would accept, of course. Or would she? It wasn't the first time in the past few days that she had felt a little uncertain of her love for him. She had hated Chris when he had told her that she had a father fixation. Was it at all possible that there was any truth in it? She knew in her heart that since they had been in Japan her affections towards Tom had changed. She was convinced she still loved him, but somehow he seemed different from the way he had seemed to her in London. Was it that here in Japan where he had once loved the Japanese girl Eiko so passionately he had reverted to that love almost to the exclusion of her, Beth's, presence?

They were upsetting, disturbing thoughts. She tried to put them out of her mind. She glanced at her wristwatch. What was keeping Michiko? It was almost time for the dinner gong. She began to be worried and as the minutes ticked by her worry increased. Michiko might have returned and be down in the lounge talking with her foster mother.

She went down into the lounge wearing the Japanese kimono with the jade-green obi. But there was no one there. Finally Hanako sounded the brass dinner gong in the hall. There was the scurry of rushing feet as the students, always hungry, went into the dining room.

She followed them, thinking she might find Michiko there. All the student boarders were already squatted around the table with Mr. Ito. But Michiko wasn't there and neither was her foster-mother.

Mr. Ito apologised for his wife's temporary absence and said she would be with them presently.

'Isn't Michiko coming in to dinner?' Beth asked him.

'I do not know,' Mr. Ito said in his precise difficult English. 'My wife will undoubtedly tell you when she comes in to dinner. She was delayed and has only just returned to the house.'

She saw that John Chao was looking at her sympathetically through his thick-lensed glasses. She felt that in him at least she had a friend, and she felt badly in need of a friend in this alien household.

19

Beth felt in her bones that something had happened to Michiko. She didn't know what but she was dreadfully worried. Apart from her own genuine affection for the girl, she wondered, if anything had happened to Michiko, how she could break the news to Tom.

Dinner went on the same as it had on the previous night, with Hanako kneeling beside each of them as she served the main dish. Tonight it was *sushi*, a succulent dish which was composed of small hand-pressed wads of rice, topped with smaller pieces of raw fish.

Was it Beth's imagination or were the students gathered about the table less festive and talkative than they had been the night before? They ate mainly in silence though now and again she saw one whisper to another. They seemed to avoid not only talking to her directly but even to avoid her glance. Though the dish was excellent, Beth found she had no appetite for it.

Dr. Frank was also missing from the meal. For a time she hoped that he and Michiko were somewhere together, but when she finally plucked up courage and asked Mr. Ito where he was the Japanese man told her that this was the night he operated at the hospital. Michiko's absence was all the more disturbing, especially when halfway through the meal Mrs. Ito appeared without the girl. She looked stern and uncompromising. Somehow Beth didn't have the courage to ask her where Michiko was; not in front of all the others. But at the end of the meal she followed Mrs. Ito into the lounge. For the moment they were alone in the room.

'Where is Michiko-san tonight?' she asked.

The elder woman gave her a hard stare. 'Is that any business of yours, Miss Rainer?'

Beth found herself taken aback.

'I only wondered. Michiko-san didn't tell me she would be out tonight.'

'Why should she acquaint you of her movements?' Mrs. Ito asked, almost rudely.

Beth forced herself to answer politely, 'There is no reason, of course, Mrs. Ito. I only wondered . . . I wanted to show Michiko-san my new kimono.'

'Very attractive,' Mrs. Ito said in a voice which said she intended to finish the conversation.

By now Beth was thoroughly alarmed.

'Will Michiko be in later this evening?'

'My daughter has gone away,' Mrs. Ito said finally. 'I have no idea when she will return.'

'She has gone away?' Beth stammered. 'But Michiko-san said nothing to me about going away!'

'Were you so much in her confidence? I may be wrong, but I understood that you only met her yesterday evening.' Her voice was caustic.

'I know we only met yesterday,' Beth said. 'But last night we became very friendly. I am sure if she had intended going away Michiko-san would have told me.'

'*I* am telling you now she has gone away,' and again Mrs. Ito's voice was rude. 'You will oblige me by not asking any more questions. Do you wish to sit in here or will you go to your room? Maybe you are expecting one of your American friends to call for you.'

'My American friends?' Beth stammered.

'You did not fool me, Miss Rainer — at least you did not fool me for long,' Mrs. Ito said angrily. 'You were seen lunching with Americans today at the Imperial Hotel, and later sitting in the lounge having coffee. I never believed from the first that you were a genuine student of the Japanese language. I thought — we all thought — you had been sent here for some purpose. You were followed today from the moment you left the house. Your actions confirmed the truth of what we had thought. Why should you pay me for board and lodging when you have a room at the Imperial Hotel registered in your name? I know you went today to the language centre, but that, I am sure, is merely a blind. We are convinced in this household that you have come here to spy upon us. We do not like spies. Moreover we know how to deal with them. Now you had better go to your room. You can wait there until I send for you.'

Beth had gone very white. 'You cannot stop me leaving this house if I wish to, Mrs. Ito.'

'Oh, yes, we can stop you — quite easily,' the Japanese woman said with a curious hissing sound in her voice.

'We do not intend that you shall go and tittle-tattle to your American friends about Michiko's disappearance.' The elder woman's voice was quiet, but somehow its very quietness made her threat seem even more menacing.

Beth didn't doubt that Mrs. Ito could do as she threatened. If she herself could not forcibly prevent the girl leaving the house, she had only to summon her husband and nephew and possibly some of the other students. Beth had no doubt now but that they were all members of some secret organisation and that they believed, as John Chao had hinted, that she had been sent into the house as a spy. Michiko might have helped her, but Michiko had suddenly and mysteriously disappeared. Was it at all possible to find out where the girl had gone or where she had been taken, or even — and an awful shudder ran down Beth's spine again — if she were alive. Michiko had been attacked before as a warning. All the same, last night she had talked to Beth. Undoubtedly she had told her more than she should have, but then she had been under deep emotional stress. But did someone else know that she had talked? Had they really been footsteps they had heard or thought they had heard creeping silently down the corridor away from the closed door of their room?

Beth had been sure that the door had been closed, but the Japanese doors were paper-thin. That conversation of theirs in the still hours of the night might easily have been overheard. John Chao had hinted and Mrs. Ito had said bluntly that she had been sent to this house to spy upon them. Could she make a run for it and get to a telephone so that she could call Tom or Chris?

But this house was in a very isolated position. It was extremely doubtful if she could reach the telephone before they caught up with her. Besides, even if she herself managed to escape she would be no nearer to finding out the truth of what had happened to Michiko. She felt if she deserted now with the mystery of Michiko's disappearance unsolved, Tom would never forgive her.

And Chris? But did it really matter what Chris thought of her? He was probably now in Sally's arms, having asked her to marry him in the romantic surroundings of Ueno Park.

Why should that thought upset her so much? Chris was a friend, maybe a passionate friend, but still just a friend.

'Very well, Mrs. Ito, I shall go to my room, since you wish me to,' Beth said. She added impulsively, unable to restrain herself, 'But I do wish you would tell me whether or not Michiko-san is alive and well?'

'She is out of harm's way; that is all I can tell you,' Mrs. Ito said stiffly. 'She is where neither you nor your American friends can possibly find her, nor that good-for-nothing young doctor, who works mainly for charities. Bah! I despise him. A man is put into this world to earn good money for his womenfolk. Our *nakado* or go-between has an excellent husband lined up for Michiko but the stupid girl will not hear of a marriage which would be a good one and a prosperous one.'

'But surely if Michiko-san loves Dr. Frank you would not object, Mrs. Ito?'

'In my days, and even now in the best Japanese families, such things are arranged by the parents of the bride and groom through a *nakado*. But I do not see that the man Michiko marries has anything to do with you, Miss Rainer, unless,' her dark eyes narrowed to thin slits, 'you are here on behalf of her father — that no-good American soldier who deserted her mother and then the child.'

Beth cried out angrily, unable to control herself any longer, 'That isn't true, Mrs. Ito. You must know it isn't true! But it's a story you have been feeding Michiko-san for years; a bad wicked lie you have made her believe. Mr. Dillan wanted to marry Eiko, Michiko-san's mother, but he was under age and the army and his parents refused him permission. He was sent back to the States and before he could return the tornado had struck the town in which she was living.'

'You are telling me a pack of lies!' Mrs. Ito cried furiously. 'I know the truth from Eiko-san's elder aunt, who gave Michiko into my care when she was a baby. I have cared for her like a mother. She is my child, *my* child. Do you think I would dream of handing her over to a rotten American who had not the decency to marry her mother and make an honest woman of her?'

'If you believe that, Michiko-san's aunt lied to you,' Beth cried in desperation.

But Mrs. Ito clapped her hands over her ears. 'I will not listen to you. Go at once to your room and do not dare leave it again.'

Beth went to her room but she didn't go to bed. It was too early. Besides, she was too much worried over Michiko's disappearance. Hanako hadn't yet laid out the mattress nor made up the bed.

She paced up and down the room, wondering what she should do — if there was anything she could do — and especially what she was going to tell Tom on the morrow. Would he blame her for his daughter's disappearance? It was too ridiculous to think that he would, but she had an uncomfortable feeling that he might. She thought, smiling a little wryly, that at the moment his whole thoughts were centred upon his daughter to the complete exclusion of everyone else.

Had the girl found the situation was too difficult and gone away? But already she had learned that, despite her youth, Michiko had a strong determined character. It would not be easy to persuade her to go away from Tokyo, even though she might be scared. It would not be easy to persuade her to leave Dr. Frank; or was it with his approval she had gone away?

She wished she knew where his surgery was. She knew he had a flat above it. But she had been forbidden by Mrs. Ito to leave the house. Besides, she had learned that the young doctor would be operating at the hospital until late into the night.

Her thoughts turned to John Chao. He had warned her at the institute not to return to the Itos' house. He seemed kindly disposed towards her because she was British as he was. He was also friendly with the other students. But perhaps, he, like Michiko, did not approve of the mass murders the student organisation was planning. At least he might tell her where Michiko was and if there was any chance of her, Beth, getting in touch with the girl. But she didn't know which was his room.

Presently Hanako came in to make the bed. Beth noticed that she only made up one bed that night. Obviously Michiko was not expected to return. She had discovered that though Hanako spoke very little English, she understood a great deal more.

Beth held out a book she had brought with her from the institute. 'Book belong Mr. John Chao,' she said, speaking slowly and distinctly. 'I want to return it. Which is Mr. Chao's room?'

'Chao-san? Him sleep. Little room end of corridor.'

'Thank you,' Beth murmured.

'*Doozo*,' Hanako said, bowing low to her.

She decided to wait a little longer until the house had settled down for the night. If she went to John Chao's room now, someone might see her.

But the waiting seemed interminable; the minutes and the hours went by on leaden feet. But at last the house was still and she thought it safe to creep down the corridor in her soft house-shoes to John's room.

It wasn't difficult to find his room since she discovered that all the students had their names on visiting cards attached to their doors. John's room was somewhat apart from the others, right at the end of the corridor by the back balcony.

She knocked very softly so as not to disturb any of the others, but there was no response. She knocked again, still with no result. He must be very sound asleep or else he was not in his room, she decided. She supposed all she could do was to go back to her own room and try again later in the night. But then very faintly from within the room she heard a sound which might have been a groan.

On an impulse she turned the handle, pushed open the door and went inside. John Chao was lying on the floor, groaning softly. She stared down at him in terrified horror. His eyes were closed, his thick black hair was matted with blood. Blood was trickling from the wound in his head on to the floor.

She dropped down on her knees beside him. She shook him slightly by the shoulder. 'John! John! It is I, Beth Rainer. Can you hear me? What has happened to you?'

He groaned again and she saw him open his eyes with a conscious effort. He stared at her in a glazed, glassy way, but she felt that he recognised her. 'Go — go away, Miss Rainer,' he whispered, articulating his words with the greatest difficulty. 'If they find you here, they will try to kill you too. I shall die. Leave me alone. You can do nothing.'

'But of course I am not going to leave you alone,' Beth said indignantly. 'And I'm sure you're not going to die. Who attacked you?'

'Wang Lee and Yaizu Seki, two of the leaders of the student body organisation. They saw me talking with you at the institute this afternoon; they think I betrayed them to you. I told you they think you are a spy. You must leave here at once.'

'I can't leave here,' Beth said. 'And anyhow you've got to have help at once. I'll call Mrs. Ito.'

'No, no,' he said, and with his failing strength he grasped her arm. 'She is a bad woman; she will do everything Yaizu tells her to do. They think only of their plan for bloodshed and mass murder.'

Beth voiced her own fear. 'Michiko; what has happened to her, John Chao?'

'I do not know but I think she has been taken away somewhere — or sent away by Mrs. Ito. As I told you, they tried to intimidate her when they attacked her in the kindergarten gardens. Now they have either killed her or taken her forcibly away. But I am too tired. I can tell you no more. I want to die.'

'But you mustn't die,' Beth cried hoarsely. 'I'll get help somehow.'

'No, no; they would only kill you, Miss Rainer.'

'How right you are, John Chao,' a voice said from behind Beth.

She swung round with a startled scream, which stopped abruptly as Wang Lee's hand closed over her mouth. With his other hand he gripped her throat. 'You will tell no one, you English spy,' he hissed. 'I know that you were sent here by your government or by big capitalist interests to spy upon us. They do not want the revolution; they not only fear defeat but they fear even more than death losing all their money. I knew you were a spy from the moment that you stepped into this house. But just because you are British as is that fool Chao, who is sentimental and weak, not a true son of the revolution, he tried to help you by warning you to keep away from the house — Oh, yes, we know everything about you; we had you and John Chao followed from the moment you both left the house today. We have never wholly trusted him. But now you are going to die, slowly, slowly. That is his and your punishment. A quick death is merciful, but a slow death is agonising; you have too much time to think; the will to live revives so often when death is very close, and the will to live when you are dying is hideous and torment-ing. I am going to strangle you, Miss Rainer, but very, very slowly. And John, who is still conscious but who is dying too, has not the strength to stop me. If you try to scream or make any movement, your death will be more painful.' His long cruel fingers pressed tightly into her throat.

'Your head is buzzing, isn't it? Your ears are ringing. You do not want to die. And that is good. It is no satisfaction to kill those who want to die. The spirit of killing is to kill those with a zest for life still in them. Do not stare at me like that — it will not help you. I have no pity for you. Do not try to struggle either; it would be quite, quite useless.' Once again the fingers tightened about her throat.

She found herself almost unable to breathe, she heard herself give a gasping, choking sound.

'Yes, you are slowly dying, Miss Rainer.' His hoarse, inhuman voice went on: 'I appreciate the slow agony of your death. It will be something very pleasant to remember.'

Beth summoned all her strength. She tried to kick out at him. She must have succeeded in hurting him for he gave a sharp cry of pain and momentarily his hold upon her throat slackened. But only momentarily; once again the cold fingers were about her throat, pressing even harder.

She was half unconscious. She no longer knew or cared what happened to her. This is the end, she thought dully with a last flash of consciousness. What a way to die!

And then suddenly it happened. While Wang Lee had been talking to her in his soft menacing voice, exulting in the thought of the slow and torturous death he was inflicting upon her, John Chao had somehow managed to crawl towards the door and with his shoulders forced the flimsy door open. With all the strength that was left in him, he shouted, 'Help!'

'What do you think you're doing?'

Momentarily Wang had released his grip upon her throat and he hurled himself upon the dying Chinese from Hong Kong. He whipped out a knife which was hidden in the sleeve of his kimono and moved to thrust it through the other man's body.

'No!' Beth shrieked. She stumbled towards them and then fell. Just then she heard a shot.

She did not know where the shot had come from nor who had fired the gun.

She had a strange feeling before she finally lost consciousness that a man was bending over her, that his voice was very familiar to her, that the man was Chris. But it couldn't be.

'It isn't you, Chris,' she whispered, and then she blacked out completely.

20

When she recovered consciousness she knew she was lying in a bed, that a strange man, and a woman in nurse's uniform were bending over her. Vaguely she heard the man say, 'She'll be all right now, Nurse. Just keep her quiet for the next few hours. See if she can't drink a cup of tea.'

'Yes, Doctor,' she heard the nurse reply.

'She had a lucky escape,' the doctor continued. 'We got to her just in time.'

But the effort of listening to them, of trying to think where she was, was almost too much. She closed her eyes again and drifted into a semi-conscious state, lying prone on the bed, half sleeping, half waking. She tried mentally to place the events of the night in their proper sequence, but at the moment everything that had happened seemed like a jigsaw puzzle.

But gradually her mind began to clear and the events of the past night took shape. Michiko had disappeared and she had gone and knocked at John Chao's door to see if he could tell her what had happened to the girl. She remembered pushing open the door and finding him lying on the floor in a dying condition, his head bashed in. Even now she could see the blood from the wound in his head trickling on to the floor, and she shuddered. She remembered bending over him and slowly she remembered everything he had said to her. She had sprung to her feet to go for help, but although neither had heard the door open, Wang Lee must have entered the room noiselessly.

Her throat still ached where his long thin fingers had closed about it, slowly choking the life out of her. He had said he wanted her to die slowly, slowly; he had said he wanted her to be aware that she was dying, that there was no hope for her.

She didn't know how John Chao had managed to get to the door and almost with his dying breath cry out for help. She had seen Wang Lee take the knife out of the sleeve of his kimono. She had tried to intercede but somehow she had fallen to the floor. Had Wang Lee finally killed Chao with the long cruel knife? She didn't know. All she could remember after that was a blurred impression of Chris bending over her. But that, of course, was sheer imagination. Chris could have been nowhere near the Itos' home. It must have been wishful thinking on her part. But why should she wish that it had been *Chris* bending over her? Wasn't it more logical to wish it had been Tom? But she felt too tired to bother trying to find an explanation at the moment. She relaxed her tired, still aching, body and let her thoughts drift away.

She must have slept for some considerable time for when she woke again the room was full of bright spring sunshine and she felt much better, almost herself again, though there was still a painful throbbing in her throat. She saw the little nurse in a white dress and flowing cap moving about the room. It was a familiar room, and then she realised that it was her own room at the Imperial Hotel.

'Nurse, what has happened?' she asked.

The nurse was Japanese but she spoke English fluently. She had trained in London. She smiled at Beth. 'Shush!' she said. 'You're not to talk. Dr. Inglis said you were to stay very quiet.'

'I feel better,' Beth said, 'and I really must know what has happened, Nurse.'

'I'm afraid there's not much I can tell you,' the little nurse said in a pretty, kindly voice. 'You were brought here in an ambulance. Dr. Inglis, an English doctor who lives in the hotel, was summoned. I have often worked as his special nurse, and he telephoned for me. We were told that someone had tried to strangle you. But that is all I know.' She smiled and added, 'Honestly.'

Beth accepted that. It was unlikely that the little nurse knew anything more. But she was greatly concerned for John Chao's safety.

'You haven't heard if there is another person here, a young Chinese man from Hong Kong?'

The nurse frowned slightly. 'I did hear something about another patient having been taken to the hospital, but I did not listen much. Both Dr. Inglis and I were fully occupied with you. Now you must be quiet. You have had a narrow escape, Miss Rainer. I understand that someone tried to murder you and that the police are investigating.'

'The police?' Beth asked. 'But how did the police come into it?' Was it they who had fired the shot she had vaguely heard? Had it been a policeman bending over her? But no, she was convinced that the face she remembered vaguely hadn't been Japanese.

'Do you think you could try some tea or hot milk?' the nurse asked. 'And you must go to sleep again.'

'I'd love some tea,' Beth said. 'And I don't feel sleepy any longer, honestly, Nurse.'

'Well, after you've had your tea you must try to relax, anyhow,' the nurse said.

Beth drank the tea and finally she must have drifted off to sleep because it was well on in the morning when once again she wakened.

She opened her eyes and smiled at the nurse. 'I feel perfectly all right now, honestly.'

'Do you feel strong enough to see visitors?' the nurse asked. 'There are several people waiting to see you.'

'Oh, yes, I feel quite strong enough,' Beth smiled and added, 'Will you hand me my bedjacket?'

It was an attractive bedjacket of palest blue nylon.

'Who is waiting to see me?'

'Mr. Dillan has phoned repeatedly and so has Mr. Christopher Landour,' the nurse said. 'There was also a call from a Miss Sally Hyman and one from a man who gave his name as Dr. Frank Rickard, who said he could be contacted at his surgery.'

'I'll see them all,' Beth said. 'I no longer feel the least wuzzy in the head.'

'Good.' The little nurse smiled back at her. 'Whom do you want to see first, Miss Rainer?'

But of course she would want to see Tom first. And yet once again she had a vivid picture of Chris's face bending over hers before she lost consciousness. She must know if it had been he and how on earth he had been at the Itos' house.

'I'd like to see Mr. Landour first,' she murmured.

'He gave me his private number,' the nurse said. 'I'll phone him immediately.'

As she dialled the number Beth felt both angry at herself and guilty. Obviously Tom was the person she should see first. She was not only still in his employ but he was here in the hotel. Besides, she loved him — or did she? But she felt too tired at the moment to answer that question.

After the nurse had replaced the receiver she brought Beth over a box of powder and a lipstick. 'You'll want to pretty yourself up as you're receiving gentlemen,' the nurse said and giggled behind her hand.

It wasn't far from the Marunouchi quarter to the Imperial Hotel. Chris must have dropped all the business he had on hand, for he was there almost immediately.

She looked up at the tall lean figure, the thin arresting face with the sharply etched features, the very dark hair and those surprisingly blue eyes. Her heartbeat quickened — dangerously so. For a moment she found it difficult to speak.

'I'm glad you're better, Beth,' Chris said conventionally.

'Yes, I feel much better. The throbbing in my throat has eased. Chris,' she stretched out a hand and touched his arm, 'am I completely mad or was it really you bending over me at the Itos' house last night after Wang had attacked me?'

'It was I, all right,' he said, grinning half shamefacedly. 'And I'm darned glad I got to you in time. Another few minutes and you would have been completely finished.'

'But I don't understand how you got there.'

'It's really quite simple.' He shrugged slightly. 'I never was easy about your being in that house, as you know. I got in contact with the police, told them the whole story and last night a couple of stout Japanese policemen and I kept watch outside the house.'

'But I thought you were going to the Noh drama with Sally?'

He grinned again. 'You shouldn't think these things, Beth. You should know better. That suggestion of Sally and my going to the Noh drama was merely a blind.' He went on: 'We stood there for hours it seemed, everything was very quiet and still. We were almost on the point of going away when suddenly we heard a faint call for help. We didn't wait upon ceremony, I tell you; we barged straight into the house and up the staircase from where we thought the cry had come. We burst open every door and finally we found John Chao and you lying on the floor. The other Chinese made an effort to stab us with his knife. It was then that one of the cops shot him through the arm. I bent over you; you smiled at me and then you lost consciousness.'

'So I was right after all,' she breathed. 'It *was* you, Chris?'

'I was there the previous night as well,' he said. 'I was determined that nothing should happen to you in that household.'

Her hand upon his arm tightened. 'You're very sweet, Chris.' There was a half-broken note in her voice.

'Someone's got to look after you,' he said gruffly. 'You're capable of getting into the most impossible situations.'

'Michiko isn't as anti-American as her foster-mother is,' Beth said slowly. 'I think she's quite prepared to meet her father. But where is she? She didn't come home to dinner last night. She wasn't home when I went down to John Chao's room. That's why I went down — to find out if he had any news of her.'

'Michiko's all right,' Chris said. 'The police arrested Mrs. Ito and put her through the Japanese third degree. She has confessed she had sent the girl down to her parents' home in Kyoto to get her away from you.'

Beth breathed a sigh of relief. 'Tom must be relieved?'

'He's relieved both about you and Michiko.'

'And John Chao?' she asked urgently. 'Is he still alive?'

'Only just, but he's fighting gamely. We should have further news of him later on today, and I hope it will be good news. Both Mrs. Ito's nephew and a Chinese called Wang Lee have been arrested for attempted murder. I understand there is another even graver charge. Tom is all for flying down to Kyoto to get in touch with Michiko. Directly you feel well enough, Beth, I suggest we make it a foursome and go down. You remember I suggested it before?'

She nodded. 'I know, but Tom wasn't keen. He didn't want to leave Tokyo because of Michiko. Does Sally like the idea?'

'Why shouldn't she? She'll see both Kyoto and Nara, and they are two of the most interesting towns in the whole of Japan. Both towns are famous for their supremely beautiful shrines and temples and cherry blossom. I've always longed to show you Kyoto and Nara, Beth.'

She was surprised at the intensity of feeling in his voice as though it meant something to him that he should show those two famous beauty spots to her.

'I'd love to go, of course,' she smiled back at him.

'That's settled. When do you think you'll be ready to travel? I'll make aeroplane reservations.'

'I feel fine now. I am sure I'll be ready to go tomorrow.' She turned towards the little Japanese nurse: 'Don't you think so, Nurse?'

'If one's heart is set upon a thing it is always wise to go,' the little nurse said and smiled in a slightly cryptic way.

'That's settled then. I'll see Tom about it,' he said determinedly.

She moved her head slightly on the pillow in a negative gesture. 'No, Chris; let Tom suggest it himself. I'd rather he didn't know I'd seen you.'

'You mean you haven't seen him already?'

'I haven't. But I shouldn't like him to know that.'

'The ways of women,' he shrugged and smiled broadly. 'You love 'em or hate 'em, but you never can trust them. All right, I'll leave it all to you, Little Miss Fix-it. You don't feel well enough for lunching today?'

'Could I, Nurse?' She looked towards the little nurse hopefully.

Reluctantly the girl shook her head. 'No, you must stay in bed today, Miss Rainer. But tomorrow, if you wish. I think you will be quite well enough to fly down to Kyoto.'

Again Chris gave that half-lopsided smile. 'I'll have to fall back on Sally.'

She laughed. 'I don't think that'll hurt you over-much, Chris.'

He merely said, 'You'd be surprised,' and, after promising to let her know about the flight reservations, he took his leave.

She saw Tom a little later. He was deeply concerned for her but she saw too that the knowledge that Michiko was alive and well was foremost in his thoughts.

'I saw Chris here a few moments ago. He suggested we all fly down to Kyoto. After what the police learned from Mrs. Ito about where she had hidden Michiko, my first impulse was to fly down to Kyoto at once. But then I thought it better to wait until you were fully recovered. You know Michiko; you will be able to intercede for me.'

'I will do my best,' Beth promised. 'I do not think from what the girl said to me it will be difficult for me to persuade her to see you.'

'Bless you.' He touched her hair. 'I can never thank you enough for what you've done for me, and I wish I could do something nice for you. When Michiko goes into our Western way of life she will need some older girl to guide her. Have you ever thought of it?'

She almost laughed out loud. This was the time, if ever, when she should say to him, 'Of course I've thought about it. I've thought about marrying you, Tom, for the past two years. Don't you know I love you?' But somehow she didn't say it. She knew suddenly that the words, even if she said them, wouldn't be true.

'I have thought about marriage, Tom,' she said presently, 'but I'd have to love the man I married very much.'

He smiled down at her faintly. 'You couldn't think of me in the role of a husband, Beth?'

'I don't know,' she said. 'Please don't ask me now, Tom.'

'I understand. You're not at all well. I shouldn't ask you to make decisions at this juncture. Sometime later I'll ask you again, Beth, and I hope — I'll pray — you'll give me the answer I am longing for.'

She stared at the door after he had closed it behind him. It couldn't be that Tom had actually proposed to her and that she, if not actually rejecting him, had asked him to wait for her answer?

I must be going off my head, she thought. Perhaps I'm much more ill than I think I am.

But the two conversations had left her more exhausted than she had imagined.

'If you wouldn't mind pulling the blind, Nurse, I think I'll go to sleep,' she said.

21

The four of them were on the plane for Kyoto the following evening.

'When Chris settles his mind upon a thing he certainly hustles,' Beth thought.

Her throat felt better and it was with a great sense of happiness that she had learned that John Chao was no longer on the danger list.

Tom and she sat together and Sally and Chris in the seats immediately behind them. They were served an excellent dinner and while they are they talked. Chris told them that Kyoto, which he had visited before, was the ancient capital of Japan and had been the centre of her civilisation for over a thousand years. It teemed with histori-cal tradition and was noted as the birthplace of those arts and crafts of old Japan which have won the world's admiration. 'It has thirteen hundred

Buddhist temples and four hundred Shinto shrines,' he told them, laughing. 'That means if you stayed in the city for over a year and visited four temples and one shrine every day, even then you couldn't see them all.'

It was also a modern city with pachinko parlours, a game dearly loved by the Japanese, four hundred modern movie theatres, numerous large stores and very modern hotels. But Chris told them that he had booked them into the famous Miyako Hotel, which offered modern Westernised comforts but also a Japanese atmosphere. It was fifteen minutes' drive from Kyoto and gave a magnificent view of the surrounding countryside.

Tom listened to all Chris had to say and then he gave a short laugh. 'But I didn't come down here to see Kyoto; I came down here with only one purpose — to find my daughter.'

'You'll find her all right,' Chris nodded. 'The police gave you the address, didn't they?'

'Some people named Matsuano,' Tom said. 'I can't wait to get down there and see Michiko.'

'We'll be arriving late and it may not be convenient for you to call at such a time,' Chris warned him. 'I think you'd better put off the reunion until tomorrow.' He added with a half-smile, 'Everything seems less dramatic in the daytime, anyhow.'

'I suppose you're right, Chris,' Tom said reluctantly. 'But I know I shan't sleep tonight.'

'I've a feeling the more cool and collected you are in the morning the better your prospects with Michiko will be.'

They picked up a taxi at the station and were driven out to the Miyako Hotel. Chris had been quite right in saying that it was set in a lovely environment. The surrounding hills were capped in moonlight. There were deep valleys and the smell of the cherry blossom trees around the hotel was almost overpowering. They had already dined on the plane so they had a brief drink in the lounge and went to bed.

For a moment Chris and Beth were alone in the lounge.

'Could you get up early in the morning, Beth?' he suggested, 'and let me take you on a sightseeing tour? I want to show you the old Imperial Palace. It's beautiful at this season when not only the cherry blossoms and apricot blossoms but the azaleas, wisteria, peonies and irises are in full bloom. Lord only knows what will happen afterwards when Tom has seen his daughter. Tom is completely unpredictable,' he added whimsically.

Beth answered seriously, 'Yes, I'd like that, Chris. Tom may decide we should return to Tokyo at once. But I fancy from now on his wishes will be Michiko's, and I know she will be eager to get back to Dr. Frank.'

He smiled across at her. 'Then don't let's waste a beautiful morning. Can you be ready by half past six?'

She smiled back at him. 'Easily, Chris.'

She slept well that night full of a pleasant sense of anticipation of what the early morning would hold for her.

It was six forty-five when she finally met Chris down in the lounge. Chris had hired a car and they were driven through the lovely countryside between the mountains to the enchanting garden which surrounds the Imperial Palace. The old palace had repeatedly been destroyed by fire; the present building dated from 1855 but it was modelled on the old structure, a palace of great beauty, surrounded by the formal gardens so dearly loved in Japan.

Chris said he did not want an interpreter; he had been there so often before.

Beth especially loved the *Seiryôden* or 'Serene and Cool Chamber,' so called from the stream drawn from Lake Biwa running under the steps. The hall is partitioned off into several apartments, the main apartment containing a matted dais where the emperors sat on ceremonial occasions;

the seat was covered with a silk canopy and the hangings were of red, white and black. The *Seiryôden* is sixty-nine feet long and fifty-one feet wide, and is built of *hinoki*, Japanese cypresses. It was originally intended for the living room of the emperor but it soon came to be used for ceremonial occasions only. The *Kogosho*, or minor palace, is approached from the *shishinden* by another corridor. It consists of three audience chambers used for small receptions, and with its pictures with poems attached, its polished metal ornaments, its regal hangings, its large doors which open out on to a beautiful landscape garden, it makes one of the many sights of Kyoto.

Beth was never to forget her first visit to the Imperial Palace, nor the moment when beside the ornamental pond Chris took her in his arms and kissed her lips.

'I love you,' he said very quietly. 'I love you, Beth.'

But what of Sally? Did he make love

to every girl? But why had he brought her, Beth, upon this outing instead of Sally? She couldn't ask him for an explanation and he made no attempt to explain. For a time, like two children, they wandered about the vast grounds, hand-in-hand, intoxicated not only with the beauty of the scene but with each other's company.

But presently Beth said they must go back. Tom and Sally would wonder what had become of them. Chris agreed without demur, and it was as well they had left when they did for Tom was in the front hall.

'What on earth has happened to you two?' he demanded. 'I've been searching the hotel grounds and the surrounding countryside.'

'We took a drive,' Beth said. 'Chris wanted to show me the Imperial Palace.'

'You might have left a note for me,' Tom grumbled. 'It's getting late and I want to see Michiko. Don't you realise how much I want to see her? I scarcely slept a wink all night.' His voice was edged and ragged.

'You could have gone and seen her yourself this morning,' Chris suggested mildly.

'But I want Beth to be with me. I want her to see Michiko first. If she doesn't intercede for me, Michiko may refuse to see me. Are you ready to come with me now, Beth?'

Chris interposed again. 'Have a heart, Tom. Beth hasn't had any breakfast yet. I could eat a horse and I bet she feels hungry too. Michiko won't run away; for where could she run to? Where is Sally, by the way?'

'I inquired at the reception desk,' Tom said. 'She rang down for her breakfast in bed half an hour ago.'

'Good. Then I don't have to worry about her.' Chris sounded relieved. 'Have you breakfasted, Tom?'

'I'm far too excited to think about breakfast,' he snapped, showing the raw state of his nerves.

'I won't be long having breakfast,'

Beth said. 'And then I'll be ready to go with you, Tom.'

'Fine, fine. I'll take a stroll around the grounds and smoke a cigarette while I'm waiting.'

'I think it would be better if you had a good breakfast yourself,' Chris advised. But Tom merely snorted and walked off in the opposite direction.

'Michiko has become an obsession with him,' Chris remarked as they sat in the breakfast room waiting to be served. 'I only hope he's not disappointed once he's reunited with her.'

'She's sweet and charming. No one could possibly be disappointed in Michiko,' Beth said warmly.

'But what about this young doctor I heard about?' Chris asked.

'Dr. Frank? He's a pleasant and extremely likeable young man, and Michiko is very much in love with him. I don't see what Tom could possibly have to object to in him.'

Chris shook his head. 'You never know how a father will feel; most of them have had their daughter's company from babyhood. Tom has been denied all that. He will probably try and make up for everything he has missed. As I said, Michiko has become an obsession with him.'

Beth looked grave and thoughtful. 'I hope he doesn't try interfering too much in Michiko's life. The girl has had enough interference from Mrs. Ito. She is desperately in love with Dr. Frank and she deserves her happiness.'

They finished breakfast. Sally had not as yet put in an appearance. Beth expected that Chris would wait for her at the hotel. But when Tom finally came into the breakfast room to ask rather testily if they were through, Chris announced that he intended coming with them.

Tom looked doubtful and rather annoyed. 'I don't see that this is any business of yours, Chris.'

'You don't?' Chris raised one dark eyebrow. 'Think of all the spade work I put in for you, Tom. After all, if it hadn't been for me, you would never have succeeded in getting in touch with Michiko.'

'I agree to all that,' Tom said testily, 'but still I don't see why you want to come along.'

'I have my reasons,' Chris said. 'Well, are we going?' He was apparently determined to come with them and Tom said nothing more to try to dissuade him.

The hire car Chris had used earlier that morning was still waiting for them. It drove them through the main section of the town and along the riverbank to the district surrounding the Nigo Bash, a bridge which crossed the river to the other side near the Okazaki Park and Zoological Gardens, where the Matsunos lived. It was an attractive house, fairly recently built with a fine view over the Okazaki Park.

It was decided that Beth should go in first to warn the girl that her father had come to see her. The others would wait outside in the car. Beth opened the gate, went up through the small ornamental garden to the front door, changed her shoes to slippers and rang the bell.

A neat little kimonoed maid opened the door and fell on her knees before Beth, her head touching the floor. Obviously the Matsunos, like their daughter, Mrs. Ito, followed the traditional customs and insisted upon their observance in the house.

'*Konnichi wa!*' Beth said, proud that she had managed to master a few words of Japanese. 'Michiko-san, *doozo.*'

The little maid burst into a flood of Japanese. '*Hakkiri to wakari-masen,*' Beth said. It was a sentence Chris had taught her meaning that she did not understand.

The maid looked helplessly at her and in the pause Beth walked into the house and stood inside the hall. 'Michiko-san, *doozo,*' she repeated, and at that moment, as though by some lucky chance, Michiko came out into the hall.

'Elizabeth-san!' she exclaimed happily. 'Oh, it is good to see you. But what brings you here?'

'I came to see you, Michiko-san. I have a message.'

'From Mamma-san?'

Beth shook her head.

'From Dr. Frank?' The girl's voice trembled slightly.

'No, not from Dr. Frank. Could I talk to you alone, Michiko-san?'

The girl spoke in Japanese to the maid, who bowed low and disappeared.

'Come into the lounge,' Michiko said. 'My grandmother and grandfather are out of the house. We can be undisturbed. From whom do you bring me a message, Elizabeth-san?'

'From your father,' Beth said.

'From my father?' Michiko cried in a startled unbelieving voice. 'But how would he know where to find me, Elizabeth-san? How did you know? Mamma-san would never divulge my address here. Especially not to my father.'

'She was questioned by the police. They got the address from her,' Beth said, and went on to tell Michiko as briefly as possible the events of the night before last at the Itos' home in Tokyo.

'I never liked Wang Lee, but that he should actually have tried to murder John Chao and you is unbelievable,' she cried.

'John Chao tried to warn me,' Beth said. 'I think Wang Lee looked upon him as a traitor.'

'It is horrible, horrible,' Michiko said, wringing her hands. 'I feel as though I never wanted to go back into that household.'

'But you needn't go back,' Beth said. 'Your father wants you very much, Michiko-san. Won't you at least see him? He has come half across the world to see you.'

But Michiko still needed a great deal of persuasion before she would finally consent to see her father. Directly she capitulated Beth ran out hastily to bring in Tom before the girl could change her mind.

'This is your father, Michiko,' she

said as she drew Tom into the room.

There was a brief pause. Tom stared at the beautiful dark-haired girl with the light complexion and the grey eyes like his, who was his daughter.

'Eiko!' he said. 'Eiko!'

The girl ran into his outstretched arms: 'Father-san,' she whispered.

Beth left the room. She knew that Tom had seen a ghost when he saw his daughter. She reminded him in every way of his long-lost love, his only love.

Beth stumbled a little as she made her way down the path; she was crying quietly.

Chris was with her in a moment, one of his arms tight about her shoulders. 'Darling, darling, what has happened? Why are you crying?'

'Tom acted as though he had seen a ghost. I know now that he will never love anyone as he loved Eiko. I don't believe he would ever be happy married to anyone else.'

'Thank God you've found that out at last,' Chris said quietly. 'Let's sit in the car and wait for the others.'

It was a fairly long wait, not that they minded that.

'I love you,' Chris told Beth very gently. 'I've loved you from the first moment I saw you, Beth. But because of Tom I didn't think I stood a donkey's chance. You do love me, don't you?'

She nodded soberly.

'I knew you loved me,' he said exaltedly. 'I knew it from the moment when I held you in my arms at the Japanese inn and kissed your lips and your throat and you kissed me back. But you're a stubborn little thing. You wouldn't admit it, even to yourself; you still clung to the idea that you were in love with Tom.'

'But what about Sally?' Beth asked during one of the pauses when he had ceased kissing her.

'Sally's always been as a sister to me. She wouldn't want it any other way, and I wouldn't either.'

She pouted. 'But you did flirt with her.'

He laughed. 'Did that make you mad? It was her idea. She said you needed to be a little jealous so that you could learn to make up your own mind. But you do know your own mind at last; you know you love me.' He said it triumphantly, exultantly.

She smiled and rested her head against his shoulder. 'I do love you, Chris, but I'll never forgive you for trying to fool me about Sally.'

They were still in each other's arms when Tom came out of the house with Michiko. She was dressed in Western-ised clothes and Tom was carrying her suitcase. He didn't comment upon Chris's beaming happiness, nor Beth's somewhat tousled appearance. He seemed too happy being reunited with his daughter to worry about anything else.

'If I really loved him, I would be madly jealous,' Beth thought. 'Thank God I know now that I've been in love with Chris, almost from the first.'

The four of them climbed into the back of the limousine together, the two men sitting on small occasional seats facing the two girls.

'Michiko is coming back to England with me for a year,' Tom told them. 'After that, if Michiko still wishes it she can come back to Japan to marry Dr. Frank. I haven't met him yet but I'm looking forward to the meeting.'

'You'll like him, Father-san,' Michiko said shyly. 'I love him so very much.'

Tom grinned. 'Then I'll try to love him, too. But don't expect the impossible, Michiko.'

'So long as I know that eventually I can marry him, I am content to wait,' Michiko said.

'When you come back you can come and stay with Beth and me. I'll guarantee we'll give you a slap-bang wedding.'

For the first time Tom seemed to register that something had happened between Chris and his pretty young secretary. 'Beth and you,' he exclaimed. 'But Beth will be with me in England.'

'I'll say she won't be,' Chris said

determinedly. 'While you were in with Michiko, Tom, Beth and I decided to be married. We'll be married at once and she'll stay out here. I'm not going to take the risk of letting her fly back to England until we go there as man and wife. Beth wants her mother to be at the ceremony. I'll send her an air ticket to fly over here.'

'Well,' Tom said and let out a deep breath. 'I don't suppose there's much that I can say.'

'Nothing at all. Nothing at all,' Chris repeated happily.

'Oh, Elizabeth-san, I am so very happy for you,' Michiko threw both her arms about the other girl and hugged her impulsively. 'From the moment I met you, I have loved you like a sister, and it is through you that I have got to know my father once again and to realise what a fine man he is. I am so very happy.'

'I guess we're all pretty happy,' Chris said. 'My, won't we have a celebration tonight!'

'In Tokyo?' Tom suggested.

Chris shook his head. 'You and Michiko can go back to Tokyo if you want, but I am not going to let Beth leave Kyoto until I have shown her some more of the sights, especially the Horyuji Temple near Nara, the oldest in Japan. Nowhere else in this world will you see such beautiful wooden statues surrounded by the most magnificent scenery.'

'Have it your own way,' Tom said. 'We'll all stay over for a few days and make a special visit to Nara.'

Sally seemed almost as pleased as they were when she was told of Chris's and Beth's engagement. 'Goody, goody,' she cried. 'I was right after all, wasn't I, Chris?'

'Trust a woman,' he said, grinning, and told her of the excursion to Nara they had planned for that day.

They stopped on the way to see the famous deer in the park near Nara. The deer are so tame they come up and eat out of your hand. It is a huge park, the largest of its kind in Japan. It is beautifully wooded with huge Japanese cedars, oaks and wisterias. Most of the famous sites and classical records of the past of this ancient city are within close range of the park.

Chris said that he and Beth would stroll through the park and meet them later at the Nara Hotel for lunch. They wandered happily about the park under the trees and wisteria-covered arbours.

'We can take in the shrines and temples in the afternoon,' Chris said. 'At the moment all I want is to be alone with you.' He smiled down at her and she laughed up into his face.

'Is it brazen to say I want the same thing, Chris?'

'Now you're asking for it,' he said, and took her closely into his arms, kissing her lips, loving her with his hands. 'When shall we be married? Tomorrow, darling?'

She laughed again. 'I haven't a word to say in protest, Chris.'

We do hope that you have enjoyed reading this large print book.

Did you know that all of our titles are available for purchase?

We publish a wide range of high quality large print books including:
Romances, Mysteries, Classics
General Fiction
Non Fiction and Westerns

Special interest titles available in large print are:
The Little Oxford Dictionary
Music Book, Song Book
Hymn Book, Service Book

Also available from us courtesy of Oxford University Press:
Young Readers' Dictionary
(large print edition)
Young Readers' Thesaurus
(large print edition)

For further information or a free brochure, please contact us at:
Ulverscroft Large Print Books Ltd.,
The Green, Bradgate Road, Anstey,
Leicester, LE7 7FU, England.
Tel: (00 44) **0116 236 4325**
Fax: (00 44) **0116 234 0205**

SO NEAR TO LOVE

Gillian Kaye

Despite Emma's dislike of Mr Peirstone, schoolmaster in Ellerdale, she is forced to go to School House to look after his children. There she meets his son, Adam, and falls in love. But Adam's circumstances don't allow for marriage. Then Mr Peirstone dies unexpectedly and Emma goes to work for Dr Redman and his wife, Amy, in Ravendale. The doctor schemes to matchmake Emma and Adam . . . but can there ever be a happy ending for the young couple?